Evil awaited them...

The entrance soon loomed before them, a cavernous hole framed by timber that looked older than Michael.

"The timber's not *that* old," he said, half smiling as he handed her the flashlight. "Here, hold this."

She shined the beam at the entrance. The light penetrated only a few feet of darkness before being swallowed. But it was enough to see the footprints. Michael squatted on his heels and ran his fingers around the outline of the prints.

"Zombies," he said, indicating a scuffed section on one print. "See? Their step is heavy, and they drag their feet. Jasper would leave no prints, and he would have carried Jake in."

"We knew he'd have traps waiting." So why hadn't her psychic senses kicked in and warned her?

"They won't." Michael stood and brushed the dirt off his hands. "Jasper's using the psychic net again—I can feel it pulsing. It's shielding this entire area, and probably interfering with your abilities."

Yet the watch still beat between her fingers. "I can still feel Jake."

"Only because Jasper wants you to find him."

She shivered. "Then the rest of my abilities will be useless?"

"Probably. You can't find out without trying, and the net will catch you if you do."

Her stomach twisted. While she'd often wished to be normal, to be free of the gifts that had somehow always set her apart, she'd known deep down that she relied on them too much to ever let them go. And her brief time with Jasper had proven just how useless she was without them.

Michael wrapped his fingers around hers. "You're not alone, Nikki."

She closed her eyes, fighting the warmth that sprang through her body. It wasn't right to want someone as much as she wanted Michael. Wasn't right to need his touch, the comfort of his arms to chase the demons away.

"I'll always be alone," she said, and stepped away from him. It couldn't be any other way. Not when her love was a curse of death. Michael might be a vampire, but that didn't make him invincible. Monica had proven that vampires could die as fast as any human. "Let's go."

For Pete,
who supported my dreams
when so few did.

Dancing with the Devil

***

Keri Arthur

DANCING WITH THE DEVIL
Published by ImaJinn Books, a division of ImaJinn

ISBN: 1-893896-59-5

10 9 8 7 6 5 4 3 2 1

PUBLISHER'S NOTE:
This book is a work of fiction. Names, characters, places and incidents are products of the author's imagination or are used fictitiously. Any resemblance to actual events or locales or persons, living or dead, is entirely coincidental.

Books are available at quantity discounts when used to promote products or services. For information please write to: Marketing Division, ImaJinn Books, P.O. Box 545, Canon City, CO 81215-0545, or call toll free 1-877-625-3592.

Cover design by Patricia Lazarus

ImaJinn Books, a division of ImaJinn
P.O. Box 545, Canon City, CO 81215-0545
Toll Free: 1-877-625-3592
http://www.imajinnbooks.com

One

Someone followed her.

Someone she couldn't see or hear through any normal means, but whose presence fairly vibrated across her psychic senses.

Someone whose mission was death.

The wind stirred, running chill fingers across the back of her neck. Nikki shivered and eyed the surrounding shadows uneasily. She'd never been afraid of the dark before—had, in fact, found it something of an ally, especially in the wilder days of her youth. But tonight there was an edge to the silence, a hint of menace in the slowly swirling fog.

People disappeared on nights like this. At least they did here in Lyndhurst.

She returned her gaze to the slender figure just ahead. This was the fourth night in a row Monica Trevgard had come to the park after midnight. So far, it was to do nothing more than sit on a bench for an hour before slowly returning home.

Nikki had no idea why. If the teenager had a reason for coming here, she sure as hell hadn't found any evidence of it. Her actions to date made very little sense. The only child of one of Lyndhurst's—and possibly America's—richest men, Monica had spent most of her life rebelling against her family and their wealth. And yet, ironically, it was only thanks to her father's money that she was free to walk the streets tonight. Though nothing had ever been proven, it was a generally conceded fact that John Trevgard had at least one judge and several police officers on his payroll.

Nikki smiled grimly. Trevgard would probably have been better off keeping his hand in his pocket and letting his only child spend some time in jail. Maybe a day or so locked behind uncompromising concrete walls would shock some sense into the girl.

It sure as hell had with *her*.

Shoving cold hands into the pockets of her old leather jacket, Nikki let her gaze roam across the fog-shrouded trees to her left.

He was still there, still following her. The man with

darkness in his heart and murder on his mind. Not her murder, not even Monica's. Someone else's entirely.

She bit her lip. With two knives strapped to her wrists and her psychic abilities to fall back on, she was well enough protected. At least under normal circumstances. But the man out there in the darkness was far from normal, and something told her none of her weapons would be good enough if he chose to attack.

Maybe *she* was as mad as Monica. Four women had already disappeared from this particular area. She should play it safe and go home, let Jake take over the case. A teenager looking for trouble was going to find it, no matter how many people her father hired to follow and protect her.

Only Jake had enough on his plate already, and his night sight wasn't particularly good, anyway.

The sound of running water broke through the heavy silence. Though the fog half-hid the old fountain from sight, Nikki knew it well enough to describe every chipped detail, from the wickedly grinning cherub at the top to the embracing lovers near the bottom. It was amazing what became interesting when you had nothing else to do but watch a teenager watch the water.

Only Monica didn't stop at the fountain.

Didn't even look at it. Instead, she glanced quickly over her shoulder, a casual move that raised the hairs on the back of Nikki's neck.

Monica knew she was being followed. Tonight, she didn't just wander. Tonight she was the bait to catch the watcher.

The bitter breeze stirred, seeming to blow right through her soul. Nikki swore softly and ran a hand through her hair. It was nights like this, when she was caught between common sense and past promises, that she really hated being psychic. Had it not been for the gifts warning that death would claim Monika's soul if she weren't protected tonight, Nikki would have run a mile away from here.

But she couldn't stand the weight of another death on her conscience and had no real choice but to follow.

They neared the far edge of the park. Streetlights glimmered, forlorn wisps of brightness barely visible through the trees and the fog. Nikki's unease increased.

Monica wasn't heading for the street or the lights, but rather toward the old mansion on the far edge of the park. The place had a reputation for being haunted, and though she didn't particularly believe in ghosts, the one night she'd spent there as a kid had sent her running from the place. Ghosts may not exist, but evil sure as hell did.

The mansion was steeped in it.

Monica squeezed through a small gap in the fence and cast another quick look over her shoulder. There was no doubt about it—the kid definitely wanted to be followed.

Nikki stopped and watched her walk up the steps to the back door. Common sense told her not to follow. Psychic sense told her danger waited inside. She clenched her fists. She could do this. *Had* to do this.

She stepped forward, then froze. No sound had disturbed the dark silence. Even the breeze had faded, and the fog sat still and heavy on the ground. Yet something had moved behind her. Something not quite human.

Throat dry, Nikki turned. Out of the corner of her eye, she caught a hint of movement—a hand, emerging from darkness, reaching out to touch her...

Yelping in fright, she jumped back and lashed out with kinetic energy. Something heavy hit a nearby oak, accompanied by a grunt of pain. She stared at the tree. Despite the sound, there was nothing or nobody at its base.

Something had to be there. It didn't make any sense—bodies just didn't disappear like that. She swallowed and ran trembling fingers through her hair. Disembodied hands couldn't emerge from the darkness, either.

Had it just been her imagination, finally reacting to the overwhelming sensation of being followed? No. Something *had* been there. Was still there, even if she couldn't see it.

Not that *that* made a whole lot of sense. She turned and studied the dark house. Trouble waited inside that place. But so did Monica.

She climbed through the fence and ran across the shadowed yard. Edging up the steps, she slipped a small flashlight from her pocket and shone the light through the open doorway.

The entrance hall was small, laden with dust and cobwebs that shimmered like ice in the beam of light. Faded crimson and gold wallpaper hung in eerie strips from the walls, rustling lightly in the breeze that drifted past her legs. The house really hadn't changed much in the ten years since she'd last been there.

Motes of dust danced across the light, stirred to life in the wake of Monica's passing. She directed the beam towards the stairs. Monica appeared to have gone upwards. Up to where the evil lived.

Gripping the flashlight tightly, Nikki walked through the dust towards the stairs. The air smelled of decay and unwashed bodies. Obviously, it was still a haunt for those forced to scratch a living off the streets. It was odd, though, that there was no one here now—no one but Monica and whoever it was she'd come here for.

A floorboard creaked beneath Nikki's weight, the sound as loud as thunder in the silence. She winced and hesitated. After several heartbeats, someone moved on the floor above.

It wasn't Monica. The footfalls were too heavy.

Reaching into her pocket, she turned on her mobile. If things started to go bad, she'd call for help. Trevgard might not like the publicity a call to the cops would raise, but if it meant the difference between life or death—*her* life or death—he could go to hell.

The staircase loomed out of the shadows. Nikki shone the light upwards. Something growled; a low sound almost lost against the thunder of her heart. She hesitated, staring up into the darkness.

It had sounded like some sort of animal. But what animal made such an odd, rasping noise?

One hand on the banister, the other clutching the flashlight so tightly her knuckles began to ache, she continued on. The growl cut across the silence again.

It was definitely no animal.

She reached the landing and stopped. The odd-sounding snarl seemed much closer this time. Sweat trickled down her face. The flashlight flickered slightly, its beam fading, allowing the darkness to close in on her. Nikki swore and gave it a quick shake. The last thing she needed right now was the light to give up the ghost. Being stranded in total darkness was not a prospect she looked forward to.

The light flickered again, then became brighter. She

moved on but kept close to the wall, just in case. At least she could use it as a guide, even if the peeling remains of the wallpaper felt like dead skin against her fingertips.

The hallway ended in a T-intersection. Moonlight washed through the shattered window at the end of the left-hand corridor. On her right, there was darkness so complete it almost appeared solid.

Monica was in there somewhere. Of that she had no doubt. But that odd sound had come from the left. Whatever it was, she had to check it out first. There was no way in hell she'd run the risk of being attacked from behind in a place like this. She turned left. Two doors waited ahead. One open, one closed.

Was it just fear or instinct that warned against entering either room?

The wind whispered forlornly through the shattered window, accompanied by a low moan that raced goose bumps across her skin.

It was definitely human more than animal. And it wasn't Monica. The teenager still waited in the darkness of the right corridor. Edging forward, she peered around the door frame. Nothing moved in the moon-washed darkness, but something was in there, nevertheless. The sense of malevolence was so overwhelming she could barely breathe.

So why do you not turn around and run?

The thought whispered into her brain, feather light but hinting at anger. Nikki froze, fear squeezing her throat tight. Just for an instant, her mind linked with another. She tasted darkness and concern and the need to kill. This was the man she'd half seen near the fence—the man who'd followed her through the fog.

Turn around and leave. You cannot help the child now.

No. Why could she hear this man's thoughts? Telepathy had never been one of her talents, even though she'd been able to receive Tommy's thoughts well enough. *And who the hell are you to tell me what to do?*

I merely try to save your life. You will not like what you find. Not in that room, and not with the teenager.

Yeah right. Who was this weirdo? A would-be prophet of doom? *I have never run from anything in my life, and I don't intend to start now.*

The lie gave her courage. She took a deep breath and

stepped into the room.

***

Michael Kelly hit the fence in frustration. The little fool had entered the room, despite his warning. Perhaps because of it.

She knew danger waited—he could taste the fear in her thoughts, despite the distance between them. So why wouldn't she run? Why did she continue this fruitless quest for the teenager? Given the strength of her psychic talents, she had to know the child was well beyond salvation.

He let his gaze roam to the far end of the house. Hidden by the darkness, evil waited for his next meal, ably served by his young companion. Unless *he* intervened, Nikki James would become the fifth woman to go missing in this area.

Had it been anyone else, he wouldn't have particularly cared. His task here tonight was to trap and kill a murderer, not save lives. But her abilities added a dangerous dimension to his task. It was for those abilities, more than her blood, that Jasper hunted her.

He turned and walked to the end of the fence. The sudden movement caused pain to shoot through his head, but he resisted the urge to rub the lump forming near his temple. He had deserved that, and more, for being so careless. But he just hadn't expected the fool to use her kinetic abilities against him. Why he hadn't, he couldn't say. He smiled grimly. Maybe senility was finally setting in.

He stopped and studied the houses opposite. Like the area in general, the homes appeared deserted, forgotten. Yet several of the nearest were occupied; he could see the slight haze of life through the walls. Though he couldn't actually enter the main buildings, such restrictions didn't seem to hold when it came to garages. If he could find a container of some kind, he could siphon the gas from the cars.

Michael glanced back up to the house. Jasper hated fire. Feared it.

It might be enough to save Nikki James.

***

The room smelled awful—a putrid mix of stale urine, excrement and death all rolled up into one breath-withering mix. She cupped a hand over her nose and mouth and tried not to gag as she swept the flashlight's beam across the room.

Something shied away from the light's touch—a hunched, humanoid shape that smelled like death.

Nikki backed away. She didn't know what hid in the shadows and didn't really care to find out. She'd learned long ago that some things were best left unexplored; this was certainly one of those times. Perhaps if she closed the door, the thing would leave her alone. She knew from past experience that all the doors in this old house creaked; it was one of the things that had spooked her as a teenager. At the very least, it would give her some warning if the thing decided to move.

She half turned away, then stopped. A prickle of warning ran across the back of her neck. The shadows parted, revealing a mass of hair and pale, naked flesh.

It was definitely human. And yet not.

Fear slammed through her heart. *What the hell...?*

The grotesque figure lunged at her. Stumbling backwards, Nikki threw out her hand, thrusting the creature away kinetically. It slammed into the back wall, grunting in surprise. No sooner had it hit the floor than it was scrambling to its feet, its agility surprising.

Glimpsing movement to her left, Nikki whirled. A second creature ran out of the shadows, its face a mocking image of humanity. She reached again for kinetic energy. The heavy steps of the first creature were an express train drawing close. Sweat trickled down the back of her neck. She thrust the second creature back through the doorway, then flicked a wrist knife into her palm. Spinning, she met the charge of the first, stabbing at it wildly. The blade cut through its skin as easily as butter and her fist slammed into the creature's pale flesh—flesh that was as cold as ice.

Or death.

Nausea rose, tightening her throat. Nikki swallowed and tried to back away, but her feet wouldn't move fast enough. The creature lashed out, connecting hard. The blow flung her backwards. Her back hit the wall, and for a moment she saw stars. Blood spurted from the creature's wound, spraying hot droplets across her face. Nikki gagged, scrubbing at it with the sleeve of her jacket.

The creature made a second grab for her. Dropping the flashlight, Nikki scrambled away, but it caught her shoulder and pulled her back. Talon-like fingers tore into her arm, burning pain down to her fingertips. She gasped, fighting the sudden wash of nausea. The creature snarled; its breath was fetid, full of death, full of decay. Nikki shuddered and slammed the heel of her hand into its face. For a spilt second, its hold weakened. She reached quickly for kinetic energy. A sliver of pain ran through her mind, a warning that she was pushing her psychic strength too far. She ignored it and forced the heavy creature away from her. It flew across the room and smashed through the window, tumbling out backwards with a guttural cry of surprise.

Moonlight fanned across the darkness, lifting the shadows and touching the face of the second creature as it lumbered back into the room. For an instant, it almost looked pretty. Nikki backed away. *What on earth were these things?*

It snarled, and any illusion of prettiness shattered. The creature took one ponderous step forward, then stopped. Nikki readied another kinetic lance. The glimmer of pain in her head became an ache. She was going to have a hell of a headache tomorrow—if she survived tonight.

Blood ran past her clenched fingers and dripped to the floor near her feet. She had no choice but to ignore it. One move, no matter how small, and the creature would attack.

Why wasn't it attacking now? It simply stood in the doorway, shaking its head and snarling softly. It was almost as if the creature was fighting a leash of some kind.

She had absolutely no desire to find out just who, or what, held the end of that invisible leash.

The creature snarled again, an angry, sullen sound. Then turned and leaped out the nearest window.

The retreat sent a chill up her spine. She waited tensely for something else to happen. The breeze stirred the dust from the corner shadows, and the heavy silence returned.

After several heartbeats, she sank down against the wall and drew her knees close. For a minute she simply sat there, breathing deeply and letting the silence run over her.

Why had the creature retreated? The desire, maybe even the need, to shed blood had been all too evident in its eyes. But it had left.

Because it had been ordered to.

Moonlight played across the glass that lay scattered all around her. Glass that was stained with bright splashes of red. She wasn't sure if the blood belonged to the creatures or to her, and knew in the end it wouldn't really matter. *He* would come for the blood. *He* would smell it and come for her.

Who *he* was, she didn't really know. Or care. She had to get out of this crazy house, had to escape, while she still could...

The thought stalled. What about Monica? Did she really want to leave the teenager to face fate alone?

Yes.

No.

She took another deep breath and pushed upright. At sixteen, Monica had barely begun to live. She had so much yet to learn, so much more of the world to see.

Ten years before, Nikki had left another teenager to his fate. He'd been a hell of a lot more capable of taking care of himself than Monica ever would be, and still he had died. This time around, she was not letting fate get the upper hand.

She eased off her jacket and studied the wound on her forearm. While the three gashes bled profusely, the creature's talons obviously hadn't severed anything vital. She could still move her fingers, even if it did hurt like hell. Digging a handkerchief out of her pocket, she wrapped it around the wound. Hopefully it would stem the flow of blood long enough to find Monica and get out of this house.

Putting her jacket back on, she walked across to retrieve her flashlight, only to discover it no longer worked. She gave it a quick shake and heard a slight tinkle coming from the globe area. It must have smashed when she'd dropped it.

"That's just great," she muttered, thrusting it back in her pocket. Now she'd have to cross the threshold of utter darkness with only instinct to guide her.

Instinct that had proven somewhat unreliable in the past.

The hallway was quiet. Her gaze was drawn to the darkness at the far end of the hall. Monica had to be down there somewhere. But so was the presence that tasted so evil.

She took a deep, calming breath, then walked back to the T-intersection. A tingle of awareness ran across the back of her neck as she neared the stairs. She hesitated, studied the shadows that hid the staircase. The stranger had entered the house. *Michael Kelly*, Nikki thought. *His name is Michael Kelly.*

Nikki rubbed the back of her neck. Why could she read this stranger's mind? And why had he entered the house? Was he here to help her, or did he have something more sinister in mind?

No answers came from the darkness, and the spark of awareness flickered and died. Nikki frowned but continued on. The rapid beat of her heart seemed abnormally loud in the strange silence. Her senses warned of another door, even though she couldn't see it. She ran her fingers along the wall and touched a door frame, then the cold metal of a doorknob. Stopping, she listened to the silence.

Evil was near, maybe even in the room beyond this door. She clenched the doorknob so tightly her knuckles practically glowed, and wondered why in hell she was doing this.

The answer was easy enough to find. Monica reminded her of Tommy, the teenager she'd left to die so long ago. To appease his ghost, to appease the guilt in her heart, she'd follow Monica through the flames of hell if that's what it took to save her soul—simply because she'd been unable to save Tommy's.

Swallowing, she opened the door. Laughter greeted her, laughter that was young and sweet, and yet somehow cold.

Monica.

The teenager stepped out of the shadows, her smile easy to see despite the shadows that hid her face.

"If you wish to talk to me," she said, her voice melodious, yet holding a touch of menace. "First you must follow me."

She turned and walked into another room. Instinct told Nikki not to follow—told her to run as far and as fast as she could. Told her Monica wasn't worth dying for.

Told her if she ran, Monica would die in her place. That was a weight she just couldn't bear. Taking a deep breath, Nikki followed the teenager.

Straight into the arms of the devil himself.

Two

The creature moved too fast to avoid. Michael slammed a fist deep into its gut, but the blow failed to halt its charge. The two of them went down in a fighting tangle of arms and legs.

Michael swore viciously. Every second he wasted with these creatures left Nikki James another second closer to death. The little fool had entered the room. His enemy's hunger was palpable, a beast that filled the darkness.

Anger surged through him; a deep, dark fury he desperately tried to control. He needed a clear head, not a mind ruled by blood rage. The creature wrapped its hands around his neck and squeezed hard. Michael laughed harshly; the stupidity of these things was beyond belief. He reached up and wrenched loose its fingers. Holding them away from his neck, he gave a quick thrust with his knees, throwing the creature back over his head. It smashed through the front doorway and disappeared down the steps.

He scrambled to his feet, then swung, sensing the approach of a second creature. Instead of charging, the beast slithered to a halt—in that instant he saw the silver blade the creature held.

He backed away. The beast followed him, the blade an argent flame promising death.

Foreboding ran through him. He had no time for this. The web of darkness was closing in around Nikki. He should have stopped her in the park, should have seized control of her mind and ordered her away from the child and this house.

But she was different from most others. While he could read her surface thoughts easily enough, he doubted he'd be able to reach far enough into her mind to achieve any sort of real control. Her gifts were too strong—for him, and more than likely, for Jasper. But after death, it was a whole new ball game. Jasper had the ability to call his victims from the grave. Death wouldn't kill her abilities. Not while there was flesh on her bones, at any rate.

The creature lunged at him. Michael dodged the thrust of the knife then grabbed the creature's wrist. Squeezing tight, he forced the blade from its grip, then thrust an elbow into its face, shattering its nose. It howled, a high keening sound of distress. Michael cursed softly. The creature was an abomination, but who was the greater horror? The dead or the man who forced them from their graves?

He might not be able to kill Jasper right now, but he could give this creature final peace. Gripping its head, he snapped it hard sideways, breaking its neck. It fell to a lifeless heap at his feet. One down, five to go, if he included Jasper and the teenager.

Michael kicked the blade away with his foot then retrieved the can of gas. Undoing the lid, he sloshed the contents round the floor and up the walls. Anywhere and everywhere. It didn't matter, as long as it burned.

Throwing the empty can into a corner, he dug a box of matches out of his pocket. The old house was tinder dry. With the gas he'd splashed around, it would ignite like wildfire. But there was no one in the house except the four of them. Jasper wouldn't burn—he'd run the minute he smelled the flames. If Monica was too stupid to follow, then that was just too bad. Nikki was the one he had to get out. She'd be too dangerous a weapon in Jasper's hands.

Michael lit the match and flicked it in the direction of the can. Then he turned and ran for the stairs.

***

The door slammed shut behind her. Nikki spun but knew there was no escape. Childish laughter echoed through the silence, mocking her.

Monica, in league with the devil himself.

"You have done well, my pet."

The soft voice was powerful. Hypnotic. It filled the room with its warmth, and yet her skin crawled in terror of its touch. Instinct warned her not to move, told the slightest show of fear would quickly bring death. But the beat of her heart was a drum that filled the silence. He had to know—had to feel—her fear.

The air stirred. She stepped back quickly. The presence laughed, a low sound of amusement. Nikki clenched her fists. Energy tingled across her fingertips, but she didn't release it, instead retreating another step. Her back hit the wall, but she felt no better for its protection. If she could get to the door...   "There is no escape for you now." The stranger's tone was oddly gentle, yet filled with the certainty of death.

Nikki edged sideways, one hand outstretched, searching desperately for the doorknob. It had to be close; she hadn't walked that far into the room, for Christ's sake.

"Look at me," The voice changed, became deeper, more alluring. "Look at me..."

Blue fire flared in the darkness. Nikki stared, mesmerized, as the flame grew brighter, transforming itself into a pair of sapphire eyes.

So beautiful.

So very deadly.

Nikki swallowed and tore her gaze away. Her fingers touched the doorknob, clenched convulsively around it.

"No," he whispered. "Stay with me."

His words wrapped around her, seductive and compelling. Blue fire pinned her. She couldn't tear herself free of the commanding beauty of his gaze.

"Be mine."

Memories rose unbidden, and Nikki saw another time, another man, uttering the same words.

"No," she said and flung out her arm, releasing the pent-up kinetic energy. The sapphire gaze disappeared, then something heavy hit the far wall.

Anger hissed across the darkness. Nikki slammed the door open and ran for the hall.

Smoke swirled through the darkness, a stench that caught in her throat, making her cough. *Christ, there's a fire somewhere.* But she couldn't stop. Not with evil so close to her heels. She reached the door leading out into the hall and flung it open.

Only to be greeted by hell. Wallpaper dripped fiery tears to the floor, and the stairs were lost to an inferno of red heat. Smoke curled around her, stinging her eyes and making it difficult to breathe. She coughed, and dashed the tears away from her eyes. What was she going to do now?

Wood creaked behind her.

Run, she thought, and leaped into the hall, slamming the door shut behind her.

The heat was fierce, scorching her clothes and searing her skin. Heart pounding with fear, Nikki spun, not sure where to go. The smoke did a mad dance around her, making it difficult to get her bearings. If she couldn't use the stairs, she'd have to run down the hall...but which way was safest?

"This way," a voice said behind her.

Nikki jumped then turned. A figure emerged from the swirling darkness. Something deep within quivered in recognition. This was Michael Kelly, the man she'd sensed earlier.

"Trust me," he said and held out his hand.

She hesitated, despite the danger of doing so. The dancing brightness of the flames revealed the finely chiseled planes of his cheeks, and a nose that hinted of exotic blood. It was a handsome face. A haunted face. One she could trust—at least for now.

She placed her hand in his. His fingers closed around hers, wrapping them in a heat that was fiercer than any flame.

He led her quickly through the fire and into another room. She kicked the door shut, then saw the only exit was the large window to her left. They'd have to jump.

Shit. Nikki thrust kinetically at the window. The glass burst outwards, glittering like a thousand bright stars as it fell earthward.

Wind rushed into the void, slapping her face like a bucket of cold water. She blinked, and looked at the ground far below. It was a long, long way down...

As if sensing her sudden reluctance, Michael grabbed her, swinging her into his arms.

"No!" she screamed, then shut her eyes as he ran toward the window.

He leaped out into the night. The wind whipped around them, and, just for an instant, it felt as if they were flying. The illusion shattered when they hit the ground. The impact wrenched her from Michael's hold and pitched her roughly forward. She rolled down a slight incline and through several plants before coming to an abrupt halt against a fence, rear half buried in the garden bed and legs pointing skyward.

For several seconds she just lay there, too stunned to move, just thankful to be alive. She'd bitten her tongue sometime during the fall and could taste blood in her mouth, but other than that, everything seemed in working order.

At least she was free from the house, and the immediate threat of evil. But the man with the hypnotic sapphire eyes was still near—she could feel his presence, hunting her. She'd better get away from this area—fast.

She slowly lowered her legs from the fence. Pain shot along her back, and she groaned softly. No doubt she'd have a colorful array of bruises to parade tomorrow.

"Take my hand."

Every nerve in her aching body jumped. Her heart in her mouth, she glanced up. Michael's form flowed out of the night and found substance. Just like a ghost, Nikki thought with a shiver. Her gaze swept from the blackness of his clothing to his face. Instinct might be telling her to trust this man, but there was something in his eyes that made her wary.

And yet he'd undoubtedly saved her life. "If you were going to throw me out a window," she muttered. "You could have at least arranged a softer landing."

Though his eyebrows rose in surprise, a hint of a smile touched his generous mouth. Nikki ignored his outstretched hand, and pushed herself into a sitting position. Her stomach churned, and she took several deep breaths, battling the urge to be sick.

"We have no time," he said, concern touching the soft tones of his voice. "Please, take my hand and let's go."

Nikki studied him for a moment, then looked back at the house. Bright flames were leaping from the ground floor windows, hungrily reaching skyward. She had no sense of Monica, but the evil was on the move.

She took his hand. He pulled her up easily, his strength at odds with his lean build. Surprisingly, he stood only three or four inches above her five-four. In the flame-filled confines of the hall, he'd appeared a lot bigger.

"He hunts us," Michael stated softly. Though he still held her hand, he'd turned slightly to study the house. "We must keep moving."

"What about Monica?"

Michael glanced at her. His eyes were ancient, endless pools of ebony. You could lose yourself forever in those depths, Nikki thought, and glanced away uneasily.

"The child accompanies her master. You were a fool to go in after her."

"She would have died if I didn't." Nikki took her hand from his, and briskly rubbed a tender hip.

His smile was grim. "Death is one thing that child no longer fears."

She frowned at him. "What do you mean?"

"Nothing." He shrugged gracefully. "Ready to move?"

She returned her gaze to the house, then nodded.

Michael led the way forward. He was quiet, as one with the night. A ghost, she thought uneasily. She glanced at her fingers, remembering the gentle strength of his hand in hers. If he was a ghost, he was certainly a solid one.

"I am as real as you, Nikki," he said softly. His dark gaze touched hers briefly before returning to study the surrounding night.

She'd forgotten he could read her thoughts—just like Tommy had, so many years ago. Fear stirred, along with old guilt. So why did she trust him? She couldn't say, and that worried her.

"They follow us."

Nikki looked over her shoulder. A dark shape lumbered after them. "Should we run?"

"No. They can run faster than you ever could."

But not, she surmised from his tone, faster than he could. So why was he still here, offering his protection?

There was a flash of movement to her left. Before she could react, Michael thrust her sideways and spun to meet the charge of a second creature.

She hit the ground, tasting dirt. Spitting it out and cursing him fluently, she rolled back to her feet. The creature attacking Michael held a knife, the blade a blue-white flame against the night.

Michael seemed wary of it, something that struck her as odd. Certainly it wasn't what she'd considered a large knife, not when compared with what the street kids used these days. She grabbed a rock near her feet and threw at the creature. It hit with enough force to make the creature stop and shake its head in confusion. Then it snarled and charged her. Somehow, Michael was in front of it again, his movements so fast he appeared to blur. He spun, kicking the creature in the head. It screamed and staggered sideways.

It was the sound of a woman in pain. A chill ran through her. What *were* these things?

The creature lunged again. Nikki reached for kinetic energy. Despite the ache in her head, it surged in response. She focused it on the knife in the creature's hand. At the same time, she heard footsteps behind her.

She tore the blade from the creature's grasp then spun, hurling the knife at the approaching figure.

And saw that it was Monica.

Frantically, she flung another bolt of energy at the blade. The weapon flared brightly, as if in protest, then quivered and changed direction. It thudded hilt-deep into a tree trunk several feet to Monica's left.

The teenager took no notice. Nikki frowned. Despite the crackling of the flames that consumed the old house, the night was strangely quiet. The creature had to be dead, or surely it would still be attacking.

Michael stood behind her, not touching and yet close enough that the warmth of his breath whispered past her cheek. Under normal circumstances, she would have stepped away. But the night had become something more than normal, and she had a feeling she would need his protection before it was over.

Monica stopped several paces away. Nikki cleared her throat softly. "Your father wants to speak—"

"I don't care what my father wants. Tell him to leave me alone, or he'll regret it. So will you if you don't stop following me."

The words themselves weren't overly threatening. It was the lack of life in Monica's eyes, the emptiness in her voice, that chilled. As if she were nothing more than a blank canvas ready to be filled by an unknown painter.

"Not as far from the truth as you might think," Michael said softly, obviously reading her thoughts again.

She crossed her arms, trying to ward off a sudden chill.

"And if you even try to answer *his* call," Monica continued, gesturing towards the park. "I'll kill you myself."

There wasn't a doubt in her mind that Monica *would* carry out the threat. Just for an instant, evil flared in the girl's eyes. It was old, centuries old. It was the same evil that now stood in the park, in the shape of a man. Nikki rubbed her arms. Maybe she was far too late to save Monica's soul.

The teenager walked away, a slim shadow against the brightness of the flames beginning to leap from the upper floor windows.

"We must go, " Michael said quietly. "The fire department is on its way."

She glanced at the nearby houses. People were lined up near their fences, watching them. If the fire department was on the way, then so were the police. She grimaced and returned her gaze to Michael. The wind tugged at his hair, blowing the midnight-colored strands across his face.

"What were those things that attacked us?" she said, shoving her hands in her pockets to keep them warm.

He hesitated, then shrugged. "They go by many names."

Word games were the last thing she felt like playing right now. Her head ached. Her arm ached. In fact, everything ached. She stunk of smoke and sweat and fear, and wanted nothing more than to go home and soak in a nice hot bath.

But she couldn't. Not until she'd talked to her boss. To do that, she had to first make some sense of the night's madness. "So what in hell do *you* call them?"

He looked past her. She resisted the temptation to turn around, sensing if she did, he'd be gone.

"I suppose it's best to call them zombies," he said after a moment, his eyes dark pools of ebony anger when they met her gaze again. "They answer to the man who attacked you inside the house."

She laughed at the absurdity of it, but her amusement quickly fled under his watchful silence. Swallowing, she remembered the wash of fetid breath across her face, the chill of flaccid flesh against her palm.

Remembered her own impression that the creatures were dead, and yet not.

Zombies. *Hells bells.* Monica was into something far weirder than any of them had realized.

A siren wailed into the silence, and she glanced over her shoulder. A fire engine came around the corner and drove towards them. They must have taken the shortcut through the park to get here so fast. "So how do we explain the presence of zombies to the fire department?"

"We do not," Michael said, his gaze on the approaching engine. "They will only find charred remains. The others have already left. As should we."

"If the fire's been reported, no doubt someone's reported seeing us out front. I'd better stay here and wait."

"I cannot." He looked past her again, then stepped back. "We will meet again."

"Wait!" she said, reaching out to stop him, not wanting to lose the comfort of his presence. " I...I don't even know your name."

He smiled and caught her hand, his fingers gliding across hers. An odd tremble ran up her arm. She wasn't sure whether its cause was the unusual warmth of his touch or simply the caress of his palm against hers.

"You lie, Nikki James. And you will see me again." He raised her hand, brushing a delicate kiss over her fingers.

She quickly pulled her hand away. He was a stranger, an unknown. She should be responding with wariness, not...fascination. She'd traveled that path once before, and it had ended with blood on her hands.

His smile faded. "The fire department is almost upon us. You should be safe enough. The man you fear has left the immediate area, anyway."

His words drew her attention back to the park. The touch of evil had left. So had Monica. Yet she knew the danger was far from over. She still had a client who wanted to see his daughter, whatever the cost.

"He may have left the area, but I doubt he's left my life." Her voice faded.

Michael had completely disappeared.

Three

The scent of his enemy swirled around him, but it was faint, distant. Michael crossed the street then hesitated, glancing back at Nikki.

Even now, he could taste her fear. Oddly enough, it wasn't so much fear of Jasper that he sensed, but fear of death. Monica's death, more than her own. She'd pursued the teenager beyond all common sense, as if, in some way, she owed it to the child.

Certainly she was an intriguing enigma. There was something of the streets in her mannerisms, and yet it was tempered by an odd sort of innocence.

If he'd had more time, he might have tried to get to know her better. The rapport that had flared between them, if only briefly, was something he hadn't experienced for a very long time. He grimaced and thrust a hand through his hair. And maybe after that he'd fly to the moon. What the hell was he thinking?

He'd see her again, of that he had no doubt. She might have escaped Jasper's trap tonight, but Jasper had tasted her abilities, and would not let her go so easily.

But *his* association with her could never amount to anything more than friendship. And certainly it could last no longer than the time it took him to stop Jasper. He could not change who he was or what he did. And truth was, he'd use anything or anyone he could to destroy the likes of Jasper.

He turned and followed Jasper's fading trail north. For tonight at least, Nikki was safe. Dawn was less than an hour away, and the only thing Jasper would be hunting right now was a safe place to wait out the day.

The wind gusted around Michael, its touch chill, thick with the promise of rain. Frowning, he cast his senses forward, searching for the scent of his enemy. Nothing. The fiend had escaped him yet again.

The next time he would not be so easy to find. Jasper would have sensed him tonight and be more wary.

Which left Nikki as his only real hope of finding Jasper fast.

The sound of high heels clicking against the pavement

ahead made him slow down. The red haze of life flared
before him—a prostitute plying her trade along the street.

Darkness stirred. Hunger rose, eager to taste the sweet
offering of life. The woman was alone, unprotected. It would
be so easy to reach out and take what his body craved...

Michael clenched his fists and closed his eyes, taking
a deep breath. *Never again.* He ignored the need pounding
through his veins and crossed the street. He would feed,
but not now, not tonight.

And definitely not on anything human.

He'd booked a room in the old hotel up the street. It
was the kind of establishment frequented mainly by
prostitutes and junkies needing a cheap place to crash. A
place where no questions were asked, the proprietor not
caring who rented the rooms as long as they paid up front.
Certainly not an establishment he'd normally choose, but
he had little real choice here. Jasper liked easy prey. An
area like this provided an effortless hunting ground.

Michael walked through the entrance and up the stairs.
On the third floor he stopped and scanned the area, more
out of habit than from any sense of danger. The red heat of
life flared in several of the rooms down from his own but
everything else was still.

He continued on. The threadbare carpet did little to
muffle his steps, and the floorboards creaked under his
weight. At least Jasper, or anyone else, for that matter,
couldn't sneak up on him. He opened the door to his room
and quickly looked around. Everything was as he had left
it.

Retrieving the bottle of wine he'd placed in the small
refrigerator earlier, he found a corkscrew and glass, then
moved back to the center of the room. Sitting cross-legged
on the carpet, he relaxed his mind.

Contact was instant.

You arrived safely.

The harsh whisper winged into his mind and made
him wince. Would Seline never realize the power of her
mind voice?

Yesterday. He absently opened the wine and poured
himself a glass.

The situation as bad as we thought?

Michael tried to remember a time when the situation

was actually better than they'd thought. *He's up to his old tricks again.*

Not good. Do you need help?

Images of Jasper and his teenage lover ran through Michael's mind, as did the twisted images of the two remaining zombies. Four deadly beings against one. Michael grimaced. If he'd been a betting man, he knew whom he'd place his money on. And if Jasper called any more of the dead to life...

Even if I did, dare we risk anyone else's life? Jasper's killed two of our number already, and knows I'm in Lyndhurst. He'll be watching for backup.

He heard Seline's sharp intake of breath. Concern ran like wildfire through the link.

You will never find him. He may even leave.

This battle has been brewing for a long time, Seline. He won't leave.

How will you find him? Lyndhurst is a big town.

Michael smiled grimly. It was big all right. But Jasper wouldn't run. Or hide. The game was over. This time the battle would be final. The prize would be life—or death—for one of them.

I have bait.

Oh? Who?

He had a sudden image of Nikki's eyes—they were such an unusual color—a warm, smoky amber that seemed to reflect the intensity of her emotions.

Nikki James. She's a private investigator following Jasper's current girlfriend. She's a strong psychic—very strong, in fact.

And Jasper craves power. He will kill, then retrieve her.

Anger rose at the thought of Nikki as one of Jasper's lumbering creatures. And yet, he had to acknowledge the image as one possible outcome. Nor would it stop him from using her as bait.

He took of quick gulp of wine. *I'm going to befriend her. Hopefully, Jasper will turn up pretty quickly, and I can get rid of him before he kills again.*

Take care, Michael. You're playing with fire on this one.

Michael frowned. He had an odd feeling Seline knew more about the situation, or at least about Nikki, than she was letting on. But he also knew there was no point in questioning the old witch. She'd tell him what she thought he needed to know and nothing more. There was little more to add, so he bid her good night and broke the contact. Yawning, he stretched his legs, trying to relax the tension cramping his muscles.

Picking up his glass, he rose and walked across to the window. The blinds were open, and the pale light of the rising dawn streamed in through glass. Michael leaned a shoulder against the window frame and sipped slowly at the wine.

The sun had killed many of his kind, and it was a pleasure he'd long thought lost to him. Only time had taught him otherwise. He lifted his glass to the dawn's light and watched it reflect through the pale amber liquid. Wine was another pleasure he'd thought lost. He'd been told he could only survive by taking the life of others—that anything else would kill him. More lies. His changed metabolism might mean he could consume no food, but it didn't prevent him from taking fluids. Wine would never sustain him, but it couldn't kill him, either.

He took another sip and wondered what had happened to the woman who had turned him. Dublin in the 17th century had been an unforgiving place, and he'd fallen under Elizabeth's spell so very easily. Perhaps he'd just been desperate to escape the emptiness of his existence—even now, he wasn't entirely sure. He had a sudden vision of Nikki, her delicate features and smoky amber eyes, surrounded by a halo of dark hair. In very many ways, she reminded him of Elizabeth.

The sun's light grew stronger. He swallowed the remaining wine in one swift gulp and closed the curtains. As much as he would have liked to watch the flags of dawn color the sky, he had to sleep. There was much to do when night next fell.

***

Nikki drove her old car into the first available parking space near the office. Climbing out was difficult; every battered muscle protested fiercely against movement. Taking a deep breath, she leaned against the car for a moment, waiting for the various aches to subside. The painkillers the doctors had given her were about as useful as a sun hat in a thunderstorm. What she really needed was a nice hot bath and some sleep—nothing too long, just three or four days. She grimaced and turned. Yeah right, that was likely to happen.

A long, white limousine dominated several parking spots out front of the single story building that housed the agency. Monica's father. She grimaced. Just what she needed to finish the perfect evening.

The cool breeze ran around her, rich with aromas from the bakery down the road. She took a deep breath, then sighed in pleasure. Fresh, hot donuts. Was there a better smell on this earth, other than chocolate?

Maybe it was just what she needed. And if nothing else, it would delay the confrontation with Trevgard a good ten minutes.

Besides, she hadn't yet decided what she was going to tell the old fart. Shoving her hands in her pockets, she headed off to the bakery and ordered half a dozen donuts. No doubt Jake would need some form of sweetening if he'd been entertaining Trevgard for any length of time.

Energy boost ready, she finally walked back to the agency.

"Where the hell is my daughter?"

Trevgard's demand hit her the moment she opened the door. His fury hit a second later, as breathtaking as a punch in the gut. Yet behind the bluster, she sensed concern. Trevgard might look and act like an ogre, but right now, he was a man very worried about his daughter.

She shrugged and slammed the door shut. "I don't know." Though it was an honest enough answer, it was one Trevgard was not likely to appreciate.

"Why not? I'm paying this agency damn good money to keep tabs on her."

"Now, John, relax." Jake's voice was at it mildest. A sure sign he'd reached the end of his tether. "Rest assured that we want to find Monica as quickly as you do. Just give Nikki a chance to explain what happened last night."

She dropped the donut box on her desk and walked across to the counter that held the percolator. "For a start," she said, pouring herself a coffee into a mug that had seen better days, "I did find her. She wants be left alone."

"What? Why didn't you—"

"John," Jake warned quietly.

She flashed him a smile of thanks. Trevgard on the warpath was not something she needed right now. The ache in her head was bad enough already.

"I told you before I wouldn't take photos. And I couldn't drag her back with me because she wasn't alone. Her friends were a bit protective."

To emphasize her point, she put down her coffee and took off her jacket. The white blob of the bandages stood out like a sore thumb. Trevgard's rotund face paled, thin mouth twitching slightly. His worry level rose several notches. She wondered how he'd react if she told him four of those protectors were zombies. Yeah, right. After he'd stopped laughing, he'd probably arrange to have her locked away somewhere.

"Are you all right?" Jake leaned forward, blue eyes concerned.

She nodded absently, her attention still on Trevgard. The sooner she could get rid of him, the better. There was a lot she had to tell Jake, and if she didn't get some rest soon, she'd fall where she stood.

"I'll find her again tonight." What she would do when she found her was an entirely different matter.

"And how will you achieve this miracle?" Trevgard asked, tapping stubby fingers against the desktop. "It's taken you nearly a week to get this far."

She raised an eyebrow and glanced at Jake. This one he could field. She wasn't about to explain that their problem hadn't been finding Monica, but rather keeping track of her long enough to talk to her. Their reputation was on the edge where Trevgard was concerned. Any further, and there was a very real possibility he could ruin them. All it took was a word or two in the right places— and Trevgard had them all in his pocket.

"Lyndhurst is a big place, John." Jake's deep voice was calm, despite the flicker of annoyance she saw in his eyes. "We've been using conventional methods up until now to try to track her. Tomorrow night, we'll try something different."

"Like what?"

His gaze shifted between the two of them, distrust evident. But then, he hadn't become a multimillionaire by naively trusting the world. He'd made his money the hard way, trusting few, working long hours and saving every penny. It was a pity his daughter wasn't a little more like him, at least when it came to trusting. Maybe then she wouldn't have gotten so involved with evil.

The image of sapphire blue eyes swam briefly through her mind, and her hand shook, splashing coffee across the carpet. She sat down quickly, hoping Jake hadn't noticed. It would only lead to questions she couldn't possibly answer.

"We'll need something of Monica's. Something she wore quite a lot," Jake said quietly.

"Why?" The older man's question was gruff, full of suspicion.

"Have you ever heard of psychometry?"

"No." Trevgard's gaze narrowed. "Why?"

Jake's smile was so bland, she had to sip her coffee to hide her grin.

"Not many have," he continued. "Psychometry is the ability to hold an object and sense some history of the owner. If the link is strong enough, you can sometimes use the object to trace people."

"Yes? So?"

"So, Nikki has that ability. We think we can use it to trace your daughter."

"Right. And my left foot plays 'Jingle Bells.' What are you two trying to pull?" Heat suffused his cheeks, making them look mottled. And him uglier, if that were possible.

Jake shrugged. "If you don't believe us, why don't you go see Anita Coll? Nikki found her daughter alive and well, two days after the cops had given up looking for her."

Trevgard suddenly looked thoughtful. Definitely no fool, despite outward appearances. He might not like the agency, or their methods, but he would use them—or anyone else— in order to bring his wayward daughter back.

He nodded abruptly. "All right. There's a charm bracelet Monica wore up until a week ago. I'll go get it—but if you think I'm going to let it out of my sight..."

"Fine," Jake interrupted smoothly. "You can be here when Nikki makes the attempt to find Monica."

Nikki opened her mouth to protest, but snapped it shut when Jake glared at her. She sipped her coffee and seethed in silence. Did Jake really expect her to find Monica with

Trevgard breathing down her neck? Her talent wasn't always reliable, and distractions only made matters worse.

Trevgard rose. "I'll go fetch it now, then."

"Fine. But don't bring it back until..." Jake hesitated and she held up her fingers. "About six this evening. Nikki has to rest before she tries this."

The older man grunted and strode to the door, his steps powerful despite his short legs.

"Phew," she said, once he'd gone. "Talk about a powder keg."

"He's worried, believe it or not. But he's definitely in line for a heart attack if he keeps going. " Jake relaxed back into his chair. "And don't say the world would be better off. It's not polite."

"Neither am I." She yawned. "Sorry. It's been a long night."

"So tell me what really happened tonight, then you can go home and rest."

"It's a long story, boss." And not one she was sure she could really explain.

"I have all day, kiddo."

She smiled wryly. That was a lie, and they both knew it. In his early forties, Jake didn't fit the typical image of private investigator. Absent were the scruffy looks, clothes in serious need of an iron and scuffed shoes. Jake's image was more the successful businessman. Not only did it make his clients more at ease, it gave him an extra advantage on the job. His look at the office was never the one he used in the streets.

She dug out a couple of donuts then tossed the box across to him. He caught it deftly and munched in silence as she gave him an edited version of the night's events. The zombies she left out, not sure if she could convince him they really existed. Jake had a hard time believing anything he couldn't see for himself.

He whistled softly when she'd finished. "Sounds like Monica's got herself into something serious."

"It's more than serious. The man she's with...he's evil, Jake. Pure evil." She leaned back in her chair, shuddering at the seductive memory of fiery blue eyes. "I don't think we have a hope of getting her away from him."

He shrugged. "We have to try."

She bit into her doughnut. Yeah, they had to try, but she didn't hold much hope of succeeding. Evil had too strong a grip on Monica now.

Jake rose and poured himself a cup of coffee. "And this man that helped you, Michael Kelly? Where does he fit in?" he asked.

She shrugged. "I don't know."

"There's too much going on here that we just don't understand. I don't like it, Nik."

She struggled to smother another yawn. "Neither do I. Not a lot we can do about it, though."

"I could take you off the case."

"And just who would take it over? You?" She grinned at him. "You're so busy now, you don't have time to scratch."

"This is true." He shrugged. "One of these days I'm going to have to hire myself another investigator." He gave her a sympathetic look as the yawn she'd been fighting broke free. "Why don't you go home and get some sleep? You look dead on your feet."

His words revived memories of the fetid breath and cold flesh of the creatures. She shuddered and rose quickly. "It's an offer I can't refuse. I'll leave the rest of the donuts, in case you want them."

"An offer I can't refuse." He grinned, and helped himself to another donut. "Just make damn sure you're back by six. I might be tempted to murder our client if I have to put up with him for any amount of time tonight."

"Then I'll make sure I'm late," she replied sweetly and stepped out the door before he could throw something at her.

***

In the end, exhaustion and a broken alarm clock made her late getting back to the office.

"And what happened to six o'clock?" Trevgard said the minute she opened the door.

His voice was mild given the anger she could sense in him. She looked at the clock. It was nearing six-thirty, so he had every right to be annoyed.

"What happened?" Jake asked, his irritation undisguised.

She grimaced. "Alarm clock."

Jake just shook his head. He'd been telling her for weeks to replace the damn thing, but she hadn't considered it a priority.

She glanced at Trevgard. "I'm sorry to keep you waiting. Did you bring the bracelet?"

He nodded. "Yes. Jake has it."

Jake gave her the bracelet, sealed in a plastic bag. He knew from past experience that too many people handling an object spoiled her ability to get a strong reading.

She sat down, stomach suddenly churning. She'd done this a hundred times before. It was simple.

Easy.

But never before had her life been at risk.

She frowned at the thought and tore open the plastic, dropping the delicate gold bracelet into her hand. Her skin tingled as she closed her fingers around the charms, pressing them into her palm. Shutting her eyes, she reached for the place in her mind that could call forth the images locked within the bracelet.

Gradually, they came.

A factory. Three floors. Broken windows. Dark. Her mind seized the pictures, storing them for examination at a later point. She had to go with the flow or lose it. She didn't have the strength for a second try.

The smell of the sea...creak of boats. Inside...evil. She recoiled. *Oh God, he's here!*

Panic seized control, and for an instant, the images faltered. Now she understood her earlier intuition. Evil was here in the darkness—and hunting her. Her fingers twitched against the bracelet, but she fought the instinct to break the contact. Time was running out for Monica. She had to find her quickly, and this was the only way of doing it.

And surely the man she feared couldn't harm her spirit. Could he? Sweat broke out across her brow, but she reached again for the images.

Stairs...a basement. Two rooms, three. In the fourth one, Monica. Naked. Unconscious but alive.

Something hit Nikki hard, drawing her into darkness, snaring the very essence of her soul as securely as a fly in a web.

And the spider laughed in demonic delight.

Four

Only the harsh notes of her breathing broke the silence. There was nothing to see, nothing beyond a deep void of darkness. Yet something or someone was near. She rubbed her palms down her thighs and wondered what sort of game was about to be played.

Soft laughter stirred the satin cover of night, filling the void with its corruption.

She closed her eyes. He was here—in the cage that had captured her spirit—and there was no escape. Energy pulsed above her head, a net of power that somehow held her prisoner. If she stayed here too long, she would die.

Was that his aim?

Sweat trickled down her back. Fists clenched, she watched a golden shaft of light spread across the darkness. It revealed a makeshift bed. On it lay Monica.

There was no sense of death, yet she could see no sign of life. It was almost as if the teenager hovered somewhere between the two. Shivering in apprehension, she wondered what other surprises her abductor had in store for her.

As if in answer to her question, laughter slid around her. Heart working overtime, she turned.

He flowed into existence from a patch of midnight, a maneuver that reminded her oddly of Michael. But the man before her now—no, he was more a boy, albeit boy with the physique of a body builder. He appeared maybe fifteen, sixteen years old, but he was strong. Powerful. Hauntingly beautiful...and totally evil.

"Monica is mine."

His whisper sliced through her. "Why are you doing this to her? To me?" Her voice came out high, almost childlike. She swallowed, trying to ease the aching dryness in her throat.

"She has what she wanted." His blue eyes began to change. Began to burn with a sapphire flame.

She licked her lips. "And that is?"

He moved a step closer. Horror held her immobile.

"What do all the vain rich want?" he replied. "Power. Eternal life."

His answer made no sense. "And me?" she asked,

fearing the answer.

"You, my pretty, are the first to ever elude my call."

He reached out, brushing her cheek with a feverish hand. Her skin stung and bile rose in her throat. She longed to run, but even the simple act of breathing had become suddenly difficult. His hand slid lightly down her neck and across her breast. She closed her eyes, digging her nails into her palms to stop herself from screaming. She'd be damned if she'd give him *that* pleasure.

He laughed. Her eyes flew open. Hunger stirred deep in the bright heart of his eyes.

"So brave," he whispered. "So very brave. Our association will be an interesting one indeed."

She shuddered, her mind screaming a denial her lips refused to utter. His gaze became a sapphire blaze.

So bright.

So blue.

She watched, enthralled, as death closed in.

***

Night had settled across cloudy skies when Michael made his way through the last of the stockyards. The cattle had stilled their restless stirring now that he no longer walked among them, and the distant rumble of traffic made little impact on the hush surrounding him.

He reached the last fence and stopped, leaning his arms against the rough railings. The red flare of life burned in the buildings opposite, and his hunger, though sated, stirred sluggishly. He grimaced. Would the desire for the sweet strength of human blood ever leave him? Three centuries had passed, and still the yearning ran through his veins, an addiction that refused to die.

Four men worked within the building, their life forces visible through the large windows. The man he sought was not among them. Not that he expected Jasper to be hiding on the outskirts of the city. His foe had a taste for the high life, even if he hunted easy prey in the poorer areas. Monica was not the first young woman turned by a gentle dance with the devil.

He climbed through the railings, then broke into a run, moving quickly along the road that would take him back to the heart of Lyndhurst. A quick check earlier in the day had revealed that Lyndhurst had five detective agencies.

After three calls, he'd found Nikki's. He glanced at his watch. It was nearly six-thirty—she should be there by now.

What he did then depended very much on Nikki's reaction to him. But one way or another, willing or unwilling, she *would* become his bait.

The sounds and smell of humanity swirled around him as he approached the business district. The streets became crowded, forcing him to slow. He might be able to prevent most people from seeing him, but he couldn't prevent them from feeling the impact of his body if he ran into them. The last thing he needed right now was to stir more hysteria. The recent disappearances of four women had caused enough trouble. Too much more, and Jasper might just leave. Despite his assurance to Seline, he knew Jasper wasn't stupid enough to stick around if hunting became too difficult. There was always another city, another time. Their final battle might be long overdue, but Jasper had time to spare. He would wait until the time was right and the odds on his side.

The building where Nikki worked came into sight. Lights shone brightly through the windows. Nikki was...He stopped abruptly, a cold sensation he might once have named fear running through him.

Energy shimmered across his skin—a powerful cord of evil that held Nikki's mind captive. He took the steps two at a time and opened the door. Two men looked up as he entered. One stood near a desk, the other kneeling beside to Nikki, one hand reaching out—

"Don't touch her!"

"What do you mean, don't touch her?" The blond stranger glared at him. Though he hunched over Nikki protectively, he made no further attempt to touch her.

No fool, this one, he thought and knelt on the opposite side of Nikki's prone body.

"You might kill her," he said tersely, running his right hand a whisper above her body, searching for some chink in the powerful energy shield surrounding her.

He heard the man's sharp intake of breath, but paid him little heed. Nikki's breathing was shallow and erratic, her heart straining under the increasing pressure. A body could survive only so long without the will, the essence, of its being.

If she died, she would be Jasper's.

Power pulsed against his skin like a thousand dancing fireflies. He narrowed his eyes and watched the bright promenade, studying its rhythm. Urgency beat through his heart, but he ignored it. She could die if he hurried—and die if he didn't.

The tempo of the dance faltered, weakening slightly, allowing him access. He reached out to her mind, swiftly following the psychic cord through the darkness.

Fear hit him again when he realized that Jasper was also attempting a mind lock...and that he was close to succeeding.

Nikki, Nikki, don't look at his eyes! He charged the mental shout with all the power he could. He had to break the magnetic hold his enemy had on her mind.

Why?

Her reply was weak, vague. She was so close to giving in, yet in her own way, still fighting. It was a miracle she'd held out as long as she had.

His eyes are so very...beautiful.

No! Nikki, look away!

Confusion stirred through the link, and hope soared within him. The more she fought against the net holding her captive, the weaker it would get. But Jasper was more powerful than he'd realized, if the fiend could hold this net in place and still have the strength to attempt the possession of a mind as strong as Nikki's.

Fight him!

The net trembled, weakening with every second. Yet so was she. Psychic energy burned through him, but he held his weapon in check, denying the impulse to assault the net and destroy his enemy. He didn't understand how the net entwined her mind, and if he tried to destroy it, he might destroy her. He didn't want to do that unless it was absolutely necessary. He would just have to wait, and catch her when she came free. If she came free.

Don't give in, Nikki!

Michael?

Her response was stronger this time. Wisps of urgency shimmered across the net, testing its boundaries, its strength.

A desperate surge of energy ran through the lattice of power, yet Jasper was faltering. A small tear appeared in its fabric. More energy flared through the net, but it was no longer enough to hold her.

Reaching out, Michael pulled her clear. Her spirit entwined with his for an instant, a gentle yet intense caress that shocked him. Then she was gone, and he was back in his body, left with an odd sense of regret.

He opened his eyes and lowered his hand, gently stroking sweaty strands of dark hair away from her closed eyes. That caress...It could get them both into trouble. Whether she knew it or not, she'd created a link that would not be easily broken. It could make things awkward, given that he had no intention of doing anything more than using her to capture Jasper.

She opened her eyes and stared at him blankly. Just for an instant, he saw an echo of evil in the smoky amber depths. How far had Jasper succeeded in his mind lock? There was no way to tell, no way to know until his enemy made his next move.

"Michael?"

"You're safe," he replied softly.

"Need to rest," she murmured, closing her eyes again.

He wasn't surprised. After what she'd just endured, she should sleep a week.

"How is she? Will she be okay?" the blond stranger asked anxiously.

Michael ignored him, focusing instead on the big man near the desk. Frustration, fear and worry were evident in his thoughts, and he was about ready to explode. Slipping into the old man's mind, he ordered him to be silent. Nikki needed attention. He didn't have the time to be involved in a war of words.

"She's fine," he said, returning his gaze to the blond man. "She just needs to rest."

"We'll put her in the room behind you. By the way," he said, "I'm Jake Morgan."

"Michael Kelly." He shook the offered hand impatiently. "Thought you might be. How long will she be out?"

Michael shrugged. "Minimum, a couple of hours. I shall stay and keep watch over her." And what better way to start gaining her trust than by being here, guarding her, when she woke?

Jake nodded, not asking the questions Michael could see in his mind. Instead, he rose and crossed the room to speak to the older man.

Michael slipped his arms under her body and carefully lifted. She was light. Too light, really. How in hell did she manage to maintain the energy needed to feed her psychic gifts when there was so little of her?

He took her into the next room and laid her carefully on the old couch that dominated one wall of the small storeroom. She stirred and opened her eyes.

"Don't leave me," she murmured.

Her gaze was filled with shadows and fear. He smiled and sat beside her. She shifted slightly, using his leg as a pillow. Closing his eyes, Michael carefully reached into her mind, calming the surface turmoil, stilling her fears—at least enough to allow her to sleep peacefully for several hours. That he could do this without her knowing spoke of her desperate need for rest.

He opened his eyes and gazed at her. She looked so young lying there, almost childlike. Yet he'd caught the occasional whisper of thought that spoke of a harsh past. He caressed her forehead, her skin like satin against his fingertips. Though he knew he could not afford to get more involved than he was, he found himself wishing again that he had the time to learn more about her.

But that was a freedom he'd lost long ago, and it was too late now for regrets.

***

Darkness drifted through her dreams. It filled her mind, washing corruption through her soul. She fought it, desperate to be free. Yet she couldn't break the chains holding her captive.

In the distance she heard a voice whisper her name. She turned toward the sound, following it desperately through the darkness.

Awareness surfaced. A door slammed in the front office. Trevgard, Nikki thought, and knew by the sudden leap of tension in the main office that both his patience and his temper were growing thin. She also became aware of Michael, of the firmness of his thigh against her cheek, the gentleness of his fingers caressing her forehead. Of his scent, an odd mixture of spice and earthiness.

Much too aware.

She sat up abruptly. Averting her gaze from his, she pushed her hair back behind her ears. How did you react to a man who had saved your life and yet was still so much of an enigma?

"A simple thank you would be sufficient," he said quietly.

She glanced up sharply. "I've never met anyone who can read my thoughts as easily as you appear able to." Tommy *had* been able to read her thoughts, but not so easily, unless she'd been angry or tired.

Michael shrugged, ebony eyes regarding her warily. "Telepathy is a strong gift in my family. Over the years, I've honed its use."

She had an odd feeling he wasn't speaking of blood relatives when he spoke of family. She frowned, but turned at the sound of approaching footsteps. Jake opened the door and entered the room

"Thought I heard voices," he commented, stopping just inside the doorway. "I hate to have to rush you, Nik, but—"

"Trevgard's getting anxious," she finished with a sigh.

"I just made a fresh pot of coffee. Want a cup?"

"Yes." She tried to ignore the ache that ran through nearly every muscle and pushed to her feet. "Michael?"

"If it's strong and black, I'll drink it."

He stood quickly, touching her elbow as she swayed slightly. She smiled her thanks and moved into the office, aware of Michael close behind her. Ready to catch her if she fell, she thought wryly, though her weakness was no joke.

Jake placed her coffee on the desk. Michael accepted his cup with a nod and sat on the edge of her desk.

Trevgard swung around to face her as Jake returned the coffeepot to the hot plate. "So tell me, did you find Monica or not?"

Nikki sighed. "Yes, I found her." She didn't mention the fact that Monica might be dead. She didn't have the strength to face the old man's fury right now.

"And?" he demanded.

"And I'll try to bring her back with me."

Not alone, you won't.

She looked at Michael warily, wishing she knew more about him. Instinct told her to trust him, yet there was something about him that made her uneasy. She would not refuse his help, however. Nothing on this earth could make her go into that building alone to find Monica. Not with a young madman on the loose, wanting her.

"Then you really can find my daughter?" Trevgard's voice was an odd mixture of hope and anger.

She returned her attention to him. "I think so. I've got a general idea of direction; it's just a matter of driving around until I find the right building."

"Then what went wrong before?" Jake asked, moving back to his desk.

"Ever heard of out-of-body experiences?"

Jake nodded. "Never believed them, of course."

She smiled. He hadn't believed in psychic talents, either, until they'd saved his life. "It was something akin to that. Except my spirit, soul, metaphysical body—whatever you want to call it—was forcibly drawn away from my body and trapped."

"How?"

"I honestly don't know." But she wished she did, so she could prevent it from happening again.

"It took a lot of psychic power to create and hold that net," Michael commented quietly.

Nikki regarded him thoughtfully. "And a lot strength to pull me in. Yet he still had enough left to hold the intensity of the web as long as he did."

Jake's eyebrows rose. "Web?"

She took a sip of her coffee, then nodded. "Yes. A net of some sort held me captive. I don't know what he was trying to achieve. I wasn't really there. He couldn't physically harm me."

Though he could have killed her, had he held the net long enough.

"Control." Michael's expression was grim when it met hers. "He was after control."

"So I wouldn't be able to fight him if we ever met." Cold fear ran down her spine. She had come so close.

"The man's a fiend," Jake swore and rubbed the back of his neck. "I don't suppose you can give a description to the police?"

"Yes. Whether they'll believe it is another matter."

Jake grimaced. "Our reputation's not exactly solid where they're concerned."

Trevgard made no comment, but she knew from the look in his eyes that their reputation was not one hundred per cent where he was concerned, either.

Smiling grimly, she said, "And it's not a man we're after, Jake. It's a boy."

Only Michael showed no surprise. Nikki had a feeling he'd known about the madman's youth long before she had.

"A boy?" Jake asked incredulously.

She nodded. "All of maybe sixteen. As solid as a brick wall and as mad as a March hare."

Jake sighed and scratched at the ginger stubble lining his chin. "Just what we need. Another psychotic in Lyndhurst."

"Lyndhurst specializes in this sort of thing, does it?" Michael asked, the mild amusement in his voice at odds with the sudden interest in his face.

Jake gave him a sour look. "Lately it seems to."

"Enough!" Trevgard's gravely voice cut in. "This is not doing anything to find my daughter."

Though she hated admitting it, he was right. She finished her coffee and rose. Trevgard took several steps forward, his body radiating the anger she could feel in his thoughts. He was ready for a confrontation. Wanted it.

"I'm coming," he announced. "I'll not run the risk of losing her a second time."

His company was the last thing she needed. She'd be too aware of his anger and disbelief to concentrate on the fragile images that would lead her to Monica.

"No," Jake said. "Leave this to the experts."

"And I suppose he's an expert?" Trevgard sneered, jutting his chin in Michael's direction.

"Well, he's not someone I'd tackle on a dark and gloomy night," Jake replied with a wry grin.

Trevgard grunted and looked away. She glanced across at Michael. He stood beside her desk, arms crossed as he regarded Trevgard thoughtfully. He looked casual, yet there was something menacing about him, something that spoke of a fighter ready to step into the ring. He certainly wasn't someone she'd want to tackle on a dark night, either. He met her gaze and raised an eyebrow, a slight smile tugging one edge of his generous mouth. She licked her lips and looked away. Damn. She'd have to remember to watch what she was thinking.

She grabbed her keys and jacket and walked towards the door.

"Remember, use the damn phone," Jake called. "Let me know what's happening."

She acknowledged his order with a wave of her hand, and stepped outside. A blast of wintry air greeted her. She shivered and quickly put on her jacket. Michael stopped beside her, his gaze searching the streets, as if looking for someone. And while the light cotton sweater he wore emphasized the width of his shoulders very nicely, it couldn't have held much warmth. She frowned and hurried down the steps to her car. Lots of people didn't feel the cold, so why was she bothered by the fact that he didn't?

"Would you prefer it if I drove?" Michael asked as she opened the passenger's door.

She hesitated. If he drove she could concentrate on finding the right building, and Monica. Nodding, she handed him the keys, then climbed in and fastened the seat belt.

"Where to?" he asked, starting the car.

She closed her eyes and tried to pin down the elusive images. "Head for the docks. I'll know more when we get there."

"That's not where I expected him to be." He swung the car around and headed east.

An odd prickle of unease ran down her spine. Michael knew her attacker. Knew him well enough to know his habits. "Why?"

He shrugged, "No reason. I just didn't expect him to be there."

"It sounds as if you know him."

"We've met before."

His voice gave little away, and the shadows hid any reaction there might have been in his face. "Then why in hell haven't you said anything before now? You might know something that could have helped Monica—"

"Nothing can help Monica. The child has chosen her own path."

"But before—"

"Was still too late."

"Will you let me finish a damn sentence!" she demanded in exasperation.

Michael smiled slightly but didn't respond.

She chewed her lip absently and studied the street ahead. "Why are you in Lyndhurst?" she asked after a moment.

"I came to Lyndhurst to stop the boy." He met her gaze briefly. "As you have already guessed."

By stop, she knew he meant kill. She shuddered. Was this the darkness she sensed—an ability to kill as easily as he breathed?

"Trust me, Nikki," he said gently. "I'll explain when I am able."

Yeah right, she thought. *Heard that one before.* "Then tell me about yourself."

He hesitated, and in that instant, she sensed he'd give her nothing but lies. He was here for the boy and nothing else mattered. Not her, not anyone.

"I am a bounty hunter, of sorts. I have been on the boy's trail for several years now."

"Why?"

He shrugged. "Because he is a killer who must be stopped."

She frowned. The slight edge in his voice suggested the reason was something more personal. But it was also a warning to go no further.

She returned her gaze to the street, and her stomach lurched. They were nearing the docks. Taking a deep breath, she closed her eyes, reaching for the images of the old building. The certainty of its position came instantly, and with it, fear. *He* was there, waiting for her.

"Turn right into the next street," she murmured, letting her instincts take control. "Then left. We're nearly there."

The smooth surface of the road gave way to uneven bitumen, then the rough timbers of an old wharf. The shadows of the nearby buildings drew close, crowding the narrowing alley. Michael eased the car past a row of Dumpsters then stopped. A building sat before them, squat and ugly.

This was it.

He touched her hand, entwining his fingers briefly in hers. Heat flowed, warming the ice in her veins. "I can go in alone," he said.

She shook her head. She'd never felt afraid of the darkness before, and the boy had somehow taken that from her. One way or another, she had to get it back.

She grabbed the flashlight out of the glove compartment and slowly got out of the car. The wind was bitter, tainted with the smell of fish and putrid rubbish. She dragged the zipper all the way up on her jacket and joined Michael at the front of the car.

Tin rattled noisily along the building's roof, and the wind whistled through the shattered windows lining the first two levels. The distant sounds of traffic were muted, veiled. They might well have been the only two people alive in this part of the world.

"I'll go first, if you like," Michael said, his voice oddly in tune with the strangeness of the night.

"No. Let me lead. I'll feel danger before it approaches."

"I'm not without some abilities of my own."

"But mine—"

"Just follow me, Nikki," he stated in a voice that brooked no argument. "For once in your life let someone else take control."

Anger surged. She clenched her fists, somehow resisting the temptation to throw him in the nearby ocean. "Don't you dare say something like that to me. You know nothing about me—not who I am, or what I've been through."

He studied her for a minute, then nodded. "Fair enough. I apologize. I still intend to lead, however."

She bit back her retort. He'd already moved ahead of her, anyway.

She followed him into the shadows encasing the worn building. It loomed above them like some misbegotten troll frozen in darkness. The forlorn moan of the wind chased goose bumps across her skin. Perhaps it cried for the soul of the teenager locked within. Perhaps it cried for them.

She shivered and rubbed her arms. There was no sense of life within the building. No sense of death, either. She turned on the flashlight. Shattered glass gleamed diamond-bright in the light. Nothing moved except the rubbish sent tumbling along the decaying brick walls.

Yet something waited.

"Nothing waits except the darkness and Monica, Nikki."

He was wrong. Evil had visited this building, even if he wasn't still inside. "I think he's set a trap of some kind."

"Perhaps." His fingers clasped hers gently. "Why don't you remain with the car?"

His hand burned against hers. She squeezed his fingers lightly and shook her head. "I'm no coward."

"I wasn't suggesting you were."

"I know. But I can't back away from this. I won't let him beat me."

Michael nodded and glanced at the doorway. "Shall we go on?"

No.

He looked at her, one dark eyebrow raised in query. She took a deep breath, then smiled. "Lead on."

He didn't let go of her hand, and for that she was grateful. They climbed the front steps. The door opened without a sound, revealing the warehouse's dark interior. The air that rushed out to greet them smelled musty, full of decay. Michael tugged her forward, his steps sure despite the darkness. The flashlight did little good. The night might have been a solid object, for all the impact it had.

After several minutes, she saw a faint gleam of silver in the darkness. Stairs, leading down to a deeper pit of darkness.

Michael hesitated on the top step. Stopping just behind him, she had a sudden sense of him searching the darkness below. Wisps of energy ran through her mind, powerful enough to burn if she tried to capture them.

It was the first time she had some hint of his power, and it made her own seem small by comparison. A man with that much psychic energy could do anything— anything he wanted. An odd sense of foreboding ran through her.

"Monica's downstairs," he murmured after a moment. "Do you still want to go on?"

"Yes." There wasn't a hope in Hades she'd stay *here* alone.

Their footsteps echoed on the metal stairs, a sound

that scraped uneasily across the night. The flashlight flared against the sea of black, yet gave away no secrets.

"Last step," Michael warned softly.

Her foot hit the floor; the wood underneath seemed to give, and she tensed.

"Old flooring," he commented, squeezing her fingers lightly. "It's probably rotted. You'd better wait here while I check it out."

She bit back an instinctive denial and tried to ignore the sense of loss when the warmth of his hand left hers. Holding onto the banister instead, she listened to the soft sound of his footsteps moving away.

"I've found Monica," he called out after a few moments.

She could tell by his tone that he wasn't happy. She swept the flashlight in the direction of his voice but couldn't see anything. "And?"

"She's still warm."

Warm but dead, she knew without asking. She closed her eyes and took a deep breath. If she hadn't been such a coward last night, the teenager might still be alive, safe in her father's house.

"Neither of us had much choice last night, Nikki. Do not condemn yourself for matters that cannot be controlled."

His words failed to ease the guilty ache in her heart. She could have tried harder. Should have tried harder.

"How did she die?" she asked, edging towards the sound of his voice.

His reply was terse. "Blood loss."

The floorboards moved a second time. Frowning, she stopped. Apprehension crawled up her spine, but she thrust it away. Michael had walked across this same floor only a few moments ago. If they had held his weight, surely they'd hold hers.

"He's mutilated her?" she said, praying it wasn't so.

"No."

She took another step. "Then how did she die?"

The floor buckled. Wood groaned, as if ready to collapse. Imagination, she told herself fiercely, and took another step.

The floor bowed again, this time accompanied by an odd cracking sound. Sweat broke out across her brow. She cleared her throat. "Michael, I think something's wrong here."

"What?" His voice was sharp, alert.

"The floor." She frowned and took another small step. The boards seemed to bow even further.

"It's an old building," he reminded her gently. "Who knows what condition the supporting pylons are in."

A plausible enough explanation, but not the answer here. She had the horrible feeling the whole lot was about to disappear beneath her. "It's more than that."

"Don't move, then. I'm coming back."

She swung the flashlight round in a tight circle. There was nothing to see but years of dust, stirred to sluggish life in the wake of Michael's passing. She bit her lip and took one more step.

It was one step too many.

Without warning, everything gave way, and she dropped like a stone into darkness.

Five

Her scream became a grunt when she hit something solid. She gripped the old crossbeam that had stopped her fall, and hoped like hell it would hold. Far below she could hear the cry of the ocean, a siren's song that promised death.

She couldn't swim. Could barely even dog paddle.

There was another crack, then everything around her began to fall again, heading for the deeper pit of darkness opening near her feet

She let go of the flashlight and dove forward, reaching for something, anything, to stop her slide into oblivion. Her hands scraped against wood; she grabbed at it wildly. It shifted under the force of her weight, slipping several feet forward. For one heart-stopping moment, she hung motionless above the black pit, barely daring to breathe.

The wood cracked. She swung forward, desperate to find a more secure hold. Jagged splinters tore at her hands and offered no hope.

"Michael!" Her hands slipped further down the old piece of timber. It cracked again, dropping her several inches closer to the pit and death.

"Nikki!"

She glanced up. He leaned over the pit, reaching for her. She shifted her grip on the timber then lunged for his outstretched fingers. His hand caught hers as more flooring shifted and dropped away.

"Your other arm," he ordered, voice hoarse.

She released the timber and swung towards him. He caught her other hand, his grip like iron as she swung wildly around. The sound of the ocean far below grew stronger.

Inch by precious inch, Michael moved backwards, pulling her with him. As her feet came over the edge of the hole, he stood and dragged her upright. The night whirled briefly, and she closed her eyes, willing the sensation away.

He placed his hand under her elbow and guided her to safety. Dark laughter flickered through her mind. She shivered. Jasper's trap might have failed, but he wasn't finished with her yet. Lord, she felt so cold—not externally. Internally, deep inside her heart and soul.

Michael stopped, forcing her to do the same.

"Are you all right?" He raised her hand, gently running his fingers over hers.

She flinched when he touched several splinters. "Battered and shaking, but otherwise in one piece." Her voice shook slightly, and she took a deep breath, trying to calm the desperate racing of her heart.

"Thank you," she added softly. "That's the second time you've saved my life."

"One more time, and you're mine."

The odd seriousness behind the light remark made her uneasy. She wished she could see his eyes. Wished she could see his thoughts and know what he meant.

"You're bleeding," he said, lightly touching her middle finger.

She frowned. While she had no doubt that she was, how could he tell in the darkness?

"You should go back to the car and tend to these straight away," he continued softly, "or you might risk infection."

"A couple more minutes won't matter. Can you pull the splinters out?"

"I could, but I think it might be wiser if you went back to the car."

Why was he suddenly so determined to get rid of her? "No. I want to see to Monica first."

"There's nothing to see, Nikki. Go back to the car and tend to your hands."

"No." Besides, something warned her not to leave the girl's body with this man. Warned that she might not find it again if she did. An odd thought indeed—what in hell would Michael want with a dead teenager?

"You're a stubborn woman, Nikki James."

She smiled at the hint of exasperation in his voice. He'd only known her twenty-four hours, and already he'd come to that realization. It usually took people far longer to see beneath her polite veneer.

"And this is one of my good days," she replied lightly. "Now, would you please remove the damn splinters?"

"As you wish."

She stared into the darkness and tried counting to one hundred. It didn't work. She could no more ignore the sting in her hands than the warm brush of his body against hers.

"There," he said after a moment. "All gone."

"Good. Now we can go find Monica."

He smiled, though she couldn't say how she knew this. Perhaps it was little more than a quick caress of laughter in her mind. Or wishful thinking.

He placed a hand under her elbow again and led her forward. The smell of decay tainted the air, a smell that had nothing to do with the sea or the rotting rubbish she kept tripping over. It was the smell of death. If only she hadn't dropped her flashlight...

Ahead, moonlight flickered through a few broken wallboards. The darkness shifted slightly, becoming less intense. Shapes loomed—old crates and half-destroyed internal walls. Michael stepped through a shattered doorway then stopped. Monica lay before them, serene and quiet on a battered old mattress.

She looked at peace, Nikki thought. Innocent. Strange how death could be so deceiving.

She knelt beside the teenager's body and gently touched her neck. Though she didn't doubt Michael's word, she couldn't help hoping that perhaps he was wrong.

He wasn't.

Guilt washed through her. This death was partly her fault. If she hadn't given in to fear, the teenager might still be alive.

"Monica chose her fate. Nothing you could have done would have prevented this," Michael stated, kneeling on the opposite side of the body.

She raised an eyebrow at the anger in his voice. Yet she sensed the anger had been aimed at himself, not her. He moved his hand, drawing her gaze back to Monica.

"We should check her body."

"Why? Monica's dead, and as you pointed out, there's nothing much we can do about it now. Let's call the police and let them deal with her."

"I don't think that would be wise right now."

She sighed and rubbed her temples wearily. She had a horrible feeling the night's surprises were not over yet. "Why not?"

"Once I examine the body, I'll explain."

The thought of touching the dead girl any further made Nikki's skin crawl. "What are you looking for?"

He gave her an enigmatic smile, shrugging one shoulder. "Odd marks. A recent knife wound."

She raised an eyebrow and made no comment. Michael brushed the teenager's long hair to one side and bent to study her neck. His frown suggested he wasn't happy with what he found.

She rubbed her arms. "Why are odd marks so important?"

"If I find them, I'll explain." He hesitated and glanced up. "It'll be done a lot quicker if you helped."

Though his tone was even, his irritation seared her mind. She bit her lip, then reached down, gingerly lifting Monica's right arm. The smooth flesh felt cool, like meat just taken out of the fridge. Her stomach turned. They shouldn't be doing this. It was a violation of the dead.

"If she's dead, she can't mind," Michael said.

"Keep out of my thoughts," she snapped, then frowned. "What do you mean, if she's dead?"

"Nothing yet. Keep checking."

"This is definitely not a sharing environment you're creating here, you know," she muttered.

"I never said it would be," he said. "I'm here to catch a killer, nothing more."

And she and Monica were merely the means to the end. The thought annoyed her more than it should have. Lowering Monica's arm to her side, she continued her examination.

No unusual marks appeared to mar the creamy perfection of the teenager's skin. Nikki sat back on her heels. While she would have loved to get out of this building and the death it held so peacefully, she owed it to Trevgard to find out the truth. If she couldn't have prevented Monica's death, she could at least find out why she died—and maybe bring her killer to justice.

The image of sapphire-ringed eyes rose in her mind, and she shivered. If Monica's killer and her own hunter were one and the same, what would she do?

"You'd better come around here and have a look at

what I've found," Michael commented softly.

His face was emotionless, giving no indication of what to expect. She rose and walked around to his side. "Look at what?"

"Her wrist for starters."

He pointed to Monica's wrist; a two-inch cut marred her skin. But the pale color of the scar indicated the wound was at least a week old. She couldn't see how it was related to Monica's death. "And?"

"Now look at her neck."

She squatted by his side. Two small puncture wounds spoiled the white skin. Dried blood ran a dark trail from the wounds and disappeared behind Monica's pale blonde hair.

She froze.

Michael had commented earlier that Monica had died from blood loss, yet there was very little blood near the body and no other obvious sign of injury apart from the wrist and these two wounds. Wounds that looked an awful lot like bite marks. But not from an animal. Not from anything she knew.

She closed her eyes, unable to voice the fear in her mind.

"From a vampire," Michael finished for her.

A fear as ancient as time itself rose, threatening to overwhelm her. She took a deep breath and tried to control the turmoil running panicked circles in her mind. It couldn't be true. Vampires didn't exist, damn it! They were a product of fiction and imagination, *not* reality.

"Just as psychic powers don't exist?" Michael said, voice gentle.

She glanced at him sharply. There was an odd expression on his face, as if her reaction was important in some way. "That isn't the same thing!"

"Why? Many people believe psychic powers to be in the same reality as vampires. Does not believing in them make them any less real?"

"No. But vampires?"

"Look at her neck, Nikki. Remember the man she was with, remember his evil."

She didn't need to remember. All she had to do was close her eyes and his image was there. "Being evil doesn't necessarily make him a vampire."

"No. Drinking blood to survive does that."

She shuddered. Monica looked so young, so peaceful. So very dead. But if what Michael said was true, she would soon become a vampire. All it had taken was one little bite.

"Being the victim of a vampire doesn't mean you become one," he commented softly.

"It does in the movies." She rested back on her heels and rubbed her arms, wondering why the room had suddenly become so cold.

"In real life, one becomes a vampire by sharing the vampire's blood through a special ceremony." Michael shrugged. "And only with consent on both sides."

"Are you saying Monica *wanted* to become a vampire?"

"To some, the lure of eternal life is powerful."

"Not powerful enough, thank you very much." Yet she remembered Jasper's mocking assessment of the rich, and wondered. "Besides, we can't be sure Monica went through this ceremony."

"No. But that cut on her wrist looks ominous."

She studied the half-healed wound. How could you tell an attempted suicide from an incision made during a special ceremony?

"You can't." Michael's voice was grim. "And that is why we must make sure she is dead."

She understood the intent behind his words well enough, even if he didn't come straight out and say it. "Why?"

"If she shared blood, she merely rests, waiting while her body undergoes the transformation."

"And have the movies got the methods of killing a vampire wrong, as well?"

He hesitated fractionally, then shook his head. "No. A stake through the heart will usually kill, as will the midday sun. Decapitation is the best method, though."

She raised an eyebrow. "And this is what you intend for Monica?"

His gaze searched her face. She wondered why. If he read her mind so easily, surely he could taste her anger.

"It is for the best," he said after a moment.

Once again he wasn't telling her everything. "Best for

whom? You, or Monica? What right have you to declare such a judgment on her?"

"I am a hunter of evil, Nikki. I track it and kill it, and in the process make the night a safer place for people like you to walk."

"Don't give me that sanctimonious crap. You haven't the right to touch Monica."

"I must, or she will rise to aid Jasper." This time a hint of impatience colored his quiet words.

Her anger rose another notch. "That is, I gather, the name of the man who is after me."

He hesitated again. She swore and pushed upright, moving to stand near the wall. Wintry air rushed through the shattered window above her head, but it failed to cool the anger heating her cheeks or the turmoil churning her stomach. Michael knew more than just her hunter's name, so why wouldn't he divulge what he knew? A lack of trust, or something more?

She studied Monica again. At rest, the teenager looked untouched by evil. It was easy to understand why Trevgard refused to see his daughter as anything more than innocent. What would she say to him? Or to Jake? How could she face them if she allowed Monica to be mutilated? How could she face herself, in the long years of nightmares left ahead?

"I can't," she stated quietly, finally meeting Michael's watchful gaze.

His anger seared her mind.

"You can't stop me," he warned quietly.

The threat behind his soft words shook her. Though he hadn't moved a muscle, he suddenly seemed so much larger, more threatening. The shadows moved in around him, half hiding his form, making him one with the night and the sense of evil that still haunted the old warehouse. In the blink of an eye, death had stepped into the room and become her companion.

She clenched her fingers, felt energy tingle across her skin. Michael wasn't evil, not in the same sense as the man he'd called Jasper. Yet she couldn't escape the feeling he wasn't entirely on the side of the angels, either.

"Are you willing to kill me to get to Monica?" she said.

His eyes were chips of ebony ice. "Are you willing to die for the sake of evil?"

No. But she refused to stand by and let him mutilate Monica's body, either. She owed her that much, at least. "If that's what it takes, yes."

Anger danced around her. She fought to breathe normally, trying not to show the fear tying her stomach into knots. She had a feeling Michael had spent too many years on his own, owing council to few. Sensed he was a mixture of shades—light and dark, good and bad. She just had to hope the shadows in his soul didn't win here tonight.

"Nikki, if this child becomes a vampire, she will be more dangerous than the man who hunts you. Can you live with the death of innocents?"

She stared at him. How could anyone be more dangerous than the man he'd called Jasper?

"I've been hired to find Monica and take her back to her father—in one piece. I'm just trying to do my job."

"And if she does turn?"

"I'll deal with it if it happens."

A wave of fury rocked her back on her heels. The darkness crackled with energy and the sense of impending doom. She stood her ground, not giving in to fear.

"You have no real concept of what you're letting loose," Michael said, dark eyes glacial. The shadows around him began to retreat, but not the immediate feel of danger. "Perhaps it is time for you to learn."

For an instant he became something more than human, something akin to the evil that stalked her. Her heart began to pound rapidly, a cadence that filled the tense silence. Something glimmered in his eyes, an echo of the depravity she'd seen in Jasper's vibrant gaze.

Michael wasn't evil. Yet she couldn't escape the notion that her hunter and Michael were, in some way, connected. Damn it, she really had to find out more about both of them.

"What do you mean?" she asked quietly. Energy flowed across her fingers, yet she held her weapon in check. She was not about to fire the first shot and create a war she had no hope of winning.

"Nothing. We will wait, as you wish." He shrugged and looked away.

Hiding his eyes, she thought, as he rose. The shadows no longer wrapped themselves around his body, and the impending sense of doom had fled with them. Yet the night still ran with uneasy tension.

"Come," he continued. "Let's go back to your car and call the police."

Though there was no emotion in his voice, there was still an edge of violence in his actions. This man had saved her life twice, yet she knew nothing about him—nothing beyond the fact he could be very, very dangerous.

He turned to look at her, his eyes coal black wells that told her little. Yet a flicker of emotion from his mind suggested her distrust annoyed him.

"You have my word that I will not, in any way, touch or move Monica tonight. Is that enough?"

His soft tone hinted at anger, yet she heard no lie in his words. She nodded. After tonight, Monica would be in police hands. There was little he could do to her then.

"I shall lead, if you wish," he said, and offered her his hand.

Why the sudden formality? Was it anger, annoyance, or something else entirely? The warmth of his fingers enclosed around hers, but a chill raced through her heart. This man was dangerous, in more ways than one. Yet she felt oddly safe with him.

She just had to hope this wasn't one of those rare moments when her instincts made a complete and utter hash of everything.

And that he wasn't right about Monica.

***

Michael crossed his arms and watched the two men bag the body. Even from this distance he could hear the slow but steady beat of her heart. It was a gentle rhythm few humans would ever pick up, just a single beat every few minutes. His was much the same, except in times of stress or feeding. The lack of life flowing through one's body was one of the penalties of being a vampire.

He had no doubt the teenager would soon rise. Though it usually took a minimum of forty-eight hours, Monica appeared to be taking the change faster than most. She'd probably wake with the onset of the new night.

He should have killed her. What on earth had possessed him to make such a rash promise? All too often he had witnessed the bloody rampages of the newly turned. When the depth of malice and hate were as great as those he sensed in Monica, it was sheer madness to let them live. But he'd given his word to Nikki, and he intended to keep it. Whatever the consequences.

He had a sudden image of Nikki, face white and eyes wide with fear, and frowned. He'd come too close to losing control tonight. Had he been alone so long that a simple act of defiance could tip him over the edge?

Or was he so used to forcing others to obey his will that it was something of a shock to find someone who could defy him?

He sighed and rubbed a hand across his eyes. Whatever the reason, it didn't alter the fact he'd have to watch himself. He'd spent too long mastering the darkness. The last thing he needed right now was to let that control slip, especially when he was hunting someone like Jasper. The fiend would exploit any weakness he could.

The two men placed the teenager's body on a trolley and wheeled her through the door. He followed them into the alley.

Several police officers were still questioning Nikki. He moved to one side, out of her line of sight, but her awareness washed over him anyway. He leaned a shoulder against the building's concrete wall. How could she track him when few could? Was it just her extraordinary psychic abilities, or had the brief moment of their spirits touching formed a connection far stronger than he'd thought possible?

The sea breeze swirled, running chill fingers through his hair. Michael frowned and studied the distant shadows. A faint hint of evil mingled with the smell of the sea.

Jasper had returned. He fought the urge to go after the fiend, and looked at Nikki. The police officers dwarfed her, but they'd be no protection when it came to Jasper. Or the zombies. Either of them could kill her before the cops knew something was wrong.

He glanced at his watch and raised an eyebrow in surprise. It was well after four. They'd been here for nearly three hours now. How many times could the police hear the same version of the same story? Couldn't they see how tired she was? He was tempted, very tempted, to come out of the shadows and ask what in hell was going on—only the fact the police where bound to start asking *him* questions stopped him. His years of hunting evil had made him a lot of enemies. He wanted his whereabouts unknown to all except those he could trust.

The number of which he could count on one hand.

After a few more minutes, the two officers moved back towards the warehouse. He waited until they'd disappeared, then pushed away from the shadows and walked across to her.

"Have they finished?" He kept a careful eye on the old building. He didn't want the policemen suddenly returning and spotting him.

Dark rings shadowed her eyes, and her nod was barely visible. A stray wisp of hair fell across her eyes, and he had to restrain a sudden urge to tuck it back behind her ear.

"They asked me not to leave Lyndhurst. Looks like I'm a suspect, as usual."

"And a pretty grubby one, at that." He smiled at her startled look. "Do you wish to go home, or to the office?"

"Home. They let me call Jake earlier and tell him what's going on."

"Shall I drive again?"

She shook her head. "No, I'm fine."

She looked close to exhaustion, but he handed over the keys anyway. She unlocked the passenger's door, then moved around to the other side. Michael climbed in, studying the distant darkness carefully. Jasper was still there, still watching. Hopefully, he'd follow.

Nikki fired the engine and turned the car around. Across the silence came the sound of another car starting.

He smiled grimly. Jasper's behavior was sometimes too predicable. Once Nikki was safely home, Michael could resume his hunt.

"Penny for them," she said softly.

He glanced across at her. Moonlight gilded her dark chestnut hair and softened the planes of her angular features. She was truly beautiful. A jewel he could not afford to touch.

He cleared his throat and glanced out the window. "How safe is your house?"

"It's actually Jake's old house, which he divided into apartments. It has lots of locks, I can assure you."

Which Jasper could pass with ease if she uttered the

right words. "I was thinking in terms of help if Jasper's friends turn up."

She gave him a quick smile. "I can scream very loudly."

He controlled the impulse to return her smile and watched the amusement fade from her eyes.

"I have my abilities," she stated quietly. "I can protect myself."

The hint of uncertainty behind her words suggested she wasn't as confident as she sounded. "And neighbors?"

"An old couple above me and a drunk below. Not what I'd term reliable help in this sort of situation."

Not what he'd term reliable help in *any* sort of situation.

"I'll be fine," she asserted softly. "I've been in worse situations, believe me."

Her bleak tone stirred his curiosity. What could be worse than a vampire and his undead after your body and soul? "Such as?"

She glanced at him, amber eyes suddenly as unreadable as her thoughts. "When you tell me your secrets, I'll tell you mine. We're here."

She stopped the car in the driveway of an old Victorian. Michael climbed out and studied the building. A good coat of paint and a gardener could have done wonders for the look of the place. But no amount of paint could help the rot setting into the windows or the door frame. Neither would hold Jasper back for more than a minute.

"Would you like to come in for a cup of coffee? I've got some of the best Mocha you've ever..." Her voice faded, eyes widening slightly as she stared at him.

As if she'd suddenly realized her impulsive invitation had just given him unlimited access to her home.

He smiled and reached out, tucking the stray stand of hair back behind her ear. She shivered slightly at the brief caress, but didn't retreat.

"Thanks, but I'd better not. You need to rest."

"True." She gave him a smile that was more nerves than warmth, but her gaze went beyond him, studying the night.

He knew then she'd sensed Jasper's presence.

"Nikki." He touched her arm lightly, felt the tremor that ran through her body. "I'll stop him, whatever it takes. He will not touch you. Ever."

Empty words, when Jasper's darkness had touched her already. He couldn't prevent it happening again, and in many respects, didn't want to. She was still his best hope of getting Jasper quickly.

Her gaze searched his face, curious and afraid. "Why do you do this? Why do you risk your life for me?"

He shrugged. "I don't really know."

She sensed the lie. He could see it in her eyes. But he couldn't tell her the truth—that he was using her to find Jasper. He didn't want to hurt her that way.

He ran his hand down her arm and gently clasped her hand. Her pulse skipped a beat, then began to race. Fear had no part of this reaction, just as it had no part in his own. "I shall see you tomorrow evening."

He raised her fingers to his lips and kissed them gently. She smelled of honey and cinnamon. Of life.

Everything he longed for but had long ago lost. He released her hand and stepped away, moving back into the darkness of the ill-lit street. Her gaze followed him for a while, then she turned and moved silently into the house.

He stopped and spun his senses into the night. Jasper was a half block away. Michael smiled grimly and cast a final glance at Nikki's apartment. He doubted Jasper would risk an attack with the remaining two zombies, not with dawn so close, and despite his efforts earlier this evening, Jasper hadn't succeeded in getting a firm enough grip on Nikki's mind to exert any sort of control over her. Not enough to force her to utter the words that would give him access to her home, anyway. For the moment, she was safe enough.

Time to hunt the hunter.

Six

The shadows in her room were filled with demons, insubstantial creatures that mocked and threatened from the safety of the gathering darkness. Nikki swallowed and slowly reached under her pillow. Her fingers touched the blade of the old silver knife she'd left hidden there, and cold fire leaped across her skin. The demons fled the shadows, and the room became her own again.

Shifting slightly, she turned on the bedside lamp. Pale light filled the room, but did little to ease the fear sitting like a rock in the pit of her stomach. If Jasper could haunt her dreams and send images to taunt her, could he do more? Could he somehow control her?

She raised the knife still clenched in her hand. Light reflected brightly off its tarnished surface. It was part of an old setting she'd found in a second hand shop some time ago. She had no idea how much silver the knife actually contained, and no idea if it would be of any use against Jasper. Yet it had felt oddly comforting to have it under her pillow last night. She studied the shadows still crowding the far corners. There wasn't a doubt in her mind that holding it had somehow made the demons disappear. Just as it had forced Jasper's whisperings from her mind.

Shivering, she rose and padded barefoot across the dusty floorboards to open the curtains. The fading afternoon sunlight streamed into the room, chasing away the shadows and the lingering remnants of her dreams.

If the gathering clouds were anything to go by, the night was going to be a bitch. The wind stirred the nearby oak, scraping branches against the windowpane and chasing shadows across the footpath below. People wearing heavy coats hustled by, intent on getting home before the threatening rain hit.

She crossed her arms and leaned against the windowsill. If Jasper was a vampire, as Michael insisted, how was he able to send her images during the day? Weren't vampires little more than corpses during the sunlit hours?

Maybe a quick trip to the library was in order. Her knowledge of vampires amounted to little more than what she'd seen on the movie screen. Which was pretty much all crap, if Michael were to be believed.

Goose bumps chased themselves up her arms, due more to the chill in the air than the fear sitting like a lump in her stomach. She turned and grabbed her robe. What she needed right now was coffee to warm her up.

She headed for the kitchen, turning on the lights as she went. To hell with the power bill tonight. She made a coffee, then leaned against the bench, idly watching her eccentric old neighbors jog past. The light outside had almost faded. She'd have to get moving or she'd be late for work—again.

The hairs on the back of her neck prickled a warning. Smiling, she reached for the phone. "Evening Jake."

"I wish you wouldn't do that. It's very annoying."

Background noise told her he was calling from his car. She frowned and glanced at her watch. It was nearing six o'clock, so he had to be on his way home. What was so important that it couldn't wait until he got there?

"Hey, it's one of the reasons you employ me, isn't it?"

"Yes. And it's still annoying."

The tone of his voice told her it had not been one of his better days. "What's the matter?" she said lightly. "Mary threaten to divorce you again?"

"Worse. Monica Trevgard just walked out of the morgue."

Nikki closed her eyes and tried to control a sudden burst of panic. Now that the impossible had happened, what in hell was she going to do?

"Did you hear me Nikki? I said..."

"I heard." She rubbed a hand across her eyes. They had to stop Monica, obviously. But where would a newly turned vampire go?

Home.

Michael's thought cut through her mind, knife-edged with anger. Though he had every right to be, she was suddenly glad his thoughts held a hint of distance. Monica was loose because she'd refused to believe. Yet even knowing the truth, could she have stood by and let him sever the teenager's head? She shivered and thrust the image from her mind.

Why home? She asked in confusion.

Because she must...As she must kill soon.

A chill ran through her soul. It was no secret that Monica hated her father. Trevgard was in danger.

"Still with me, Nik?"

Jake's voice made her start. She clenched her fingers against the phone. "Yes. And we have big problems."

"Nothing compared to the coroner's, I'd say."

"Wrong." She rubbed her eyes again, hoping the niggling ache behind her left eye didn't mean yesterday's headache was returning. "Where are you at the moment?"

"Corner of Jackson and Pacific."

"Then you'd better swing around to my place and pick me up. We have to get to Trevgard's. I'll explain why when you get here."

Nikki, no!

She ignored Michael and hung up the phone. She finished her coffee in several gulps that burned her throat, then walked back into the bedroom to get dressed.

Damn it, woman, wait for me. You have no idea...

It's my responsibility, she reminded him, quickly strapping her spare set of knives onto her wrists.

Don't go alone. Wait for me.

No.

She collected her coat off the chair, then grabbed her keys and a small flashlight. At the front door, she hesitated, then turned and moved back into the bedroom. Rummaging quickly through her jewelry box, she found the small silver chain and cross Tommy had given her so long ago. Bitter memories rose, but she shoved them away and clipped the chain around her neck. She had no idea if a cross would offer any protection against vampires, but, like the knife earlier, she felt safer with its coldness pressed against her skin.

Jake's sleek silver Mercedes pulled up as she stepped outside.

"What in hell is going on?" he growled once she'd settled into the front seat. "Why is it so important for us to get to Trevgard's?"

She grimaced. How did you sanely approach the subject of vampires? "I left out a few details about Monica when we talked last night."

"Like what?" The look he cast her simmered with annoyance.

She hesitated, then shrugged. Perhaps a direct approach was best. "Did the police happen to mention the manner of Monica's death when they interviewed Trevgard?"

"No."

"It was blood loss."

He gave her a quick, surprised look. "The creep cut her up?"

"No. Her body was hardly marked, in fact."

"Nikki—"

There was no avoiding the subject. "She only had two marks on her body. A small cut on her wrist that was days old and almost healed."

"And?" he prompted, when she hesitated.

"Two small puncture marks on her neck." She glanced across and met his brief, puzzled look. She must have given Michael the same sort of look.

"Am I supposed to read something significant into that statement?"

"Think, Jake. Blood loss...Puncture marks?"

"Jeez..."

The car swerved violently as he jerked around in surprise. Swearing under his breath, Jake battled to get the vehicle under control then pulled over to the side of the road.

"Now," he said, applying the hand brake before twisting around to face her. "Are you trying to tell me Monica was killed by a vampire?"

"Yes."

"A *vampire*?" He stared at her. "You really believe Monica was killed by a vampire?"

"Yes. I saw the body, Jake. Apart from the puncture marks, the only other wound was days old and almost healed. Yet there was no blood, in or out of the body."

He snorted. "Your psychic senses are now telling you how much blood someone has in their body? Give me a break, Nik."

She smiled grimly. "If you don't believe me, why not call your friend at the morgue?"

He reached for the phone. She stared out the window, watching the traffic roll past. They really had to move if they wanted to save Trevgard from his daughter's anger.

"They never had a chance to perform an autopsy," Jake said, as he hung up the phone.

"I'm afraid that's not the end of it."

"There's more?"

She nodded. "The walking dead."

"As in, zombies?"

Though his voice was flat, she could see the disbelief in his eyes. "As in. I think there are at least two running around."

"Have you been smoking funny weed or something?"

"You know I haven't smoked in years, Jake. Nor have I gone insane."

He shook his head. "Psychic abilities I can believe in. Maybe even ghosts and extraterrestrials. But vampires? Zombies? No way, Nik."

How could she possibly convince him? He had to be ready for what they might face at Trevgard's tonight. And yet, if she hadn't seen Monica's lifeless body last night, she'd probably have a hard time believing it herself.

"You've trusted my intuition before, Jake. Please, just trust me one more time."

He rubbed the back of his neck uneasily. "But Dracula's only a piece of fiction. And zombies...well, I know some Polynesian Islanders will swear to their existence, but this is Lyndhurst."

"So how do you explain the lack of blood in Monica's body?"

"There's no evidence to back up your story, Nik. And how in hell would I know anyway? But it wasn't a vampire. It just wasn't."

"There's no other reasonable explanation."

"A vampire is not what I'd term reasonable. Hell, for all we know, we've got some nut loose who enjoys draining blood from his victims."

Which was an apt enough description of Monica's lover. "So how do you explain Monica walking out of the morgue tonight?"

"I can't." His expression was determined as it met hers. "But it wasn't caused by vampirism."

Nothing she could say would convince him otherwise. He had to see it for himself. "Okay, but we still have to get to Trevgard's."

"Why?"

"She hates her father, Jake. Trevgard was probably the only person in town who didn't know it. I've got a real bad feeling that it's payback time tonight."

"Trevgard's got guards all over the place," Jake muttered, but threw the car into gear and sped off.

She sighed in relief. He might not believe her, but at least he still trusted her instincts. She just had to hope they didn't arrive too late.

"I don't suppose you brought your gun?" Jake said, after a moment.

She shook her head. "You know I won't use it. It's locked up at home. Besides, bullets don't kill vampires."

"Might if you blow their freaking' heads off," he said, voice grim. "So, where's the boyfriend tonight?"

"Michael's not my boyfriend." And never likely to be. He held far too many secrets, was too much of a loner. And far, far too much like Tommy.

"If chemistry's anything to go by, he will be. Where is he?"

She shrugged. "I don't know."

He wasn't far, though. Somewhere, somehow, he was tracking her, furious because she'd refused to wait.

"Odd that he only turns up at night." Jake gave her a sardonic look. "He's not a vampire, too, by any chance?"

"Not likely." Yet the darkness in his soul haunted her, and she couldn't help shivering.

It took them ten minutes to get to Trevgard's. Jake turned into the driveway then stopped. Nikki bit her lip and studied the dark gates before them.

"No lights," Jake commented, peering through the windshield.

"No guard." She stared at the gatehouse, as dark as the night itself. "I've got a very bad feeling about this."

She wished Jake would just turn around and drive away, before it was too late. But it was her fault Monica was loose. If she had allowed Michael his way last night...the thought stalled. No, she'd had no option last night, just as she had none now. Jake couldn't go in alone, and the police had no idea what they were up against. Even if she told them, they'd never believe her.

"I guess we'd better check it out," she said softly.

He nodded. "Gloves on. We don't want the police finding our prints if things have gone bad in there."

She dug her spare pair out of the glove compartment. Slipping them on, she slowly climbed out of the car. The gentle purr of the engine had little impact on the blanket of silence holding the night captive. Jake slipped his gun from its holster and held it by his side. She followed, energy crackling around her fingertips, ready to use.

Jake tapped lightly on the glass front of the guard's box. "Anybody home?"

No one answered. The wind whistled lightly through the darkness, rattling the branches in the nearby trees. Where the heck was the guard? Had he answered a distress call from Trevgard, and if he had, why weren't the lights on ahead?

Jake nudged her then pointed to the left. She nodded and edged carefully around the small building, every sense alert to the slightest movement. But there was no sign of life, no sign of activity. She found the door. Locked.

After a few seconds, Jake joined her.

"The gate's locked."

"So's this door. Shall we break in?"

"It's either the door or the gates." He shrugged and met her gaze. "I'm beginning to agree with your very bad feeling. I don't think we can wait for the cops."

She nodded and sent a bolt of kinetic energy at the door. It crashed back on its hinges.

"Handy little trick," Jake said. "But it would be nice if you could learn to make a little less noise."

"Sorry. It's just nerves." She shrugged and waved him through first. After all, he had the gun.

He stepped through almost tentatively. "I can't see anyone. Let's find some lights and see what's going on."

She lurched forward and grabbed his arm. "Don't. Car lights Monica might ignore if they go no further than the drive. These lights are a different matter."

Yet if Monica really were a vampire, wouldn't she sense their presence anyway? Just how close to reality did the movies come? She released his arm. "I have a flashlight."

Though it was little more than palm size, it provided enough light to see why no one made a fuss about them breaking in. The guard was here, all right, but dead.

Nikki handed Jake the light and shoved her hands in her pockets to hide their sudden shaking.

"If this is Monica's handiwork, she's one angry teenager," he said, kneeling next to the body.

He pointed the light towards the guard's neck—or what remained of it. She swallowed and turned away.

"There's not enough blood," Jake muttered. "With a wound this bad, there should be more blood."

Sweat broke out across her brow. "Monica's a vampire, remember."

"Or completely over the edge." He rose, face ashen. "We'd better move if we want to stop her. She can't be too far ahead of us."

She retreated out the door, studying the still darkness. Jake pressed one of the buttons in front of the guard's chair, and the huge gates silently opened. Hell, making them welcome.

And if the guard was any indication, the mansion had indeed become hell for its occupants.

They climbed back into the Mercedes and drove on without the headlights. The night closed in around them, oppressive and still.

Through the trees, yellow light winked, starlike, from one window on the upper floor. The rest of the mansion was dark.

"Trevgard's butler has his quarters at the far end," she commented. "Should we check that first?"

"After what she did to the guard, I'd say yes. She's obviously not being selective tonight." He stopped the car and gave her a grim look. "I'm calling the cops, too."

"Good." After discovering the guard, they had no real choice. She climbed out. Nothing moved. The night was still, and the air held the promise of rain. Her psychic senses could find no trace of life, not even in the butler's section. If Trevgard was here, he no longer lived.

"He's not here," a soft voice behind her said. "And two servant's lie dead inside that house."

Nikki jumped violently and swung around. Michael stood two feet away, arms crossed as he stared at her.

"Why didn't you wait, as I asked?" His voice was flat, devoid of the anger she could feel in his thoughts and all the more frightening because of it.

"This is my fault, and my problem to deal with." She watched him uneasily. The darkness shifted in his eyes, becoming stronger. Just how different was he from the man he chased?

Jake approached, and Nikki was suddenly glad he was there. Though she doubted he'd be much protection should Michael attack.

"Michael," he said, surprise edging his voice. "Glad you could join us."

He stopped next to her, close enough for their shoulders to rub. Nikki wondered if he could sense her uncertainty about Michael.

"I got here as soon as I could. But not soon enough, I fear."

Jake barely glanced at the house. "It would be nice to know if Monica's inside or not."

Michael's face was expressionless. "She's not here at the moment. I would sense her."

Jake raised an eyebrow. "How?"

"Nikki's not the only one with psychic abilities."

"Really? And do these said abilities make you move faster than a car? Because you certainly didn't arrive in one."

"No, I didn't." Michael's voice held an edge of annoyance. "Nor do I fly. We waste time, here. Monica's killing spree has only just begun. We have to stop her."

Nikki pushed the hair out of her eyes. "To stop her we have to find her. Unless you have some means of tracking her, I have to get inside that house and grab something of hers."

"I can trace her, to a certain extent. " Michael hesitated, then frowned. "If you enter the house, she'll know. It's home ground, the place she lived most of her life. She's still connected to it."

"Another one who believes in vampires," Jake muttered.

Nikki ignored him. "Is it true a vampire can't cross a threshold uninvited?"

Michael nodded. "Yes, but the rule doesn't work when it's your own threshold."

"Oh."

She glanced uneasily at the mansion. Monica had to be stopped before she could kill again. If she wasn't here, they had to find her. Which meant *she* had to go in and steal something still holding the teenager's psyche. She doubted Trevgard would actually lend them another bracelet.

She shoved her hands into her jacket pockets and glanced at Jake. "Let's get this over with."

They walked to the far end of the house. Jake climbed the steps and approached the side door cautiously. Something flickered through her mind, a specter of darkness, of death. She studied the brightly-lit windows above them.

The servants haven't been dead long.

Surprised, she looked at Michael. *How can you tell something like that?*

I can smell the blood.

His eyes were icy pools that somehow intensified, washing darkness through her mind. Dizzy, she reached out, catching his arm. A shock of electricity ran through her fingers, and a haze filled her vision. Suddenly, their minds merged, for an instant becoming one. She could see the bodies in the room above, feel the cooling heat of their flesh, could almost taste the sweet dark pools of blood—her stomach rose. She blanched, shuddering.

Michael shattered the contact between them. She staggered away from him, one hand held to her throat. Dear God, what sort of talent was that?

"Don't ever do that again, Nikki." His voice was gentle, but there was both surprise and anger in his expression. "It's far too dangerous for you."

He didn't explain how it had happened or why it was dangerous, and she didn't dare ask. Something told her she might not like the answers.

"The door's locked," Jake said into the silence.

She turned away from Michael and gave another mental push. The door opened gently, and Jake raised a surprised eyebrow.

She shrugged in reply and climbed the steps. Warm air rushed past her legs as she stopped in front of the open door. Light filtered down the stairs at the far end of the hall, but the rest of the house was a no-man's-land of uneasy shadows.

Jake turned on the flashlight and swung the beam left

to right, searching the darkness.

"Nothing." His voice was hushed, as if he too sensed death waiting. "I guess we'd better check upstairs."

She fought the sudden rise of her stomach. Death waited upstairs, and she really didn't want to face it again. "After you."

"I cannot go inside," Michael said quietly. "While you two can give a plausible enough excuse for being here, I can't. I'll wait here and watch for Monica."

Jake motioned her to hurry. She hesitated, glancing back at Michael. "And if she eludes you?"

"I'll warn you," he replied. "And I want you out fast. Remember, she'll be quicker than a rattlesnake and twice as deadly."

"Thanks. I really needed to know that."

He shrugged. His eyes were as frightening as the house. "Go. Just take care."

After a second's hesitation, she stepped through the doorway and followed Jake. They climbed the stairs. At the top, death waited.

"Shit," Jake said, and stopped in the doorway of the first room.

Though warned by the images she'd shared with Michael, her stomach still turned. The bodies were a twisted mass of flesh that no longer resembled anything human. Blood lay everywhere. If it hadn't been for the bits of humanity scattered about, it would have been easy to think some kid had gone wild with a can of red paint.

"Monica obviously had more than one score to settle." Jake took several steps into the room. "And for a vampire, she's damn messy."

Nikki gave him a sharp glance. His ironic half smile told her he was only trying to make a tough situation somewhat easier. Told her he still refused to believe Monica was a vampire. He picked his way through the smashed furniture and knelt next to what was left of the butler. Why, she had no idea. Certainly there was no hope of life in what was left of him.

Grab some of the wood.

She frowned. *Why in the hell would I do that?*

It's wood, Nikki. Michael's mental tone was brusque. *Deadly to vampires in any form.*

She picked up the smashed leg of a chair. A little too thick perhaps, but nicely jagged at one end...She blanched and almost dropped it. Where the hell had that thought come from?

Keep it. You have no other way to protect yourself should Monica attack.

I can run.

She is the wind.

She clutched the leg tightly. Jake rose from examination of the old man's body, his face pale.

"Well, if she used a knife to create this mess, there's certainly no immediate evidence of it." He ran a hand through his hair. "The police are going to love this."

"We have to stop her, Jake, not the cops." She motioned towards the two bodies. "They won't understand what they're dealing with."

"Nikki, we're not even sure what we're dealing with."

She shrugged. If the sight of these bodies didn't convince him, nothing would.

"We still have to find something holding Monica's vibes."

"We'd better be out of this house before the cops and Trevgard get here," Jake muttered sourly. "Or there will be hell to pay."

"Especially when he discovers his precious little daughter has become a vicious killer."

"There's no direct evidence that it's Monica, Nik. Remember that." He motioned her out the door. "If I recall rightly, the bedrooms are situated at the other end of the house."

She followed him back down the stairs, glad to be free of the room and the nauseous smell of death.

Monica's on the prowl, Michael's warned softly. *She's heading toward the house.*

Can you stop her?

Only if you want me to sacrifice Trevgard. He's cruising up the driveway.

Hell. Nikki massaged her temples. This was all they needed. *Look after Trevgard. We'll grab what we need and get out of here.*

Hurry Nikki. You haven't much time.

Jake touched her arm, and she started.

"You all right?"

She licked her lips and nodded. "Monica's heading our way."

He didn't question her certainty, which was just as well. How could she possibly explain her connection to Michael, when in all the time Jake had known her, she'd never been able to do more than read a fleeting word or emotion?

"If the kid comes near us, I'll blow her head off," Jake warned, drawing his handgun.

"The police will just love that." And there was every possibility that Jake would never even see her. Not if what Michael said about her speed was true.

"To hell with the police. The girl's a nut."

"Thought you said there was no direct evidence that she's the culprit?"

He quirked an eyebrow at her. "I did. That doesn't mean I believe she's innocent."

If what she had heard about the teenager on the streets of late were to be believed, Monica hadn't been innocent for a very long time.

The flashlight beam was faint, barely penetrating the shadows. She turned on the lights as they went through each room, knowing the time to worry about discovery had passed. Trevgard would know something was wrong; the guard and the open gates were the giveaway there. And Monica would sense them regardless. At least the light banished the shadows, made the house appear less threatening.

They made their way quickly through the house and up another flight of stairs. Nikki entered the first bedroom. It had to be Monica's—she couldn't imagine Trevgard surrounded by flowery wallpaper.

Monica's coming fast. Whatever you want to do, do it now.

Trevgard? She held out her hand, palm down, and walked past the dressing table, trying to find a response from the jewelry scattered there.

Out of action but safe. She's in the house, Nikki. Move.

She couldn't. Not till she found something to track Monica with.

You won't need it if you don't get out of there!

She ignored him. Her palm tingled when she walked

past the bed. Kneeling, she looked underneath. Something glinted in the darkness. Reaching out, she grabbed the locket from its bed of dust. Then she rose and glanced across at Jake.

"I've got what we need, but Monica's in the house."

"Then let's go." He raised his gun and led the way back into the hall.

She's near the stairs—coming up. Nikki, get out. Get out now.

How? She practically screamed the question. The stairs were the only way out.

The windows—smash a Goddamn window, just—watch out! She's...

She cut Michael from her mind and spun. A slender figure materialized behind her. Their gazes met, and Nikki stepped back. Monica's face was bloody, her mouth a thin line of rage. But her eyes were the most frightening. The bright blue depths had lost all hint of humanity.

Jake cursed and fired the gun. Faster than the wind, faster than any bullet, Monica winked out of existence.

Only to reappear behind Jake.

"Look out!" Nikki screamed, and blasted him with kinetic energy, thrusting him out of Monica's way.

The gun fired as he fell, the bullet smashing a mirror down the far end of the hall.

The teenager shrieked and lashed out at Nikki. The blow smashed her sideways. She hit the wall hard, her breath leaving in one gigantic whoosh. Blinking back tears, she shook her head and struggled into a sitting position.

Monica leaped at her. Cursing loudly, Nikki hit out with the chair leg. The teenager twisted away from the blow and threw up her arms to protect her face. The jagged edges tore into her arm. Screaming in fury, Monica leaped again. Her weight hit like a ton of bricks, pinning Nikki to the spot. Razor sharp teeth gleamed brightly in the darkness; her breath was fetid, full of death. Gagging, Nikki grabbed the teenager's arms, desperately holding the twisting, snarling girl away from her neck. Energy burned through her body. The bolt hit Monica and flung her away. As agile as a cat, she landed on her feet and surged forward again.

Nikki scrambled out of her way and reached for another

kinetic lance. But the girl stopped, eyes suddenly distant. It was almost as if she was listening to someone.

Jasper, Nikki thought with a shiver. A hint of petulance ran across Monica's face. It was an odd reminder that this was still a sixteen-year-old girl, whatever else she might have become.

With another snarl of rage, Monica turned and threw herself at Jake. They went down in a heavy tangle of arms and legs.

Nikki hit the teenager with another kinetic lance, forcing her down the stairs, away from Jake. Monica snarled, then winked out of existence.

Alarm ran through Nikki. She spun, leaping for the stake she'd dropped near the wall. She hit the carpet and rolled, gathering the stake and slashing upwards in one fluid movement. Her blow met with emerging flesh.

The wood speared Monica's abdomen. Her face twisted in agony, and she melted again from sight. The bloody stake fell free to the floor. Nikki grabbed it, then turned and ran to Jake.

"I'm all right," he muttered. "She slashed my arm open, that's all. Let's get the hell out of here."

She grabbed his good arm and helped him up. The air around them burned with fury. Monica was still nearby, watching their retreat.

But she didn't attack. It was an ominous sign that Jasper had something else in mind for them.

Seven

Nikki leaned against the front of Jake's car, lightly massaging her temples. Her headache was back with a vengeance, thanks to the long hours of questioning. And still the police didn't believe her. It was evident from the look in their eyes, the tone in their voices. They just couldn't accept a sixteen-year-old girl would be capable of such destruction.

And she hadn't even hit them with the vampire theory yet.

She eased her weight from one leg to the other and studied the brightly-lit mansion. Though Monica couldn't be seen, her pain and fury lingered. She was somewhere nearby, watching and waiting. For what, Nikki wasn't sure.

Trevgard himself could not be missed. He strode from room to room like a general marshaling his troops, taking his anger out on anyone who got in his way. Both she and Jake had withstood a good ten minutes of his tirade before the police had decided to rescue them with official questions. Her headache had probably started around that time.

A wiry figure appeared in the doorway, looking around for several seconds before moving briskly in her direction. Nikki groaned. Just what she needed—another round of questioning with Detective Col MacEwan. They'd known each other a long time—he'd arrested her several times during her early years on the streets. He was the strongest denouncer of her psychic talents, and yet, oddly enough, probably the closest thing she had to a friend on the force.

Which didn't mean they actually liked each other.

"I gave the hospital a call." He came to an abrupt halt several feet away from her, his calm tone belying the anger she could see in his brown eyes. "Jake's arm has been stitched, and they've let him go home."

She nodded her thanks and crossed her arms. MacEwan hadn't ventured outside just to say that. There would be more.

"I don't believe a word of the crap you and Jake spouted in there," he continued. "But I've no evidence to dispute it, either, so for the moment, you're free to go."

"Gee, thanks."

"I know you too well, Nikki, and I can taste a lie. When I find out what you and Jake are hiding—"

He let the threat go and glared at her a moment longer. She returned his gaze evenly. She had nothing to hide— nothing but a truth he would never believe. After a moment, he grunted and turned around, walking back to the house.

At least she could finally go home. Pushing away from the car, she moved around to the driver's side. She tugged on the door then realized it was locked. And Jake had the keys.

Damn. She'd have to walk. She kicked the tire in frustration, then turned to study the shadows. The gentle breeze held no trace of Monica, but with the teenager's speed that didn't mean much. She could be out of the scope of Nikki's psychic senses and still be well within killing range. Maybe she should ask one of the police officers for a lift.

She glanced back at the house and saw Trevgard gesturing angrily at some poor officer. *No way,* she thought, shoving her hands back into her pockets to keep them warm. There wasn't a power on this earth that could force her back in the house with Trevgard. She'd had enough of his lectures to last a lifetime.

She headed off down the drive. The noise and lights gradually faded away, and the crunch of gravel underneath her boots grew louder. She turned left out of the gates and crossed the road to the softly lit pavement. The stately mansions lining either side of the street lay wrapped in darkness, and the silence hung as heavily as the clouds in the moonless sky. Yet this time, it wasn't threatening.

Ahead, a figure rested casually against a lamppost. His dark shirt emphasized the lean strength of his chest and arms, and his jeans clung just right to his legs. Michael. He looked...nice. More than nice, really.

His sudden smile sent warmth shivering through her.

"Thought you might like to get something to eat before you go home," he said, falling into step beside her and offering her his arm.

"There aren't many places open at this hour." She tucked her arm through his.

"I'll find us something. What do you prefer?"

Her stomach rumbled noisily. He quirked an eyebrow at the sound, and she grinned. "Actually, I could go for a really big burger right now."

His look was suddenly severe, though amusement danced in his eyes. "Fried foods are full of fat, you know."

"That's all I need—a health nut." She grinned lightly and met his gaze. "What would you suggest?"

"Only the best, of course."

The look in his eyes made her pulse skip a beat. She cleared her throat and looked away. Perhaps linking arms wasn't such a great idea. The warmth of his body so close, the caress of his fingers against her arm—it was a reminder of how long it had been since anyone had simply held her. How long it had been since she had even *wanted* to be held. And it was a dangerous desire when it was centered on a man she knew next to nothing about.

"Lyndhurst doesn't have much in the way of fancy restaurants this end of town. It's residential," she said quietly.

"If I remember right, there's one not far ahead."

He meant Roslyn's, but dressed as they were, they'd never get in. "A hamburger suits me just fine. Besides, it's late. They'll be getting ready to go home."

"Then we'll just have to persuade them to remain open," he said with a smile. "What did the police say?"

She shrugged. "Usual shit. Jake and I aren't to leave town, blah, blah, blah."

"Did they believe Monica was responsible?"

"Nope. But there again, Jake wouldn't believe it either until she attacked him."

"How is his arm?"

"Stitched. The hospital's let him go home." She hesitated, and met his gaze. "You said earlier Monica had to return home? Why?"

"It's instinct for the newly turned vampire to return to the place of its birth. I think it's part of the centering process. To understand what you have truly become, first you must understand what you have lost." He shrugged. "The fledglings must also find something of the past to carry with them through eternity."

"What the hell for?"

He shrugged again. "Perhaps as a reminder that once

they too were human."

"Weird," she muttered. Then she frowned. "You seem to know an awful lot about vampires."

"I have studied them for many years."

"Why?"

He hesitated. "Because my brother was killed by one."

Jasper, Nikki thought. That would at least explain Michael's fierce determination to catch the man. Or vampire, as the case may be.

"Why didn't the wood kill her, then? I thought you said wood was deadly to vampires?"

"It is, but like any weapon, you have to hit something vital. You punctured her gut. A wound like that will be painful and can take a long time to heal, but it's definitely not deadly."

Then next time she'd aim for the heart, she thought, and shivered. "Why aren't we chasing her now? She's still back at her father's place."

"And how will you explain to the police the fact that you have stabbed Monica through the heart?"

"I thought vampire bodies turned to dust when staked?"

"Only in the movies." He smiled. "The sun will burn a vampire's flesh to dust. Otherwise, it's just a body, like any human body."

"But can they rise again? I thought it was part of the legend that vampires can heal any wound?"

"Most wounds. Which is why it is best to also decapitate. Once the head is separate, there's no chance of rejuvenation."

They approached the restaurant. Michael opened the door and ushered her inside. A waiter approached, an apologetic look on his face.

"I'm sorry, sir, but we've just closed."

"Surely you could reopen for half an hour?" Michael said, an odd edge behind the lightness of his words.

"I'm sorry-"

The waiter's words faltered. A sliver of power caressed the air, then the waiters' eyes widened, became lifeless. A chill ran through her. It was Tommy, all over again.

She dragged her arm from Michael's and punched him in the shoulder. "Stop—"

He turned, and she took an abrupt step backward.

Just for an instant his eyes held a darkness that burned her soul.

Then he blinked, and his gaze became guarded, wary. "Stop what?"

She took a deep breath. "Release the waiter. I...I don't like the meals here anyway."

He hesitated, then nodded. Power whispered around her, then the waiter cleared his throat and gave them another smile.

"I'm afraid the chef has already gone home for the night. I'm sorry, but we can't help you."

She spun and made a quick exit. The cold night air touched her fevered skin but wasn't responsible for the tremors running down her spine. Michael had controlled the waiter's mind too easily—as if it were something he did every day.

She stopped several houses down from the restaurant and took a deep breath. What kind of man so casually possessed the mind of another and then forced them to do as he asked? A man like Tommy, she thought, rubbing her arms. A man who just didn't care.

The back of her neck tingled with sudden awareness. Michael had stopped just behind her.

"I'm sorry," he said softly.

His breath brushed warmth across the back of her neck. She tensed, but made no move to turn around. "Why did you do it?"

"It's easier than arguing."

An honest enough answer. And so very similar to the excuses Tommy had used. "Could you control me as easily?"

He moved past her, his arm brushing against hers. Heat trembled across her skin. She rubbed the spot were their flesh had touched and watched him warily. His face was still, expressionless, but she sensed the turmoil beneath the calm exterior.

"I do not know," he said. "I hope I never have to try."

Tommy had tried, and sometimes succeeded.

The clock on the Town Hall tower down the road bonged into the silence. She counted the tones. Midnight, the hour when all things dark and dangerous came out of hiding.

Things like Michael, maybe. She met his gaze again,

the uneven pounding of her heart abnormally loud in the growing silence.

"If you ever do try-"

"You would never know," he said quietly. "As the waiter never knew."

She clenched her fists in impotent fury. The ease with which he'd taken the waiters' thoughts made it clear his abilities were very strong. Where Tommy had haunted her dreams, and Jasper relied on traps to snare her mind, Michael would merely walk in and take. She could so easily become a puppet to his will.

He swore softly and grabbed her arm, shaking her lightly. "I would never do such a thing to you."

Yet he wasn't averse to reading her mind. She wrenched free of his grip. "Unless you had no other choice."

She could see the truth of her statement reflected in his eyes.

"I have made a promise to keep you safe," he said softly. "Though I am a man of my word, I will not stay where I am not wanted. Do you still wish me to accompany you home?"

She opened her mouth to say no, then hesitated. Intuition whispered the warning not to let this man go. She needed the protection he offered, yet she couldn't ignore the darkness she sensed was so much a part of him.

Evil far worse waited somewhere in the night.

She shifted her stance and crossed her arms. "If you are a man of your word, will you make me a promise?"

"What do you wish?" His reply was as guarded as his expression.

"Will you vow never to try to take control of my mind or make me do anything against my will?"

Something in his stillness spoke of sudden anger. "If you trust me so little," he said, "then yes, I so vow."

There was a sudden distancing between them, though neither of them had moved. It could only be for the best, she told herself firmly. They were still strangers. Until she knew more about him, more about the subtle yet terrifying shifts in his nature, she had to keep distance between them. It was just possible her hero was no true hero after all.

***

Michael walked quietly beside Nikki, all too aware of the tension and confusion churning her thoughts. He felt the same damn way.

Perhaps something within her recognized the darkness in him. Maybe that was why she now wore the small silver cross at her neck. Why she refused to trust him.

But why was her trust suddenly so important? He was here only to find Jasper, nothing more. She was his best, and quickest, means of doing so. Trust surely played no part in any of it.

The shadows moved on the other side of the street. Michael glanced across. Only a young couple, strolling hand in hand on their way home. He looked away, studying the street ahead, unsettled by a sudden surge of envy. Just for an instant, he had shared such intimacy, and it had felt good after so many years of loneliness.

Maybe Seline was right. Two days with Nikki, and unwanted wisps of emotion were raising their ugly heads. Something he could well do without, given his job.

He frowned, remembering a whisper he'd caught from her thoughts. *Just like Tommy all over again.* Had someone in the past tried controlling her?

It was something he was never likely to attempt, and he'd had years to define and strengthen his gifts. Even Jasper would never gain full control over her—not alive, at any rate. Her psychic abilities were far too strong to ever be leashed for long.

Yet she was more terrified of Jasper's attempts to control her than of Jasper himself.

Which only made Jasper's task that much easier. He would use her fear against her, use it to beat her into submission, to bend her to his will. Then he would kill her, and she would fully be his.

Damn it, there had to be some way to get her to face the demons of her past, so the demon in her present could not get the upper hand.

And just who in hell had appointed him the keeper of her soul?

He sighed and glanced skyward. He didn't want to get involved with Nikki—not on any level. He just wanted to catch a killer, and she was his best method of finding Jasper quickly. He still had every intention of doing that. Only now, he didn't want to see her hurt in the process.

And when the time came to tell her he was a vampire?

Michael glanced at her. When the time came, he'd walk away. He couldn't change what he was, and she could not live with the darkness. Something told him there'd been far too much of it in her life already.

They continued to walk in silence, and the time slipped by. Her pace increased as they drew close to her home. He felt her anxiety to get inside, to be alone.

He stopped outside as before, scanning the dark windows. There was no hint of Jasper or any of his minions within the immediate area. Maybe she'd be safe for the rest of the night. But just to be certain, he'd stand watch across the road. He'd learned to expect the unexpected—even when it came to someone as predictable as Jasper.

She turned, her gaze meeting his. "Thank you for walking me home."

She couldn't hide the anger and confusion evident in her amber gaze. He nodded and resisted the urge to reach out and touch her. Hold her.

Something flickered in her eyes, and she stepped quickly away. Michael frowned. Just how strong was the link she'd created? If she could merge with his mind, however briefly, it was more than possible she could read his thoughts. Maybe he didn't have to tell her he was a vampire. Maybe she already knew.

He watched her quick retreat, then turned and made his way across the road.

***

Dawn's light was less than an hour away when he finally stood. The muted spark of life in Nikki's flat told him she slept. It was time to begin his hunt.

The sun was on the verge of rising by the time he arrived back at Trevgard's mansion. He walked through the fast disappearing shadows, carefully avoiding the many police officers still around.

Monica was an unseen presence, full of pain and desperate hunger. Obviously, she hadn't yet found the item she would carry through eternity. Michael glanced at his left hand. In his case, it had been a ring. Made for his father by his grandfather, carved from the soft rock that abounded on their farm. It was a reminder of the life he'd willingly forsaken; a reminder of the death he'd unwittingly caused.

It had been his father who'd discovered his body, and the discovery had caused a heart attack, leaving his mother to somehow scratch a living on land so poor even grass refused to grow. He'd returned once the blood-rage had left him, hoping to help in some way. But by then, years had passed, and the struggle to survive had all but killed her. His oldest brother, Patrick, had given up on the farm and left in search of work elsewhere, and his four sisters had found themselves husbands and homes of their own. He'd nursed his mother through her final days, and buried her next to his father. And had vowed, at the foot of her grave, never to take another innocent human life.

A vow he had kept to this day.

He stopped near the front porch and leaned against the wall, waiting. Monica would have to leave soon. The sun was on the rise, and the house offered little in the way of protection. It had too many windows, allowed too much sun to stream in. As a newborn, she needed complete darkness during the day. Resistance to sunlight came only with the onset of a century or so.

She didn't move until the last possible moment. She walked past quickly, right fist clutching a gold watch. Her father's, by the look of it. Her blue eyes were wild, her mind half-mad with thirst. She didn't sense his nearby presence—caution was the last thing on her mind. So many of the newly turned died within the first couple of days simply because they weren't careful enough.

He followed her quick steps through the half-light of morning. If he were lucky, she would lead him straight to her master. Hiding in the middle of a city as big as Lyndhurst still held special problems for the likes of Monica and Jasper. Street people already occupied many of the abandoned factories and houses. The one thing more important to a vampire than a place to wait out the sun was security.

Day sleep represented a kind of death, particularly when young in vampire years. You had to be sure you were safe in the hours when you were totally helpless. Neither Jasper nor Monica had the choice of sleeping in motels, as he did. Because of his years and lifestyle, he could wake and protect himself if threatened. The other two could not.

The skies began to brighten. Monica broke into a run, her sudden desperation reaching back to him. Only now that the sun's heat had started to itch her skin did she realize her danger.

She swung into a side street, and fled into the darkness of an old warehouse. Michael stopped, following the rest of her retreat with his senses.

As he'd expected, she fled down, not up, into the comforting darkness of the basement. Jasper waited for her there.

Michael clenched his fingers and tried to ignore the desperate urge to rush in and crush his enemy's neck. Jasper wasn't alone. Michael's old foe had gained some cunning during the years since their last encounter. People were already working on the floors above, unaware that a monster lurked below. The zombies were silent sentinels near the basement door.

He had no doubt Jasper had rigged the warehouse to explode should he be attacked. He'd done it before, and killed over one hundred people in the process.

Michael turned and walked away. He'd come back tonight, when the people in the two floors above the basement had gone home, and burn this retreat to the ground.

He glanced skyward, trying to judge the time he had left before he had to make his own retreat. At least a few hours...whistling tunelessly, he shoved his hands into his pockets and headed back to the stockyards on the outskirts of town.

Eight

Nikki absently ran the silver cross up and down its chain and watched the people hurry past the foggy office windows. Everyone was bundled up against the bitter wind that raced the clouds across the evening sky. She felt no warmer, despite the heat in the office.

Just how did you stop a vampire?

Last night had proven how difficult that might be. From the little Michael had said, she knew Jasper had been dead long enough to develop and refine the gifts vampirism endowed.

They'd never see him, let alone get near enough to kill him. She crossed her arms and tried to ignore the ice creeping through her veins. Michael was right about one thing. Jasper and Monica were evil. They would kill, and keep on killing, until they were stopped. She just wished she wasn't the one who had to stop them.

She leaned forward and grabbed her coffee cup off the desk, wrapping her hands around it to keep them warm. She turned her thoughts to Michael. She'd heard it said that the eyes were the window to the soul, so what did his ebony gaze tell her? That he was a man well versed in controlling his surroundings. That his secrets and knowledge were old. Centuries old.

She frowned and sipped her coffee. That was impossible, of course. And there was more than secrets to be seen in his eyes. There was also warmth, and a hint of passion that called to something deep inside her. She shivered lightly. Maybe it was just as well that he'd revealed a little too much last night.

The office opened. Jake stepped in, accompanied by a blast of wind that sent the loose papers on her desk scattering like confetti.

"It's cold outside," he muttered sourly. He threw his coat in the general direction of his desk and stalked across the room to the coffee pot.

"So tell me something new," she said, returning her gaze to the street. Michael was out there somewhere. While it was obvious he could take care of himself, worry gnawed at her. Last night her dreams had sent her a warning—

Jasper wove a trap around them all, with Michael's death the grand finale.

"I've sent Mary on a trip to visit her mother," Jake said into the silence.

She almost choked on a mouthful of coffee. In the ten years she'd known him, he'd never been worried enough by a case to send his wife away.

His face was bleak. "If Monica is still alive after having that stake shoved in her gut, well, she knows too much about us. She'll come after us, Nikki."

Hunter and hunted, all one and the same. Just great, she thought, and took another sip of coffee.

"At least I'm lucky that way," she said after a moment. "I have no one but me to worry about."

"You must have aunts and uncles out there, somewhere. Grandparents, even. All you have to do is find them, kiddo."

Yeah, she thought sourly. *She had them. But they didn't want to know her.* She took another sip of coffee, then met Jake's curious gaze. "Mom once told me her family refused to understand the nature of her gifts—they thought she was possessed by the devil. That's why she left when she was sixteen. And Dad's folks disowned him for marrying someone they thought no better than a gypsy."

He shrugged. "Times change. You can't be sure how they'd react to you now."

She smiled bitterly. "Yes, I can."

She bent to gather the papers from the floor, only to have them scatter further as the door opened a second time. Michael stepped inside.

"Evening," he greeted softly, his dark gaze enigmatic when it met hers.

Intuition delivered two warnings, and her pulse skipped a beat. The wall he'd raised last night would stay in place, and he had something to say she wasn't going to like. She gathered the scattered papers then sat back down.

Jake offered Michael a cup of coffee before moving back to his desk. "So," he said. "What can we do for you?"

Michael stopped near her desk. Nikki had the sudden sensation of being caught in a small pen between two charging bulls. She leaned back in her chair and eyed them both warily.

"I came to help," Michael said evenly.

"Really," Jake drawled. "I find it interesting that Nikki didn't appear to need any help until you arrived on the scene."

Her breath caught in her throat. What made Jake think that? She glanced at Michael and caught a wisp of anger—the same dark anger that had threatened her in the warehouse. He looked at her briefly, and the anger died. Yet it was obvious Michael was a man not used to having his actions questioned.

"It might also be said that she would now be dead had I not," he replied.

Jake leaned back in his chair and regarded him thoughtfully. "Why did you come to Lyndhurst, then?"

"To catch a killer—the man who now chases Nikki."

Michael sat on the edge of her desk and sipped his coffee. He appeared very relaxed, very calm. He was not. Jake's doubt infuriated him, and she wondered why.

"Why?" Jake asked bluntly. "You're certainly not a cop or FBI or anything else official. This a personal vendetta or something else?"

"Both." He hesitated and sipped at his coffee.

Deciding how much he should tell them, she thought, and wondered if there was anyone in his world whom he trusted enough to be completely honest with.

"Jasper killed my brother. A few years later he killed a close friend of mine."

The truth as far as it went, but nowhere near the full story, she thought. "I get the feeling there's more history than that between the two of you."

Michael glanced at her. His face was guarded, wary. "Ours is a battle that has been going on for many years. I have killed his brother, and I will kill him—not in retaliation, but simply because his bloodshed will not stop until he is dead."

"Which suggests there is very little difference between you and the man you hunt."

Michael's smile was bitter. "There's one big difference. I do not hunt innocents, nor do I drain the blood of my victims."

She shuddered, remembering the bloody mess Monica had made the night before. "You said you don't kill in retribution, and yet you killed his brother. Why?"

He hesitated again. "Because they were twins who hunted and worked as one. They'd killed over one hundred people before I stopped them, and Jasper has killed as many since."

Again, the truth as far as it went, and still not the whole story. "Why is he so determined to hunt me? We both know there's easier prey living on the streets."

He sipped his coffee, studying her for several seconds before answering. "Jasper hungers for things he can never have. Power, more than anything else. You have that power, Nikki."

And Jasper, who could call his victims from the dead, would control that power should she die. Bile rose in her throat, and she swallowed heavily.

I will not let that happen. I would kill you myself, if it came to that.

It was a chilling thought, and not one she found comforting.

Their gazes met and, just for an instant, the link between them surged to life. His mind embraced hers, a gentle yet intimate touch that caressed her body in a way no physical stroke ever could.

Jake softly cleared his throat. She jumped, tearing her gaze away from Michael's. What the hell was happening between them? And why did she feel like running as far and as fast as she could?

"So what do you plan to do?" Jake asked into the silence.

"I plan to kill Jasper before he can kill again."

"Not exactly legal."

"With Jasper, we have no other choice. And you know it," Michael said quietly. "You had a taste of what he will be like last night in Monica."

"Then she is a vampire."

There was no disbelief in Jake's quiet statement. Only an edge of fear she could well understand.

"Yes," Michael answered. "As Jasper is."

"Shit," Jake muttered and took a gulp coffee. "So how do we kill a vampire? Chase it with a stake and cover it in crosses and garlic?"

Michael smiled, though no humor touched his eyes.

"The cross works as a deterrent for vampires only because, historically speaking, they have always been made of the purest silver. The metal can burn vampires that touch it, particularly the newly turned. As for garlic, I suspect it is only a deterrent for those with weak stomachs."

"So what's the proper method of killing vampires?" Jake asked. "And how do you know so much about them?"

"As I've already told Nikki, a stake through the heart and decapitation are the best bet. Exposure to the noonday sun works, too. Either way, you must first find their daytime resting place."

"Why the noonday sun? I thought exposure to any amount of sun would kill?" she said in surprise.

"In most cases, yes." He paused, and shrugged. His quick look told her he wished this subject had never been brought up. "Age has a lot to do with it. The more years you have behind you, the more tolerant you become to silver and the sun."

"So how old is this Jasper?"

"As near as I can gather, just on ninety-eight years old. Not enough to give him much immunity."

And he still looked fifteen, she thought, feeling ill. "Then what about the zombies?"

"Kill their master, and they will die," he said, voice grim. "It's his life-force keeping them alive."

"Does putting salt in their mouth work?"

A shimmer of amusement spun around her. "I suppose if you shoved enough down their throats, they're likely to choke to death."

She scowled at him. "I'm being serious, here."

"So am I." His amusement fled. "Break their necks, and they will die. Otherwise, they cannot. Not until Jasper dies."

"How in hell is that possible?" she said. "How can he raise the dead and make them his slaves?"

Michael shrugged. "The ability to call the newly dead back to life—to reanimate their limbs—is a black art that often runs in families. From what we know of Jasper, both his father and grandfather were animators, as well."

Great, she thought, and wondered what other unknowns walked through the darkness, hiding from the sunlight and humanity's sight.

Be careful what you ask, Nikki, or you might just discover the answer.

A chill ran across her flesh. A premonition that perhaps it was a warning that came too late. She shivered and rubbed her arms.

"So what do you suggest we do next?" Jake said into the silence.

Grim acceptance ran through his voice. He'd finally accepted both the situation and Michael's presence.

"We must find Monica first. The newly turned tend to be unbalanced and dangerous, especially those who, when alive, had no real love for their fellow humans." Michael smiled grimly, then added, "As you've already discovered."

"Which is where Nikki comes in. Just as well we nabbed that locket."

Michael nodded. "Once Nikki finds Monica's hideout, we wait for dawn then go deal with her."

Kill her, he meant. She shuddered then frowned, studying him. She suddenly had the odd notion *she* had not been included in the *we.*

"Meaning we introduce her to the delights of sunshine." Jake frowned. "I don't know if I—"

"I'm not asking for help here. I can handle her alone."

"Monica is our client's daughter," Jake said, his voice flat. "And our responsibility. Go without us, and I'll call the cops."

If the threat fazed Michael in any way, it certainly didn't show. "Then come. Either way, I care not."

His gaze met hers. *Here it comes,* she thought. The statement she wasn't going to like.

"We should be relatively safe from attack during the day," he continued, his voice as neutral as his face. "But all the same, I think for safety's sake, that Nikki should go home and stay there."

Jake stood quickly, forestalling her anger with raised hands. "Vampires I can handle. This is beyond me. I'm off to eat." He grabbed his jacket and headed for the door. He reached for the door handle, then paused and looked at Michael. "I wish you luck. After a statement like that, you'll need it."

Michael restrained the automatic urge to stop Jake's retreat. As much as he'd counted on having the other man's support, any sign of psychic intrusion would only inflame Nikki further. As the door slammed shut, he took a sip of coffee, then braced himself to face the storm brewing on the other side of the desk.

"Who in hell do you think you are, telling me what to do?" She glared at him, cheeks flushed.

"You're a liability," he said flatly. A liability he willingly used, granted, but that didn't mean he was willing to risk her safety merely to catch the teenager. "Monica is not Jasper, and in many respects, she's more dangerous because her behavior cannot be predicted."

"So? I managed to survive her fury last night. I can do it again. Jake's more a liability in that respect than I am."

"Yes, but Jasper's not after Jake. He's after you."

"So I'm supposed to cower at home while you take care of the problem? I don't think so."

He couldn't imagine her cowering anywhere, but that wasn't what he was asking her to do. "We could walk into a trap, Nikki."

"And you'd rather risk Jasper getting his hands on Jake than on me." She snorted softly and sat back in her chair, amber eyes narrowed. "You're a cold bastard, you know that?"

Yes. And had been told it, many times. "Are you so eager to die, Nikki?"

"No."

She hesitated slightly, and something flashed through her eyes. Death, he thought, was no stranger to her, and perhaps something she would welcome, were it not for the possibility that Jasper would use her.

"And I'm even less eager for Jake to die in my place."

"I have no intention of letting that happen." If only because he didn't trust Jake's sense of honor—an honor that lay with the client, not with him. He wouldn't put it past the man to step in and stop the killing stroke in some vague attempt to reconcile the girl with her father. "I plan to use him as a guard, nothing more."

"Then why not take me? My abilities make me more useful in that department. At least I'd be able to sense the zombies before they approached."

Michael rubbed the back of his neck. She was making perfectly good sense, and they both knew it. "Nikki, I had a premonition—you come with us today, and you could fall into Jasper's hands."

"At last, some honesty." She hesitated, face grim. "How safe am I at home? Jasper may not be able to cross a threshold uninvited, but the zombies can, can't they? What if he uses Monica as bait to lure you away?"

He had to acknowledge it was a possibility, however unlikely. "I doubt whether he would make such an attempt in daylight. If things went wrong, there would be little he could do to help the situation."

"Monica is my responsibility. It's my fault she's out there now. I won't be left behind on this, Michael."

He stared at her for a long minute, then slowly, almost unwillingly, reached out, lightly cupping her cheek. She closed her eyes for a second, as if savoring his touch, then turned, brushing a kiss across his palm. Fire tingled where she touched, flared like pain deep in his heart.

"Why, Nikki?" he said, softly. "What is it about Monica that raises guilt in your heart?"

She snapped away from his touch and rose angrily to her feet. "Keep out of my goddamn mind."

"It doesn't take telepathy to realize Monica reminds you of someone. You followed her beyond all good sense the other night. There has to be a reason."

She crossed her arms and glared at him. "Maybe I'm just dedicated."

And maybe she was just plain crazy. He met her gaze. "Who's Tommy?"

She swore and spun away. She stopped at the windows, arms still crossed, shoulders tense. "Tommy died a long time ago. He has nothing to do with any of this."

The rising tide of guilt in her suggested he had everything to do with it. "Monica reminds you of him, doesn't she?"

Though she still had her back to him, her bitter smile was an ache in his heart. "Actually, Monica reminds me more of me."

He couldn't see why. They were nothing alike. "Tell me about Tommy, Nikki."

She shivered slightly. "There's nothing much to tell. He was the head of the street gang I ran with. He died when I was nearly seventeen. End of story."

Not if the pain in her heart was any indication. "Why were you on the streets? Did you run away?"

She snorted softly. "No. My parents died, and I didn't like the home the authorities tried to shove me into."

The tide of guilt rose. So her parents' deaths were also part of the reason she went after Monica. But why, if they had died before her life on the streets?

"How long were you a part of this gang?"

"Only four years." She hesitated and rubbed her arms. "It seemed an eternity longer."

"Why didn't you stay with relatives?"

She snorted softly. "Because they thought me a witch, much the same as they thought my mother. They want nothing to do with me, even now."

He scrubbed a hand across his chin. None of this made sense. He'd met street kids many times over the years, and they all had one thing in common—a fierce, do anything to survive, nature. Most had been little more than feral animals, humanity almost lost in their quest for survival. As she'd said, four years was a long time on the streets; it was an experience that should have scarred her for life. Yet there was very little evidence of it, in her words or her actions.

"How were you involved with this Tommy?"

She stiffened. "That is none of your damn business."

Her voice was curt, thoughts suddenly chaotic. In many respects, that told him all he needed to know. Her relationship with Tommy had been sexual, and for some odd reason, she felt responsible for his death.

"Why does Monica remind you of him?"

"I told you, she doesn't."

"And yet you chase Monica because of Tommy."

She didn't deny it, just stood at the window, staring out.

"Why, Nikki?"

For a moment, he didn't think she would answer.

"Because I let him die." Her voice was so soft it was a more a whisper through his thoughts than anything he could actually hear. "Because I vowed never to let it happen again."

"There was nothing you could do to save Monica. She chose her fate long before you came onto the scene."

Nikki glanced at him. "You're wrong, Michael. I could have stopped this."

The certainty in her voice made him frown. "Monica performed the ceremony over a week ago. From that point on, her fate was ordained. It was just a matter of when."

"And it was the *when* I could have changed." She hesitated, then turned to face him. "Everyone has some good in them. Sometimes all it takes is one person's belief to change the tide."

He had an odd feeling she was talking more about herself than Monica. He wondered who had turned her tide. Jake?

She lifted her chin slightly. "None of this alters the fact I will not be left behind tomorrow."

He scowled. Her tenacity annoyed the hell out of him, yet he couldn't help admiring her for it, either. "You're a stubborn wench."

"I never claimed to be perfect, Michael. And nothing you can do or say will stop me from going with you."

"I can tie you up and lock you away," he muttered.

"And I can use telekinesis to escape, then come after you."

He ran a hand through his hair. "I'm only trying to keep you safe, Nikki." Taking a sip of coffee, he watched her over the rim of the cup. If he couldn't stop her, he'd just have to find a way to keep her out of harm's way. And that wasn't going to be any easier than trying to talk her out of accompanying them.

She shrugged and gave him a rueful smile. "I know. But I've been looking after myself for a long time now. I have to finish what I start."

In that, they were very much alike. He glanced at the front door, aware of Jake's approach. The door opened, and Jake peered around at them.

"It appears safe to enter," he commented, doing so. "But it's hard to judge a winner here. The black looks are almost identical."

"Quit clowning around," Nikki growled. "I'm going."

"Ah." Jake glanced at Michael sympathetically. "She can be really difficult when it comes to doing something she doesn't want to do."

Michael smiled grimly. "I noticed."

"So, we stick to the daylight raid plan?" Jake moved over to his chair and sat down.

Michael took another sip of coffee then nodded. "It's still the safest time to try to find Monica."

Jake nodded and leaned forward, fishing through the mess in his desk. "Anyone for blackjack?" he said, producing a pack of cards.

"Just as long as you're prepared to lose your money, friend," Michael replied with a light smile. Playing cards had to be better than sitting alone with his thoughts. He could do that anytime.

"Nikki?" Jake asked.

She shook her head and turned away, staring out the window again. Michael pulled a chair across to Jake's desk and tried to close himself off from the pain he could feel in her thoughts.

But he had a notion it was not his night to win—in any way.

***

Nikki crossed her arms and leaned wearily against a metal signpost. Jake and Michael were standing several yards in front of her, barely visible through the mist of rain.

She wondered why Monica had chosen a train tunnel to hide in. There had to be more secure places about. And surely a child raised in opulent surroundings could never be comfortable with the dirt and constant noise inside the tunnel.

Not to mention the high probability of being seen, or even caught. The area was a well-known haunt for street kids. Her gang had often dared each other to race through the tunnels just as a train was due. She had no doubt kids still did today. Some brainless stunts never went out of fashion.

And unless it had changed in the last ten years, there weren't many hiding holes inside. So why come here?

Maybe Michael was right. Maybe another trap waited for them. Yet she had no sense of the evil that came with Jasper's presence, only Monica. She wrapped her fingers around the locket. The metal pulsed lightly—a single beat every few minutes. Monica's heartbeat, she knew.

Jake snapped the timetable closed. She walked across

to the two of them. "What's the verdict?"

He shrugged. "Near as we can figure, there's no train due for at least half an hour."

"I hope you're right. There's damn little room to move in there with a train going through."

Jake grimaced and studied the sky. "It's not going to get much brighter. Not with all this rain."

"It won't matter. Monica will have no choice but to rest soon," Michael said, studying the tunnel. "Are you certain Monica's inside, Nikki? No one else?"

She wondered if he could sense something that she could not. The locket pulsed in her hand, and heat washed over her skin. Heat and hunger. Monica's, not Jasper's.

"Oh yes," she replied softly. "I'm certain."

Jake switched on the flashlight and walked towards the tunnel, becoming one with the gloom. An odd prickle ran across the back of her neck.

"It's not too late to turn back, Nikki."

Yes, it is. She gripped the barrel of the flashlight tighter and walked forward. Michael kept close, and she felt safer for it. Yet instinct warned it wasn't going to be enough to save her.

She ignored the quick thrust of foreboding and watched the beam from Jake's flashlight dance across the darkness. Her own paled by comparison, barely piecing the gloom on either side. Maybe she should have stopped and bought some new batteries.

Their footsteps echoed though the silence. Would Monica hear them and flee? Would she even care?

The tunnel swung to the right, and the darkness fully encased them. Past escapades returned to haunt her, and she swung the light to the left. There had been a break in the wall near here, somewhere. She'd fled into it once in the face of an oncoming train.

Jake stopped so abruptly she almost ran into him.

"Hole in the wall," he said, shifting his grip on the stake he held. "Wait here. I'll check it out."

Shifting her weight from one foot to the other, she watched him disappear. Though she couldn't sense anyone in the hole, it was better to be sure.

Michael stood behind her, as silent and still as the darkness around them. Yet he reminded her of a coiled spring. He sensed danger ahead, like her.

Jake returned. "Nothing," he said, sounding oddly relieved. "Only rubbish."

"Monica's still ahead." She swept the light across the darkness surrounding them. She'd heard no sound, yet she had a sudden sense of movement. The forces of evil gathered out there in the darkness.

"How far ahead?" Jake's question jostled harshly against the silence.

"I'm not sure. Not far."

Jake frowned and turned, leading the way once more. The yellow beam of light danced away from the darkness, barely penetrating the thick gloom. It would be so easy to fall into a trap.

Or walk, as she sensed they were doing.

The locket in her hand pulsed again. She clenched her fingers and let her senses flare to full life. Monica was on the move, running lightly through the tunnel. Fleeing, but not in fright. Nikki bit her lip. Something was happening, something she couldn't sense or understand.

Michael's tension washed heat across her back. Maybe he could sense the presence she merely guessed at.

"Jasper's not here," he said softly. "But the zombies are. I think you and Jake should go back. I'll continue the hunt for Monica alone."

"Monica is our client's daughter," Jake reminded him. "You go nowhere without us."

"The two of you will never match Monica's inhuman speed. You'll only get in my way."

Jake turned. His flashlight pierced the darkness, almost sun-bright. "And by that are you suggesting you *can* match her inhuman speed?"

"Yes, I am." Michael hesitated. "I don't like the feel of this. Take Nikki and head back to the entrance. You'll be safe there."

He was certainly determined to keep her away from Monica. What did he fear—that she'd try to stop him? "I'm not going anywhere. I've already told you that."

"Damn it Nikki, you've encountered the zombies once already. Do you really think you and Jake can survive a sudden attack from three of them?"

Though annoyance barely touched his voice, it seared

through his thoughts, almost burning her. She stared at him several seconds. Perhaps he was right. She'd barely escaped an attack from two. Add the teenager and an extra zombie, and the odds weren't looking favorable—even with Michael on their side. Perhaps it was time to leave Monica to her fate.

Besides, she didn't like the feel of what was happening up ahead, either.

She held up her hands. "Okay, okay. I'll retreat. Jake?"

He shook his head. "I think we owe it to Trevgard to see this thing through."

Michael raised an eyebrow. "And did you not promise your wife to take no foolish chances?"

Nikki glanced at him sharply. He'd obviously been reading Jake's thoughts, to know something as intimate as that. Maybe it was only her presence that stopped him from entering Jake's mind and forcing him to obey.

Jake glared at him. "Just how in hell did you know that?"

"As I said, Nikki is not the only one with psychic abilities. She should be your main concern here, not Monica."

Jake glanced at her, his expression troubled. "All right, I'll go. But I want Monica brought out to us. I think we need to witness what happens, as much for your sake as Trevgard's."

Michael nodded, then stepped into the shadows and disappeared.

"Damn," Jake muttered. "How did he do that?"

"He moves fast," she muttered, although he hadn't. He'd only taken a dozen or so steps and had hesitated, out there in the darkness. She wondered what he sensed. "And the tunnel turns to the right a few yards away. That's why you can't see him."

Jake touched her arm lightly. "Let's head back. The darkness doesn't feel quite as safe without your sinister friend around."

He was right. It didn't. The sense of danger had increased twofold in the few minutes Michael had been gone. The quicker they got out of this tunnel, the better. Nikki rubbed her arms, then turned and followed Jake down the track.

"What's that noise?" Jake said, after a few minutes.

Energy surged in response. She clenched her fists and listened. The wind sighed past them, gathering speed. The ground began to tremble.

"Christ," Jake continued. "A train!"

She pushed him forward. "The hole's only twenty feet or so away. Head for that."

Adrenaline surged, giving her feet wings. The lights swung erratically across the darkness, and for an instant, reflected brightly in a dead blue eye. She slid to a stop.

"Jake, watch out!"

Around her, the night found form. Something grabbed her waist and swung her away into darkness. She screamed, but icy fingers covered her mouth, cutting the sound off. She tasted dirt and death, and bile rose in her throat. Struggling violently, she kicked and punched the creature that held her so tightly. Kinetic energy surged, but before she could release her weapon, something hit her head, and pain exploded.

Evil danced around her. *When my creatures bring you to me, I will make you mine.* Jasper's thoughts were soft, as if spoken from a great distance.

No! She lashed out blindly with kinetic energy, fighting the strength of the creature holding her. Though wrenched away, another quickly replaced it. Dimly, she felt the warm touch of blood on her cheek, heard a distant scream of anger not her own.

Then nothing but mocking laughter.

Nine

A slight hiss was all the warning he got. Michael dodged, but not fast enough. The dart hit his forearm, and spread fire through his veins. *Silver...the dart tip was made of silver.* Swearing softly, he wrenched it from his arm. The zombies were close, moving down a tunnel that ran parallel to his. Monica was still ahead, still running away.

It made no sense. The wind sighed past him, velocity increasing with every second. A train approached. They were running out of time. He turned and headed back.

He'd barely taken a dozen steps when dizziness hit him. He staggered for several seconds then stopped, pressing his palm against the tunnel wall. It was real and solid, and most importantly, not moving. Frowning, he squinted into the darkness. Ahead, Nikki and Jake were blurred shapes; a muted wash of red he could barely see.

He blinked and swallowed. There was a bitter taste in his mouth, and it had nothing to do with fear. *The dart had been drugged!*

The zombies came out of hiding. Nikki screamed and energy seared the air.

Something hit the side of his head. Michael dropped to his knees, battling to stay conscious as the night danced around him. Moisture ran down the side of his face. He licked it, tasting his own blood. The darkness within him rose, a demon that battled the lethargy overtaking his mind. He struggled upright, knowing time was running out. The train was almost upon them. He had to find Nikki and get out of this tunnel.

Her life force burned fiercely through the darkness. Her fear filled his soul and became his own. Michael lunged towards her, but his legs felt encased in glue. He couldn't move with any sort of speed. Jasper's distant laughter mocked him. Then darkness claimed the fire of Nikki's life force, taking her from his sight.

Taking the warmth of her thoughts from his mind.

He swore and swung around to meet the rush of a zombie.

Punching the creature in the face, he knocked it back several feet. It landed on its rear, shaking its head and growling in confusion. He turned and ran forward.

Jake was gamely battling against a second creature. Michael leaped, kicking it away, sending it staggering across the track. Grabbing Jake, he thrust him into the safety of the hole, and dived in after him. Two seconds later, the train screeched past, whirling dust and rubbish through the darkness.

Coughing, he pushed upright and leaned against the grimy wall. The sighing wind was cool, but it failed to provide any sort of comfort. He closed his eyes and sent his senses winging back across the darkness. There had to be some trace of Nikki...

Nothing. The drug slowing his responses played no part in his inability to find her. The zombies were easy enough to sense, huddled in tight balls just down the track. *Hope the bloody train severs their heads*...He took a deep breath.

So. As he'd foreseen, Nikki had been captured. He had no doubt Jasper would kill her. Then he would be forced to re-kill her, just to give her the peace of absolute death.

He'd known it was a possibility, but it wasn't one he was ready to face. Not now, not ever.

He clenched his fists in the dirt, then slowly released them. What was the life of one more human if he gained Jasper's death?

The thought chilled him, and for the first time in years, he wondered at the cost of his quest—both to himself and to others close to him. People like Nikki, who was by no means close, and yet could have been, had either of them wished it.

He rubbed a hand across his eyes. She wasn't dead yet, at least he had the comfort—or maybe that should be discomfort—of that knowledge. The connection she'd formed between them wasn't severed, just empty.

He wondered what Jasper was waiting for. He wanted Nikki's power, of that Michael had no doubt. The only way he could claim it was in her death.

"Where's Nikki?" Jake's question rasped across the silence.

Michael opened his eyes and studied him. The red haze of his blood heat was a muted glow in the night. Purple patches marred his face and torso, bruises in the making, but otherwise, he appeared unhurt.

"Gone. Jasper has her," Michael replied flatly. He blinked and switched his vision back to normal. The return of darkness was, in some ways, a blessing.

"Why the hell didn't you make her stay behind?" Jake demanded angrily. "You knew what this man was like, yet you let her come with us. It's your damn fault she's gone."

"You're her boss. Why didn't you forbid it?" Although Michael understood Jake's anger was merely his way of coping with the situation, he couldn't keep the edge of annoyance from his voice.

Jake lowered his gaze. "I'm her boss, yes. But damn it, you care for her!"

Michael stared at him in surprise. Where in hell had Jake gotten that idea? He barely knew Nikki, and while it was true there was definitely an attraction between them, he had no intention of acting on it. And by all indications, neither would she.

"What I may or may not feel gives me no right to force her to do anything against her will." And despite his noble words, he knew that had he been able to enter her mind and force her to remain behind, he would have. Even if it meant breaking his vow.

Maybe he and Jasper had a lot in common after all.

He listened to the sound of the zombies' awkward footsteps fade away into the silence, then, using the wall as a brace, rose to his feet. The drug in his system would take hours to dissipate, and, with the sun strengthening towards noon, there was little he could do now but wait.

"The creatures have gone," he said. "We'd better head back to the office."

"And make no attempt to find her?" Jake said incredulously.

"I have no other choice," Michael bit back.

So much for control, he thought bitterly and stepped out of the hole. A glint of silver caught his eye. He walked across the track, and bent to pick it up. It was Nikki's silver cross. The small amount of silver within the charm tingled against his palm, but he ignored it. At least he had something of Nikki's to hold on to. Something to remember her by in the years ahead.

He glanced across at Jake then strode through the darkness. There was nothing more they could do in the tunnel, and Jasper just might try to contact them at the office—if only to taunt them.

Tonight he would search.

And Jasper would pay when he found him.

***

The darkness stirred, coming to life.

Shifted, then disappeared.

Nikki blinked, wondering if her eyes were playing tricks on her. The night appeared silent, empty. Yet the more she stared into the darkness, the more certain she became that someone was there, watching her.

She shivered, but resisted the urge to rise from the cold concrete floor. Until she had an idea of where she was, there was no point in moving. Who knew what traps might wait in the darkness.

The minutes crept by. Sweat broke out across her brow, and fear crawled through her heart. Though there was no sign of Jasper in the uneasy darkness, he was there, somewhere. The foul scent of his evil filled the air.

She clenched her fists and tried to still the sudden rush of panic. She had to stay calm if she wanted to survive. Taking a deep breath, she tried to contact Michael through their link.

Only he wasn't there.

Nothing was.

Her psychic abilities no longer answered her call. Bile rose in her throat. She swallowed heavily. What had Jasper done to her?

Laughter rolled across the night, a rich sound that made her skin crawl with terror.

"Your lover will not hear you."

Jasper's voice spun through the darkness, entwining her in corruption. She still couldn't see him, nor did she have any sense of him. What was wrong with her?

"He's not my lover." Her voice was little more than a harsh whisper that burned against her throat's sudden dryness. She licked her lips and tried again. "And why won't he hear me?"

The night stirred, and Jasper appeared. There was an almost terrible beauty in watching his perfect body find shape from the midnight silence.

Then she realized he was naked.

Her heart skipped several beats. Closing her eyes, she tried to control the terror squeezing her throat. Despite the soreness of her limbs, she sensed Jasper hadn't touched her yet. But he would. She could feel his hunger.

He laughed. She resisted the urge to roll into a tight ball of fear and sat up instead. The concrete scraped harshly across her buttocks. Only then did she realize that she was as naked as he.

"When the form is as beautiful as ours, why cover it?"

To emphasize his point, he struck a pose, showing the muscular splendor of his body. *Mad...He has to be mad.* She wrapped her arms around her knees, drawing them close to her chest. "What do you want with me?"

"Many things." The amusement fled his features. "Mostly, I want you to help me kill the man who murdered my brother."

"Never."

He laughed softly. "Oh, you *will* help me, pretty one."

She didn't bother refuting the statement. He smiled and walked to the far corner of the room, his movements grace itself. Nikki blinked, suddenly realizing she could see. The night had begun to lift, and dawn seeped through the boarded up window to her right. Freedom. Yet she didn't dare move. She had no doubt he would kill her if she so much as blinked the wrong way right now...

He turned, holding a syringe in one hand. Relief surged. That was why her head felt so fuzzy. He was drugging her.

"This won't put you out." His smile made her edge back slightly. "Only stop you moving and cloud your gifts. I have no wish for you to call your lover so soon."

Fear held her immobile. He knelt and slid the needle into her thigh. His hand caressed her skin, his touch hot, possessive. She closed her eyes and held her breath.

Jasper laughed and rose. Her eyes jerked open, and she watched him move to the bed. He played with her, she realized grimly. Tasted her fear, fueling its flames. Savoring it.

She knew then that he wouldn't physically touch her. Not for a while, anyway. This man enjoyed violation of another kind more—the heart, the soul and the mind. Like a cat playing with its prey, he would toy with her until she broke.

Then he would use her to trap and kill Michael.

She had to escape this mad man's grasp.

Footsteps whispered through the silence. Laughter surrounded her, provocative yet chilling. Not Jasper's. Monica's.

She closed her eyes, refusing to acknowledge the teenager's presence. Bedsprings squeaked as Monica joined her lover on the bed. After several more minutes came soft moans and the rustle of sheets.

All she could do was ignore the noise of their lovemaking and try to rest. Like Jasper's word games, she knew this was meant to be some perverted form of torture. But if they hoped to shock her, hoped to encourage the first tiny cracks in her sanity, they were in for a surprise. She'd seen and heard a lot worse during her years on the streets.

Yet she couldn't help the tiny hope that daylight would quickly drive them into oblivion. Or better yet, to hell.

**

Pain woke her. Her heart pounded, racing uncomfortably in her chest. She opened her eyes. Jasper knelt beside her, warm breath kissing her skin, his gaze burning with desire as he watched...And sucked blood from her wrist.

Nikki screamed and tried to jerk her arm away. He held her still, his grip bruising as he drained her life away. There was nothing she could do to stop him.

As the realization of death hit her, he pulled away.

His razor-sharp teeth left her skin, and the hot ached eased. Smiling, still watching her every movement, he licked the remaining droplets away. His tongue danced sensually across her wrist, and the two small holes healed.

The horror of it filled every corner of her mind. It felt as if his depravity had somehow invaded her soul and left it stained. He laughed, white teeth gleaming, canines still tarnished by her blood. She closed her eyes, desperate to control the rising tide of hysteria. That's what he intended, what he wanted. It was just part of his tricks, part of his attempt to break her will.

She couldn't let him succeed. Not when Michael's life was at stake.

Jasper moved back to the bed. His bright gaze watched her steadily. There was no life, no emotion, in his eyes. It was almost as if becoming a vampire had robbed him of all humanity. And yet, she had an odd feeling that even when he had been alive, the look in his eyes would have been much the same.

She shifted uncomfortably on the cold floor, but her muscles were stiff and unresponsive. She still clasped her knees close to her chest, though the muscles along her thighs had long ago gone numb. While the protection it offered was only illusory, she didn't want her body exposed to this man.

"You have been missing for more than twenty-four hours. Do you think your lover is frantic yet?"

"He's not..." She stopped. What was the use? He'd never believe Michael and she were barely even friends, let alone lovers. Madness had control of his brain, and he refused to hear anything beyond the boundaries of what he believed to be true.

Jasper rested his forearms against his knees, face somehow more intense as he leaned forward. "He will suffer, as I suffered. And he will feel you die, as I felt my brother die."

His voice was flat, chilling in its lack of emotion. Yet his statement confused her. Why, if he was so desperate for psychic power, did he keep her alive? "I thought you wanted to get your hands on my abilities?"

Perhaps it wasn't the wisest move, asking a madman a question like that, but it was one she needed an answer to.

"I kill you now, and your lover will merely return you to death. There would be nothing to savor in such a situation."

Suddenly she understood. He thought them lovers, and wanted Michael to suffer the agony of the situation, of knowing she was a captive and yet not knowing what was being done to her. A good plan, had it not been for the fact she and Michael were little more than strangers.

Hell, Michael was probably sitting back right now wondering how to turn the situation to his advantage. She doubted if she'd waste more than a second or two in his thoughts.

Though he'd promised to keep her safe, and she had no doubt he would try and keep that promise.

"Why haven't you tried to hypnotize me again, then?" she asked after a moment. He'd come so close the first time.

"At the time, you were unaware and ripe for attack. Were it not for your lover, I would have had you. Right now, you would not be so easy a target, even with your mind so clouded. I have no wish to deplete my own reserves when fear and drugs can more easily break a spirit."

And the pain involved would give him more pleasure, she thought. He smiled, and fear curled in her stomach. There were a few too many teeth involved in that smile. She had to keep him talking. It was her only hope. Every second she could delay whatever plans he had for her was another second Michael had to find her.

"Was your brother a vampire, too?"

His gaze narrowed slightly. He knew what she was up to, yet she sensed he was prepared to play along. At least for a while.

"He was my twin. He was never strong, never certain about this gift of afterlife. He was an easy target. I've spent a long time tracking down his killer."

And probably a long time planning Michael's death. She moved her leg slightly, trying to ease the ache, but stopped when a hungry look flickered across his face. Holding still, she cleared her throat, trying to draw his attention away from her naked body. "Michael doesn't even know your name."

If he tasted her lie, he gave no sign of it.

"Then he will, before this is finished. And he will curse it long before he dies." He rose and picked up the syringe. "I must go out. Your blood, intoxicating as it was, will not contain my needs."

He slid the needle into her thigh, and she bit back a yelp of pain. White fire flashed through her veins, and her pulse began to skip. Sweat broke out across her skin, though she felt chilled to the bone. The darkness began to move, began to moan and whisper...And dancing images of every nightmare she'd ever suffered came to life in the night before her.

She closed her eyes, battling for sanity. It was only the drug. It wasn't real. Jasper's hand caressed her arm, his touch hot with desire. She shuddered, but didn't move.

Didn't dare.

"Have fun, beautiful one."

His laughter rolled through the thickening night, stirring it into a passionate dance of madness.

***

"My name is Jasper Harding."

His voice broke the numbness. She flinched, holding her knees tighter, not moving. Sweat ran in rivulets down her body, despite the dense chill gripping the room. Every heartbeat was a shudder of fear.

The darkness writhed and danced with horrors unimaginable. They filled her with their madness, twisted her soul with their evil. She'd long ago given up telling herself it was only the drug. It was more than that now. He was back.

"Repeat it. Say my name."

She bit her tongue and ignored the urge to do as he asked. The darkness ran across her skin as lightly as a spider, scalding her.

"Repeat it, and the fear will go. Everything will go."

"NO!" She dropped her head to her knees and tried to deny the growing need to do as he asked. She'd rather face insanity.

Pain flared in her thigh. More drugs. She moaned and held her trembling legs tightly. She wouldn't give in. She wouldn't...

***

Her parents' death replayed itself, over and over and over in the darkness. The look on their faces as they'd waved good-bye to her. The scream of metal as a runaway truck crushed them. Images of the twisted remains of the car entwined with blood and mangled body parts, none really distinguishable from the other.

Again and again she felt the caress of her mother's soul, her kiss of love, as she passed on.

She screamed and cried and denied the night's insistence they died because of her. Begged and pleaded for forgiveness, only to be mocked with vicious laughter.

And still the nightmare danced on.

***

Over and over she watched Tommy being beaten, her gaze hazy with the blood from a wound on her forehead.

Unable to help him, her gifts useless with the pain pounding through her brain, she could only watch the three kids kick him.

Words mocked her. Her words, spoken the night before his death. A wish for his soul to be sent to hell. She cried a denial to the darkness. The words had been spoken in anger and fear, and never meant.

The night would not listen, and the madness danced on.

She heard the distant wail of the approaching police siren that frightened the thugs away. Suffered again the agonizing crawl towards Tommy. Felt the moment of his death as she held his bloody body in her arms, the touch of his soul as it passed on its journey towards eternal darkness.

Her curse, her fault. Over and over and over...

***

"Say my name."

The chant sang through her brain. She shook her head, the movement feeble. Everything ached—her head, her muscles, her heart. The night went on forever, and time became a frozen wasteland of madness.

Resist, resist. The weak litany overran his chant, helping her ignore it. Fire touched her leg, burned through her bloodstream.

The drug. Her heart shook with fear as the craziness danced in fevered delight.

***

"Jasper Harding."

The words were torn from her. She couldn't stop herself repeating his name, though her heart wept in bitter defeat.

The darkness stilled its dance. Sweet silence filled the void.

"Repeat it," Jasper urged, elation running through his voice.

"Jasper Harding." She croaked in reply. How long had she sat here? How long had she resisted the drug? It felt like forever, but it was probably little more than a day or so.

Fatigue trembled through every muscle, but that in itself told her little. Her head swam, though she wasn't sure if the cause was lack of food or the drug. Her throat was parched, and it hurt to swallow, let alone speak. Jasper would kill her if he weren't careful.

She studied the darkness wearily. She may have lost the battle, but not the war. Jasper couldn't guard her, or control her, twenty-four hours of every day. She'd beat him yet. If there was one thing she'd learned during her years with Tommy, it was that no matter how bad things seemed, you could never give up. Hope might only be a heartbeat away.

Jasper appeared out of the darkness, a presence she felt rather than saw. She closed her eyes, refusing to acknowledge him.

"Resistance is feeble," he mocked quietly. "You are mine now."

She made no comment. The chill air caressed her sweaty flesh, making her feel colder than she'd ever thought possible.

"Open your eyes." His voice took on a commanding tone. "Look at me."

She fought the order as hard as she could. Yet her head rose, her eyes met his. Tears tracked silently down her cheeks.

Monica stood behind him, her blue eyes full of hate. Behind them both, dawn's warm light danced through the shadows.

"Get the syringe."

Her pulse leaped at his command. Jasper laughed as Monica turned to do his bidding.

"This time we merely put you to sleep. You put up a long but useless battle, pretty one. We all need our rest."

Relief surged. At least the mad dance of nightmares was at an end. He stepped away as Monica knelt beside her. Motes of sunlight played across his flesh, raising red welts that disappeared as quickly as they appeared. She remembered Michael mentioning Jasper's lack of immunity to the sun, and wondered what time it was. Something told her it could be important.

"When we are all rested," Jasper continued softly, "you will fully become mine."

She'd kill herself before she ever let him take her. But meeting his mocking gaze, she knew how futile the thought was. She had no means to fight him, for a start. The drugs they'd been pouring into her body still blocked her psychic gifts. And physically, she doubted if she'd pose a serious threat to even an ant right now.

"I shall enjoy taking your body, as I have enjoyed taking your mind."

The teenager jerked, and liquid sprayed across her leg. Nikki tensed, wondering if Monica realized...the teenager met her gaze, her blue eyes dark with anger and hate. She glanced briefly at the needle, then back at Nikki. She knew it was almost empty. In her own strange way, Monica was offering a chance to escape.

But only because she feared losing the monster she called lover.

The teenager rose and threw the empty syringe on the shelf before joining Jasper on the bed. The arm she placed around his waist was possessive. Nikki wondered how much time the teenager had left—not much, if body language was anything to go by. Her gaze met Jasper's. Malice gleamed back at her.

"Has Michael told you his secret yet?"

Nikki closed her eyes. She didn't want to hear anything else from Jasper. But not because she feared more of his lies. No, this time she feared the truth.

"Michael is one of us," Jasper said softly. "A creature of the night. A taker of blood."

"No." The denial was torn from her. Yet she knew in her heart he spoke the truth. It explained the darkness she sensed in Michael, explained how alike he and Jasper were.

But Michael was not Jasper.   Jasper laughed coldly. "Believe what you will, pretty one."

She ignored him, ignored the demons whispering doubts into her mind. It was just another game, nothing more. Sleepiness overtook her, and she welcomed its pull. She had to rest if she wanted the strength to escape and discover the truth.

***

Michael leaned wearily against the wall, impatiently watching the sun go down. For the last three days they'd followed every possible lead, yet had found no trace of Nikki or her captor. Everyone, even Monica and the zombies, seemed to have vanished off the face of the earth.

He touched the cross around his neck. The silver tingled against his skin and would, in time, burn him. He didn't care. It was Nikki's—all that he might ever be able to have of her.

He closed his eyes and reached again for the link. Darkness greeted him, a wall he could not traverse. At least she was still alive.

But until she was free of the chains holding her mind captive, there was little he could do to help her. Jasper had chosen his hiding place too well. It could take weeks to ferret him out. Indeed, the last time he had run for cover, it had taken Michael almost a year to track him down again. Nikki probably didn't have that much time left.

All he could do was wait until dusk and return to the hunt, however futile. He crossed his arms and continued to watch the late afternoon crowds rush past. A thick curtain of lace protected him from the main thrust of the afternoon's heat, but he didn't dare go any closer to the window. He wasn't suicidal.

Behind him, Jake paced the length of the office and swore into the telephone. It was a futile exercise. They both knew there was little the cops could do that the two of them hadn't already tried.

Hunger washed through him. He ignored it. There was no time to eat. The detour might mean the difference between finding some clue and not. He just couldn't take the risk.

He sighed and cast his gaze back to the skies. The day had been an appropriate one—wet and miserable. Only now did the sun begin to break the heavy blanket of clouds. He hoped it was a sign of better things to come.

Behind him, Jake slammed the phone down. "Damn those bastards."

"They're doing their best," Michael said softly.

"Well, it's not good enough!"

Nothing was good enough, he thought in bleak agreement. *Not the cop's efforts nor theirs. Nikki was still captive to evil, and God knows what he was doing to her...*He took a deep breath and shoved the thought away.

But he couldn't so easily escape the guilt. This was his fault. He should never have attempted to use her as bait. It had only led Jasper to believe she meant something to him. He was sure it was for that reason, more than the power of her gifts, that Jasper had gone after her. Though it was, perhaps, the only reason she was not yet dead.

Only now, when it didn't really matter, did Michael realize the fool he'd been.

"Damn it all, *we* should be out there ourselves." Jake swung around and snatched his coat off the back of his chair. "I can't sit here any longer. I'm going to look for her."

"I cannot."

Jake turned to face him. "Why in hell not? I thought you cared for her!"

Michael clamped down on his temper. "Whether I do or not has no bearing on the matter. I simply cannot go outside."

"Why? Afraid of the sun or something?"

"Or something," Michael muttered, then turned. It was not what he'd call an ideal time to be honest—but then, what time was? It would be so easy to just reach out and touch Jake's mind, make him trust—but he couldn't. Nikki would know.

"Jasper and I have one thing in common. We're both vampires. I'll die if I walk outside right now."

Jake stared wide-eyed at him. "You're kidding...right?

"No. While I do not take human blood, I *am* a vampire."

"But...you're standing in sunshine now."

"Diffused sunlight. Watch." He reached forward, brushing aside the curtain to let the full force of the sun fall upon his arm. Instantly his skin began to turn red. He let the curtain drop back in place before the burn became too bad. "Because I have been on this earth a long time, I can stand some sunlight. Even so, if I went out there now, I'd only last ten minutes or so."

Jake leaned against his desk and ran a hand through his pale blonde hair. Michael could hear the struggle in his thoughts. Lord, it would be so easy to reach out...He clenched his fists and waited.

"Does Nikki know?" Jake said after a moment.

It wasn't a question he'd expected. And though he could see fear in Jake's eyes, it wasn't the full-blown panic he'd half anticipated. "No. But I have no doubt Jasper will tell her."

"Hell of a way to find out." He swallowed slightly. "You don't take human blood, you say?"

"No."

"Of course, I only have your word on that."

Michael returned his gaze evenly. "If I wanted to taste your blood, you wouldn't even have time to scream."

"Well, that's just great." Jake shuddered, then ran a hand across the sandy stubble lining his chin. "In recent days I've seen zombies, and the dead walk from the morgue. I suppose it's not too much of a stretch to believe you're a vampire. Though I have to say, you don't act very vampire-like."

Michael raised an eyebrow. "And how many vampires have you met to make such a judgement?"

"Well, just Monica and Jasper, but I've seen countless Dracula movies."

"The Dracula legend was based on a man. It has very little to do with reality."

"Tell that to Monica and this Jasper of yours. They're pretty much matching the legend."

"Becoming a vampire did not make Jasper what he is today. His thirst for blood was evident well before his turning."

"But turning has made him more unkillable." Jake hesitated, eyes narrowing slightly. "Why did he really snatch Nikki? To get back at you?"

"I believe so. He thinks I care for her—"

"Which you do."

"—and he wants to make me suffer before he kills us both."

"So you and Jasper have this personal vendetta happening, and Nikki and I were unlucky enough to get in the way."

Boiled down to basics, that just about summed it up. Michael rubbed his forehead, wondering again if all the years—and all the lives lost—were worth the effort of chasing Jasper.

Then he remembered his brother, Patrick, and his friend, Jenna. And people like Monica, who was by no means innocent and yet who had still deserved more than the path of death and destruction that Jasper's seduction and lies had led her to.

"As I said before, it's more than a personal vendetta. Jasper has to be stopped. It's my job to do it."

"Why?" Jake's gaze was shrewd. "You're not in this alone, are you?"

Both were questions he wasn't prepared to answer right now. Risking his life was one thing; risking the lives of his companions by revealing too much about their organization was another. Jasper was still loose, and Jake just might be next on the hit list. The less Jake knew, the better for them both.

"Sometimes it takes a vampire to hunt a vampire."

"In other words, mind my own business." Jake flashed a toothy smile that held very little warmth. "I guess we wait, then. I hope you don't mind if I keep my distance. Being around a vampire might take a little getting used to."

Michael smiled. Jake was all right. No wonder Nikki depended on the man.

"I just feel so damn useless sitting here," Jake continued with a sigh.

"We'll find her. Don't worry."

"Yeah, right."

The disbelief in Jake's voice annoyed him. Hope was the one thing they couldn't afford to lose. But the rebuke died on his tongue. It was fear that made Jake speak like that, a fear he could well understand.

An hour crawled by, then another. Night approached. Michael pushed away from the wall. At least now he could *do* something, instead of merely waiting.

Life suddenly sparked in the darkness of the link. He stiffened, reaching out swiftly. Turmoil, fear and confusion greeted him. Nikki didn't hear him, didn't acknowledge his presence.

It didn't matter. He knew where she was.

Jasper was a dead man.

***

Puddles of yellow light splashed across the floor but did little to take the chill from the room or her body. She'd watched the gentle progress of the sun for the last few hours, lethargy holding her immobile.

But time and daylight would not wait for her. She had to move, had to get out of here before the day disappeared.

The sunlight's waning strength said it was already late afternoon. There was so little time left.

Gritting her teeth, she straightened out her right leg. Stiff muscles protested the movement, and her stomach churned. Head swimming, she gritted her teeth and slowly straightened her other leg.

Her arms were almost as difficult to move, stiff and leaden with cold. Her whole body felt numb with it, her skin icy to touch. But for the first time in ages, she felt stirrings of life in the void that had been her psychic gifts. Massaging her legs with stiff fingers, she glanced warily at the bed. Monica and Jasper lay still and silent, naked limbs entwined around each other. If they breathed, she couldn't see it.

But what interested her more was the door next to the bed. Until now, she hadn't even realized it existed. She bit her lip, then rolled over onto her hands and knees.

The effort sent the room into a swim. She took several deep breaths, her gaze never leaving the figures on the bed.

They didn't stir.

Slowly she turned and put her hands against the wall, using it for support as she stood.

No movement on the bed.

Sweat trickled down the side of her face. She turned around until her back was braced against the wall. Sick tension churned her stomach, but she ignored it, focusing instead on the padlock chaining the door closed. She lacked the time and energy for finesse; she hit the lock with all the psychic energy she could muster. It literally exploded, the noise reverberating around the room. She held her breath and watched the figures on the bed

Still no sign of movement. Maybe they were playing with her, toying with her hopes like a cat with a mouse. She had a sudden vision of reaching the door only to have Jasper reach out and grab her, destroying her last hope of freedom.

It would be the ultimate trick. The last straw. And there was nothing she could do but take the risk.

Her legs were like rubber. Every step she took felt like a mile. She kept her gaze on Jasper and prayed he didn't move.

She reached the door and pushed it open. Beyond lay

the steep ascent of stairs. Her prison, and their home, was a cellar of some kind.

Gripping the handrail, she dragged herself upward. The ache in her leg muscles became a scream, and it seemed to take forever to reach the top. When she reached the final step, she collapsed, bruising her knees and battling to catch her breath.

After a few precious seconds, she rose and staggered on, finding herself in a kitchen. Dust covered the mess time and vandals had caused. If the thickness of the dirt was any indication, the house had been abandoned for years.

Her hopes of quick rescue plummeted. She walked on, skirting shattered glass and smashed floorboards, seeking an exit. She had to hurry. Exhaustion was a huge wall threatening to topple her over.

In the next room she discovered her clothes and shoes, thrown haphazardly in a corner. Her cross wasn't among her clothes—not that it mattered. Jasper had shown no fear of it when he'd ripped it from her neck.

She stopped long enough to throw on her jacket and jeans, and slip on her shoes. The rest she left. Time was moving, and so must she.

Panic crept past her guard and filled her limbs with energy. She ran down the corridor, no longer caring about the noise she made. The front door loomed before her— locked. She pushed with kinetic energy. The door exploded outward with enough noise to wake the dead.

She felt the urge to laugh insanely, and she clamped down on it hard. Madness was no escape—and of no use to her now.

Her eyes watered against the sudden glare of bright sunlight. She threw up a hand to protect them and staggered on. It didn't really matter where she ran, as long as it was away from the house and its occupants.

Stones scurried from under her feet. The harsh sound of traffic assaulted her ears. Blinking rapidly, she recognized shops, a mall milling with people. Safety. Jasper wouldn't find her in such a crowd. Wouldn't dare kidnap her with so many witnesses.

Wouldn't have to, when all he had to do was call her name...

Heart pounding unevenly, she ran, desperate to get lost in the evening crowds and the safe oblivion they offered her mind.

Dusk began to streak the sky with crimson sheets. She reeled like a drunkard and smacked into an old man. His curse followed her as she staggered on. She had to keep going, had to escape, before he came after her.

"Nikki!"

Her heart stopped. *Oh lord, he'd found her!* Without looking back, she ran on. Somehow, Jasper had found her. Terror lent her feet wings.

Nikki!

The shout reverberated through her. She bit back a cry of terror. He was after her. She had to keep on running.

Stop! Nikki, watch it...

A screech of tires filled her ears. Too late she became aware of the road, the traffic, and the red car rushing upon her.

She tried to dodge, but the car hit her. Agony exploded as oblivion swept in.

Ten

The heavy rumbling of traffic woke her some time later. Nikki shifted slightly, and silk rustled against her skin, bunching near her thigh. A faint scent clung to the material, warm, musty and recognizable. She smiled, wondering how she'd come to be wearing Michael's shirt.

Opening her eyes, she studied the room. The sun peeped brightly behind the curtained window to her left, casting pinpoints of lights across the pale blue walls. Paint peeled from the smoke-stained ceiling above her, and from the small brown dresser next to the bed. It wasn't her room, or her dresser. Her heart skipped several beats. Where was she?

A hand rested lightly on hers, enclosing her fingers in warmth. Michael. She closed her eyes briefly and wished he'd take her in his arms, tell her that it had all been a nightmare, that everything would be all right.

But he didn't move, and maybe that was just as well.

"What time is it?" she asked softly.

"Four in the afternoon."

The weariness in his voice tore at her heart. She turned around, but even such a small movement caused pain to run down her legs. She bit her lip, fighting the sudden sting of tears.

"Gently, Nikki. Your hip and left leg were badly grazed by the car."

He sat in a chair next to the bed, bare feet propped on the mattress. He looked casual, yet there was nothing remotely casual in the way he studied her. In the dark depths of his eyes, she could see all her secrets, all her fears. All that had happened.

She swallowed uneasily, and looked away. "I guess I'm lucky it's only grazed. How did you find me?"

"Followed your thoughts."

If her thoughts were so open to him, why didn't he tell her if Jasper's mind-bending techniques had succeeded or not? "How long was I gone?"

"Three nights."

It had seemed an eternity longer. She shivered and rubbed her wrist. Though the two puncture wounds in her skin had healed, her flesh still burned. "Where are we?"

"My hotel room. It's safer than the hospital, where Jasper could come and go as he pleased."

Plus Jasper didn't know where Michael was—but would it really matter now? He could touch her thoughts any time he desired and find out where they were. There wasn't a damn thing she could do to stop him.

"How are you feeling this morning?" Michael's voice was calm as he shifted his feet and rose, but something in the way he moved spoke of violence.

She watched him pour water into a glass. His midnight colored hair was unkempt and in need of a wash, his face etched by deep lines of tiredness. His clothes were disheveled and creased, as if he hadn't slept in days.

She wanted to reach out and caress the tautness from his shoulders, kiss the tension from his lips. Instead, she clenched her fists against the blanket. Was she insane? She wanted to touch a vampire in ways she'd never wanted to touch a man before...

"Michael, why didn't you tell me?" she whispered, ignoring the glass of water he held out to her.

The muscles along his arms went taut, momentarily straining against the restriction of his rolled-up sleeves. Then he slowly lowered the glass back to the bedside table.

"I'm sorry, Nikki—" He hesitated and shrugged, momentarily avoiding her gaze. "I never meant for you to find out this way."

"Did you ever plan to tell me?"

Again he hesitated fractionally. "I don't know."

At least he was being honest with her. And if she was being honest with herself, she had never, at any stage, truly feared him. Just the darkness within him, the darkness she now could name.

A darkness he could never be free of.

He held out the glass again. Her hand shook as she brought it to her lips. The cool water did little to ease the fire in her throat.

"I would never hurt you, Nikki."

She met his dark gaze and tried to ignore the trembling deep in her soul. By not telling her the truth about himself, he'd only emphasized the fact that he didn't trust her. And that hurt more than anything Jasper could ever do to her.

Michael sat back on the chair, fingers entwined lightly
in his lap. "There are things about me that you will never
know. It's safer that way—for you, and for me. Just trust
me, Nikki."

"*Trust you?*" She couldn't help a slightly bitter laugh.
"Dear God, Michael, I've trusted you more in the last few
days than I've trusted anyone in my entire life!"

"And yet, deep down, you still fear me." His gaze met
hers, reached deep into her soul. "I have never lied to you,
Nikki—"

"No." Her voice was terse. "You just ask me to do what
you cannot, or feed me half truths when it suits you."

He slapped his hands hard against the arms of the
chair and thrust himself upright. "And would it have made
any difference if I had? " he asked sharply. "Would the
truth have stopped you from entering that tunnel after
Monica?"

"No. But it sure as hell hurts that maniac has to tell
me what you could not." She watched him walk through
the bedroom doorway into the small kitchen. "There's more
you're not telling me, isn't there? You're not in this alone,
are you?'

He glanced around, one eyebrow raised. "No, I'm not.
But they're not important, not at the moment."

He lied, and it hurt. Why wouldn't he trust her? Did he
fear Jasper's influence, or was there something more?
"Yeah. Like you being a vampire wasn't important?"

"No, not like that." He slammed a cupboard door closed.
"Are you hungry?"

Her stomach rolled at the thought of food. Considering
how little she'd eaten during the last few days, she should
have been famished. She wasn't. "As long as it's something
easy."

"I have soup simmering."

She nodded and closed her eyes, suddenly confused.
How much did her need to fight with Michael come from
Jasper's games? Would she end up betraying Michael, no
matter how hard she tried not to?

"The mere fact you ask yourself those questions
suggests his plan hasn't entirely worked."

He walked back into the room and placed a steaming
tray on the bedside table. She ignored it and sat up. "He

had me for three nights, Michael. He might still have my mind. What happens if I do betray you?"

"We'll deal with it if and when it happens." He sat on the bed beside her and placed an arm around her shoulders. She leaned into him, savoring the warmth of his body.

"We cannot undo what has been done. You must fight it, Nikki."

"And if I can't?" She rested her cheek lightly against his shoulder and tried to ignore the gentle strength with which he held her. Lord, it felt so right in his arms...

"Then we're all in trouble."

The grimness in his voice made her shiver. Just what would he do if she ever did betray him?

He sighed, a slightly bitter sound that pierced her heart. "When will you realize I would never hurt you?"

"I'm sorry." She bit her lip, regretting her thoughts the minute his arm left her shoulders. His touch fought the demons in her mind, easing the chill forming a tight knot of fear in the pit of her stomach.

He rose and retrieved the tray, placing it over her knees. "Finish the whole bowl. You need to get some nourishment back into your system. Give me a call if you want anything else."

"Why? Where are you going?" She hated the slight edge of panic in her voice, yet the thought of being alone filled her with fear.

"I'll be resting on the couch in the other room. It's been a long three days, I'm afraid."

Had he eaten...?

"I haven't." His answer was grim. "Do you think it was easy for me, knowing who had you? Imagining what he was doing?"

"I'm sorry." She hesitated, not sure what to say, not sure how to take the touch of pain in his eyes. "I just thought vampires had no choice but to sleep during the day."

"Everyone must sleep, Nikki, even those of us not quite human. Vampires do so during the day because, for the most part, the sun is deadly to us."

She remembered the sun touching Jasper's back, and the red welts it left there. "And feeding?" she asked softly, not really sure if she wanted to know the answer.

"I do not dine on human blood, Nikki. Nor do I need to feed every day, as Jasper and Monica must." He hesitated, then added in a voice heavy with bitterness. "After three hundred years of existence, you learn to do without many things."

She blinked. Had she heard him right? He was *three hundred* years old?

"Yes." He sighed, and ran a hand through his unkempt hair. "Now eat, and rest. I'll be near if you need me."

He left the room quickly. Frowning, she picked up the spoon, eating the soup without really tasting it. When she'd finished, she shoved the tray back on the bedside table and settled back down to get some sleep.

Her dreams were filled with fear and madness, haunted by an evil that teased and mocked. She woke to darkness hours later, the silk shirt twisted about her body and damp with sweat. Blinking the sleep from her eyes, she stared at the night-held room.

Something about the stillness told her she was alone, and her heart skipped several beats. But that wasn't what she feared. No, there was something else...

Like a siren's song, the call whispered through her mind, urging her into action.

Frightened, yet unable to resist the pull of the call, she threw aside the blankets and rose. Walking unsteadily across the room, she pushed the curtains to one side and stared out.

Darkness held the city in its grip. The clock tower down the street chimed four times, and the street below was silent, empty.

Then the shadows moved.

Jasper. Smiling confidently at her, sure of her response. *Come to me.*

Something deep within responded, wanting to do as he asked. She closed her eyes, fighting it, fighting him.

It's too late to fight. You are mine.

Never. I'll kill myself first.

His laughter sang through her soul, filling her with its corruption. Trembling, she crossed her arms and turned from the window. It didn't stop the treacherous whisper begging her to do whatever he wanted. She took a deep breath, trying to gather her scattered wits. *Michael, where are you? I need you.*

And if he couldn't hear her silent plea for help? Well, she wasn't helpless, no matter what the demons in her mind might say.

Do not ignore me, pretty one.

She shivered, and battled for calm and the strength to resist as she turned back to the window. *Where's Monica?*

Hunting us up some breakfast.

Images filled her—visions hot with lust and violence. Her pulse quickened, as if stirred, and she blanched, feeling sick. Lord, why was this happening? What had he done to her?

You will beg me, pretty one. As Monica begged me.

He wanted her to hunt the night with him, become a slave to darkness and death and uncontrollable blood lust. Revulsion turned her stomach. *I will never walk with you.*

Yet she could hear the uncertainty in her own assertion. Jasper was Tommy, only a hundred times stronger. If he gained control of her mind, she would never know her wish from his.

Never is a long time in my world. And I grow tired of Monica.

His laughter echoed through her mind. She clenched her fists, battling the urge to run as far as she could from the madman below. He was only toying with her, testing her nerve, her strength. And it took all the strength she had to remain still, to ignore his taunting whispers, and stare at him in silence.

***

Michael took the stairs two at a time, making no effort to keep quiet. Jasper had made little effort to conceal himself, and he would know that Nikki had called. Just as *he* knew the three zombies stationed around the hotel would move in on Nikki if he went after Jasper. He reached the third floor and ran down the corridor, only slowing when he approached his room. Even from this distance, he could feel her distress. Yet she resisted Jasper's call, and that was more than he had truly expected.

He unlocked the door and stepped inside. Psychic energy danced around him, though he doubted if she was truly aware of his presence. She was using everything she had to resist Jasper. He clenched his fingers and stopped, taking a deep, calming breath. Now was not the time to run downstairs and commit murder. Nikki needed him.

He walked to the bedroom. She stood near the window, still wearing his old black shirt. It hung to her thighs and did little to hide her slender but shapely figure. She had never looked more alluring. Or more frightened.

"Nikki?" he said softly, not wanting to scare her by suddenly appearing by her side.

She jumped anyway and turned. "He's here." Her voice was steady despite the panic he could see in her eyes. "Across the road."

He stopped beside her and slid his hand down her arm, entwining his fingers around hers. The rhythm of her heart was loud and erratic, and her hands were like ice. He drew the other curtain aside and looked out.

Jasper waved at them.

Anger spurted through him. He clamped down on it, hard. "He's an arrogant bastard."

She swallowed. "He's calling me, Michael. He wants me to go to him."

He was really going to enjoy killing this bastard. "He's only testing, Nikki. And now he knows his leash is not as strong as he had hoped."

But the man below them only teased, and she knew it. He could taste the fear in her thoughts.

"Why don't you go down there after him?"

Because he wants you dead, and the zombies are ready to complete the task should I leave your side. "I wanted to make sure you were all right first."

"Then why not go down now?"

"Because he won't be there. He is just trying to unnerve you, Nikki."

"Well, it's working." She untangled her fingers from his and wrapped her arms around her body. Though he wished he could hold her, give her the comfort she desperately needed, he didn't dare move. Jasper still watched them. "He can't hurt you unless you let him. You have your abilities. Use them to protect yourself."

She had to get past her fear. He couldn't be with her twenty-four hours a day. Besides, the best way to protect her was to kill Jasper. To do that, he had to leave her alone.

She gave him a quick glance, and he wondered if she'd heard the thought. With the link between them growing stronger by the day, it was becoming increasingly hard to keep his thoughts to himself.

"He's leaving," she stated quietly.

Michael watched him fade into the darkness, saw the blur of his body heat move quickly up the street. With dawn only a few hours away, he'd be off to hunt before retreating for the day. No doubt there would be more murders for the Lyndhurst *Mail* to report to its troubled readership.

He let the curtain fall back into place and turned, drawing her into his arms. She felt so soft and warm against him. He brushed a kiss against the top of her head and held her quietly until her tremors stopped.

"Thank you," she whispered, then pulled away slightly.

Her eyes were bright, but not with fear. He could hear the unsteady pounding of her heart and knew its rhythm matched his own

He raised a hand, gently brushing a dark strand of hair away from her cheek. Her skin was silk under his fingers. He traced the outline of her jaw, then lightly brushed her lips with his fingers. He wished he could taste their fullness, but that wouldn't be fair. Not when she was so frightened, and Jasper still ran loose.

"You should rest," he said, watching the sparkle in her amber eyes, watching the heat rise in her cheeks. God, she was beautiful.

"I want you to stay with me, Michael," she said softly. "I want you to make love to me."

He studied her, seeing the hint of desperation in her eyes, the fear in her thoughts. While he couldn't deny the attraction flaring between them, he knew it had nothing to do with her sudden desire to make love. In any other situation, any other time, he might have taken what she offered, enjoyed her company until the job was done, and then left. As he had with other women in the past. But not with Nikki, and not for the reason he could see in her heart. Somehow, it just didn't seem right for them to make love just to erase Jasper's thoughts from her mind.

But damn, she felt so good...

He bent and kissed her. He'd meant it to be brief, but her lips were soft and sweet under his, and he found himself wanting more. Her hand brushed his cheek as she moved it around his neck, and he closed his eyes, pulling her close, teasing her lips with his tongue. She made a sound that was almost a sigh, then opened her mouth, allowing him to taste her. He moved his hands down her back and cupped her buttocks, holding her softness against him.

He didn't want the moment to end, but knew it had to. No involvement, he reminded himself sharply. Let her go. He kissed her forehead lightly then stepped away.

"I cannot do this, Nikki." Because Seline was right. He was playing with a fire that, once started, he might never want to put out. "It's not the right time or situation."

A slight smile touched her warm lips. "It felt pretty right to me."

It had felt pretty right to him, as well, and that was the problem. "I am a vampire, Nikki. It's a fact that can never be changed. I live in a world of darkness and tread paths no human can ever take." He hesitated, watching her amber eyes darken. "I have made love to many women in my time, but they were little more than fleeting moments of pleasure. There can never be anything more for me. Vampire's cannot love."

The lie tasted bitter on his tongue. But it was better she think him incapable of love. It would make things easier when he walked away.

"I'm not asking for anything more than one night, Michael." Her gaze searched his for a moment. "I don't want anything more."

Maybe she didn't, he thought, studying the dark auburn highlights in her hair. But could he hold her in his arms, make love to her, then simply walk away?

"Making love will strengthen the link between us, Nikki," he said softly. "Can you risk that, when you fear the link almost as much as you fear the vampire?"

She glanced up sharply. "I don't fear you."

He smiled grimly. "No. You fear the darkness in me—the vampire. But I am not two beings, and you cannot fear one without fearing the other."

She closed her eyes and took a deep breath. "I don't care about the technicalities, Michael. I just want—"

He placed a finger against her lips, quickly silencing her. Someone approached the room. He turned and watched the heat of life approach. After a moment, he relaxed. It was only Jake.

And just in the nick of time, too.

Smiling wryly, he glanced back at Nikki. "Jake's about to knock at the door. He's angry about something."

"How can you tell?" She rubbed her hands up and down her arms, a gesture that spoke of the fear he could see in her thoughts.

"His heart is racing, and fury runs through his thoughts."

"Something's happened."

He entwined his fingers through hers and squeezed them lightly. She smiled, then motioned him towards the door when Jake knocked.

Jake's smile was anything but warm. "Have you heard the news yet?"

"No." It wasn't too hard to guess what had happened, though. He stepped aside, allowing Jake to enter. "Why?"

"Our vampires are on the loose again. There's been a triple murder in Highgate Park."

"When did this happen?"

"They figure about ten this evening." Jake grimaced and walked into the small kitchen. "But the bodies weren't discovered until two. The cops are still crawling all over the place."

"You've been there?" Nikki said, surprise in her voice.

"No. I asked Mark to let me know if anything like this happened." He glanced across at Michael and added. "Mark's the crime reporter for *The Mail.*"

Michael nodded. Jasper had been hungry when he'd left the hotel, so these murders had to be Monica's doing. He met Nikki's gaze and saw she was thinking the same thing.

"We have to stop her," she murmured.

He shook his head in exasperation. Did she never learn? Jasper was still out there, and no doubt waiting for such a move.

Her gaze was defiant. "You can't find her without me."

Maybe they could, and maybe they couldn't. It wasn't worth jeopardizing her safety to find out.

"You'll slow us down," Jake commented into the brief silence. "You're a liability, Nik. Trying to protect you might well get us all killed."

"We'll be moving in the daylight—we'll have the advantage, remember?"

"The zombies can still get around during the day," Michael reminded her. "And Jasper has proven he can move at dawn or dusk."

She lifted her chin, though he could hear the unsteady pounding of her pulse. "I'm going. I refuse to let fear rule my life."

Or anything, or anyone, else. He clamped down on a surge of anger and glanced at his watch. "It's past four now. We'll have to give it a few more hours before we move. That way we'll be sure to find them asleep—if we find them."

Jake frowned as he poured some soup into two coffee cups. "And you? Won't you be affected?"

Nikki raised an eyebrow, and Michael smiled. "As long as we avoid the sun between ten and three, I'll be fine."

Jake poured soup into two cups and handed one to Nikki. "I'll be back at eight, then. That way, we'll still have two hours to hunt around. Nice soup, by the way."

Michael walked him to the door. Jake turned the handle, then hesitated. "Don't let her come with us," he said softly.

He raised an eyebrow. "I can't really stop her."

"Find a way. Stop her. I don't care how. Just don't let that madman get his hands on her again."

This from the man who had once told him Nikki could be difficult when it came to getting her to do anything she didn't want to do. He nodded and closed the door, then turned to find her watching him. Her knuckles were almost white against the cup.

"If you intend coming with us, you'd better get some rest. Jake was right. As you are, you'll slow us down."

Her eyebrows rose in surprise, and he smiled grimly. "I don't intend to argue the point any more. If you wish to commit suicide, who am I to stop you?"

Anger glinted in her eyes, but she made no comment. She quickly drank the rest of her soup, then turned and stalked into the bedroom. He followed and leaned against the door frame, trying to ignore the slim line of her legs as she climbed into bed.

"Do you need anything?" he asked. Their thoughts touched briefly, and passion caressed his mind. He tensed and quickly broke the contact.

She sighed. "No."

"Call me if you do. I'll be resting on the sofa." He ran his fingers through his hair and turned away, moving quickly to the sofa. But he knew he wouldn't sleep. Not after the fire of her touch.

Eleven

"Nikki, wake up."

The soft words speared the madness. She shuddered and fought the dark layers clinging to her mind, desperate to reach the safety of Michael's voice.

"Nikki, let it go. Break the connection."

Warm hands touched her face, caressed her cheek. The demons of madness laughed rabidly, but retreated.

"Nikki?"

She opened her eyes, studying Michael for a heartbeat. He sat on the edge of the bed, his dark eyes full of compassion and a certain amount of wariness.

"Hold me," she whispered, pushing the blankets aside and struggling upright. "Please, just hold me."

He drew her into his arms. She leaned a cheek against the bare warmth of his chest, allowing the heat of his touch to chase the chill away. Allowed the tender caress of his thoughts to chase the last strands of darkness from her mind.

"You have to fight him, Nikki."

"How?" Her voice cracked slightly, and she bit her lip. But how could she fight Jasper when she'd never been able to fight Tommy? Jasper's evil was far more intense than Tommy's ever had been.

But she'd survived Tommy, and she'd survived three nights of Jasper's insanity. She'd survive this—any way she could.

Michael held her silently, the rock to which she clung in the ever-turbulent currents of her life. Gradually, almost unwillingly, she became aware of his scent, musky yet fresh; aware of the slight tension in the arms that held her so gently. She could hear his heart pounding as erratically as her own. She lifted her head and met his gaze. His smile made her heart do an odd little somersault.

He gently touched her cheek, then ran his fingers down to her lips. "*Not* making love to you is the hardest thing I've ever had to do."

Her pulse leapt beneath his touch. She kissed his fingers, then reached up and traced the firm line of his jaw. "I don't want your restraint, Michael. I want you."

Just touch me. Hold me. Love me. She bit her lip and looked away from the understanding in his eyes. What she was doing wasn't fair, but there wasn't any other way to drive Jasper from her thoughts. Was it too much to ask for just an hour, maybe two, of Jasper's darkness not staining her thoughts?

He sighed and closed his eyes. Fighting the needs of his body, she thought. It was a battle she didn't want him to win.

Leaning forward, she captured his lips with her own. He groaned and tightened his arms around her, his lips suddenly harsh against hers.

Then he pulled away. "Don't do this, Nikki." His voice was ragged, dark eyes troubled.

"Why not?" What was wrong with wanting to kiss him, make love to him, until the darkness ran away and there was nothing but the two of them alone?

Couldn't he see she needed this, needed to keep the darkness and insanity at bay?

"Nikki, it's wrong."

She raised an eyebrow. "Why is it wrong?"

He didn't answer. She moved closer and trailed tiny kisses around his neck, then gently bit his earlobe. He made no move to stop her, no move to encourage her, yet she could feel the tension under her fingers and wondered what he was so afraid of. Vampires might not be able to love, but they *could* make love, and that was all she was asking of him.

She ran her hand down the warm length of his body until she touched the waistband of his pants. Fingers trembling, she slowly undid his fly.

"Nikki—" he hesitated, his body tensing when she touched him. "The timing is wrong."

She closed her eyes and briefly rested her forehead against his shoulder. He was right. This was neither the time nor the place for them to make love. But what other choice did she have? She had to stop the stain of Jasper's darkness growing stronger in her mind.

"Please, Michael. Just love me."

He groaned again and crushed her to him. She kissed him fiercely, savoring the taste of his lips, his mouth. He caressed her breast, her stomach, her buttocks, his hands gentle yet his touch urgent, setting her aflame with need. She reveled in the play of muscles across his shoulders, the feel of his skin, so smooth and warm against hers.

"Lay down with me," she said softly.

Michael smiled and stretched out beside her. He ran a hand down the gentle curve of her side, watching the desire darken her amber eyes. Yet he could feel the desperation in her thoughts, the urgent need to deny Jasper's growing control over her. He touched her cheek, following the outline of her jaw down to her mouth. Her skin was soft and smelled so good, like honey and cinnamon. She captured his finger in her mouth and sucked on it gently. Heat ran through him, through the link, a smoldering fire threatening to explode.

God, there was no denying his desire for her.

"I cannot offer you anything more than this moment, Nikki." Not the words he should have said, by any stretch of the imagination. He might have been a three-hundred-year-old vampire, but in some ways, he was still very human. Something he could not deny with her so close.

Her dark amber gaze met his, and he knew that she wanted nothing more than this moment, that all she cared about was time without Jasper's intrusion in her thoughts.

It hurt somehow, though God knew it shouldn't have. She was only using him in the same manner he'd used a score of other woman during his life.

At least he would have the memory of loving her in the long nights of loneliness left ahead.

"Good." Though her voice was light, there was an edge that made him wonder if she'd heard his thoughts. "If you had stopped right now, I would've killed you."

He touched her lips, then ran his finger lightly down her neck to her breast. "The only thing likely to stop me now is a change of heart from you."

"Then stop talking," she murmured.

Power shivered between them, a gossamer touch that tugged his jeans slowly from his body. He laughed against her lips, then pulled away slightly. Using his own kinetic abilities, he eased the shirt up and over her head, then tossed it across the room.

"Now I know what the romance books mean when they say he undressed her with his mind."

Though her smile was easy, fear flickered deep in her eyes. He kissed her, savoring the sweetness of her lips as he drew her close. Their minds entwined in a gentle dance of fire, sharing each sensation, each emotion.

The chains of the link between them were drawing tighter, but right then, he didn't care. He had this moment, and he had Nikki in his arms. That was a damn sight more than he'd had in a very long time.

"I need you," he whispered and held her tightly, breathing in the scent of her hair as he battled the urgency pounding through his body, his heart.

"Then take me," she murmured, her lips trailing fire where they touched.

The gentle dance of their minds grew heated, wildfire ready to explode.

God, she felt so good, so right. How in the hell was he going to walk away from the emotions underlying the heat of all this? How could he deny the harmony of their minds? How could either of them?

Nikki ran a hand through the dark silk of his hair. "Hush, Michael. Just love me. Let tomorrow worry about itself."

Give me one night without fear, one night to remember when Jasper is gone, and you walk away. Pain flickered through her heart, but she ignored it. She had no time, no wish, to do anything more than respond to the heat of his touch, the warmth of his thoughts. Lord, it felt as if she had known him all *his* life, had been responding to him for the three hundred years he had mentioned—as though his touch and his kiss and his warmth were as vital as air. As vital as the blood that thundered through his heart and hers.

Maybe they were. But that was something she'd worry about tomorrow. She had this moment and time without Jasper in her mind. She had to make the most of it.

***

Michael gently caressed Nikki's thigh. Lord, it felt so good, lying here beside her in the warm aftermath of their lovemaking. Her thoughts were as quiet as the gentle rhythm of her heart. In a few minutes she'd be asleep. But as much as he wanted Nikki to rest, he couldn't let her, not just yet.

"Nikki, we need to talk," he said softly.

She stirred and murmured something he couldn't quite catch. He reached out, brushing silken strands of hair away from her face. "Nikki?"

Her eyes opened, and a smile twitched the corners of her mouth. Only the sudden wisp of wariness in her thoughts made him resist the impulse to kiss her.

"I gather vampires are immune to the make-love-then-collapse syndrome that seems to affect so many men."

He smiled. "No, they're not." He would have liked nothing more than to fall to sleep with her in his arms. But Jasper was out there. "We have to talk."

"What about?" A flicker of guilt ran through her thoughts, and he wondered if she were already regretting their lovemaking.

"About Tommy."

It was not what she'd expected, and her thoughts were suddenly chaotic. "Why?"

"Jasper's using your fear against you, Nikki. He's using past demons to grind down your resistance."

She tensed. "What do you mean?"

She knew what he meant. He could see the images in her mind, skittering like scared rabbits. "I mean it's time you faced the past, time for you to let go of the guilt."

She was silent for a long moment. Michael held her quietly, listening to the beat of her heart, a rhythm filled with fear.

"Tommy has nothing to do with any of this," she muttered finally. Heat crept through her cheeks as she looked away. "You've no right to know, no right to ask."

And no right to care. It was a thought that tasted bitter. But one way or another, she had to face the guilt centered around that part of her past, or she would have very little hope of resisting Jasper's final call. In many ways, Jasper represented the darker side of human existence, and guilt was part of that darkness. It drew her into Jasper's sphere of influence, made it all that much easier for him to attack her.

"Jasper wouldn't use Tommy's memory if he didn't think it would help break your spirit, Nikki. It's time you told someone what happened."

Her face was as pale as the tangled sheets beneath

them. "If I tell you, will you promise never to bring the subject up again?"

"Yes." It was an easy thing to promise, given he had no intention of staying around. He might have the *desire* to stay, but desire was something he rarely gave in to.

She stared at her feet. "I met Tommy several months after my parents' death. I was pretty messed up at the time, and on the run. The authorities wanted to place me with my grandparents, who I'd never met." She hesitated, and shrugged. "Tommy led the street gang I started running with."

No wonder she'd empathized with Monica. She'd been in much the same situation as the teenager—young and confused, with no one listening to what she wanted. An easy target for evil. Though why she thought Tommy was in the same league as Jasper, he couldn't say. Maybe it was merely a reaction to her memories, her fear.

"How did you meet him?"

She licked her lips. "I was in a store his gang was robbing. One of the kids was bashing the old guy at the register, and I stopped him."

"Kinetically?"

She nodded. "It was the first time it happened. Up until then, I hadn't really done much more than have the occasional dream."

Images of her parents' death flickered through her mind, images not faded by time or acceptance. She must have dreamed of their deaths. "How old were you?"

"Fourteen."

Fourteen years old and no doubt going through puberty. Most talents didn't fully appear before then. Add on top of that the fact she'd seen her parents die, once in her dreams and once in reality, and it was no wonder she'd been pretty messed up.

And in many respects, still was.

He might not be able to stay here with her and share his dreams or his heart, but he could give her peace. *If* he could keep her talking. "What happened?"

"Tommy happened. He'd swung around and our gazes met—" She hesitated, then shrugged. "I know it sounds corny, but at the time, it felt like I'd just met my destiny. He was gifted, like me, and seemed to know I needed help."

More than likely he'd seen the potential of her abilities and had known the power that one day would be hers. And had wanted it, as Jasper wanted it. Michael clenched his fist. Nikki glanced at him, and he forced himself to relax. "So you joined his gang?"

She nodded. "He was good to me, at least at first. He taught me how to survive the streets, taught me how to control and use my gifts."

Pain swirled around him, a gossamer veil he could almost touch. "When did it all change?" Though he could see the answer in her thoughts clearly enough, he wanted her to talk about it. Maybe then she would see that Tommy wasn't the savior she thought him to be. The bastard had done little more than take advantage of a frightened young girl.

"When I turned fifteen." She shuddered, and he had to resist the urge to hold her close and caress all the hurt away. "Everything changed. He became possessive, never letting me out of his sight. Sometimes it felt as if he was in my mind, governing my thoughts, my actions."

If Tommy's telepathy had been as strong as she seemed to think, then that was probably just what he'd been doing. Fifteen years old and barely in control of her gifts, she would have had little resistance when it came to subtle mind merging. He clenched his fingers again, then slowly straightened them out. Tommy was dead, and there was nothing he could do about the past—other than help her through the pain of it.

"When did this extend to trying to control your gifts?"

Her gaze jerked to his. "How did you know?"

He grimaced. "It wasn't hard to guess, given your reaction to our link."

Her gaze skittered away, but her thoughts were clear enough. She still wasn't comfortable with the link, still wasn't comfortable with him. Maybe she'd never be. Attraction or not, it was only the thought of Jasper invading her mind that kept her on the bed with him, kept her talking.

At least he had something to thank Jasper for.

"What happened?" he asked softly.

Fear shimmered through the link. "Tommy gave me a ring for my next birthday. He told me he loved me." She hesitated and swallowed. "What did I know of love? He was my world, all that I had left since my parents' death. But maybe he could see the doubts, because he asked me to prove what I felt for him."

"How?" The question came out more abruptly than he'd intended, and she looked up quickly. He forced a smile, though it was the last thing he felt like doing. "What did he ask you to do?"

"Merge minds. Even though I sometimes feared him, and what he could do, I saw no harm in it. It was something we'd been practicing for a while." She shuddered. "Only this time it was deeper. This time it was complete."

He could see the chaotic results in her mind. Her gifts, controlled by Tommy, had been used in violence. No wonder she now feared any sort of mind-link.

"What did you do?"

"What could I do?" Her question was almost a plea. For an instant she was very much a confused and frightened teenager, not a twenty-five-year-old woman. "I was sixteen years old and had no one I could turn to for help. Not that Tommy would have let me run. He knew my thoughts, and he could stop me, make me do things..." She paused, and a tear ran down her cheek.

The first crack in the wall, Michael thought, resisting the urge to wipe the drop away. It wasn't over yet. She had to face up to the destruction she'd unwillingly caused.

"What sort of things?"

She wouldn't look at him. He placed a finger under her chin and gently tilted her face upwards. "What did you do, Nikki?" he said, closing his heart to the pain in her eyes and her thoughts.

"Tommy pulled a bank robbery, but it went wrong." She jerked away from his touch and dashed the tears from her eyes. "I'd refused to take part, and for some reason, Tommy hadn't been able to make me. Instead, I waited a block away with a getaway car. But the police had received a tip and were waiting."

Which didn't explain the pain he could almost taste. "What happened, Nikki?"

"Tommy escaped, and the police and security guards chased him. He came straight back to me. He used my gifts to...to..."

She hesitated again, and more tears glimmered on her cheeks. He made no move, though he ached to hold her.

She took a deep breath. "He used my kinetic abilities to destroy several police cars. One of the security guards he threw through a store window. The falling glass cut the guard's throat. Another was thrown into a wall and now lives in a wheelchair. I couldn't stop him, Michael. I fought so hard, but I just couldn't stop him."

That was why she'd made him vow never to make her do anything against her will. A sob escaped her control, and he drew her into his arms and let her cry. At least she was finally letting go of the pain she'd held in check for so long. But it wasn't over yet. "How did you escape the police?"

She laughed, a bitter, brittle sound that made him wince. "I didn't. Tommy escaped. They told me later that I'd been lucky he hadn't grabbed me as a hostage. They never knew it was me who killed that guard..."

"If one man uses a gun to kill another, you blame the man who pulled the trigger, not the weapon, Nikki." And that's all she'd been, a weapon. She sniffed, but wasn't ready to let go of the past just yet. "How did he die?"

"The streets caught up with him. His violence had made him a lot of enemies, and in the end, it came back to him."

Then why did she feel so guilty about his death?

She shifted in his arms, resting her cheek against his shoulder. The warmth of her skin burned into him. He fleetingly wished they could just stay here, on this bed, and forget about everything but each other.

"Because I dreamed it was going to happen," she whispered. "And I didn't tell him."

She was reading his thoughts as clearly as he was reading hers. Link or not, she shouldn't have been able to. "Why not?" he asked, knowing that in the same situation, he would have wished the fiend to hell and laughed as he died.

But Nikki didn't have three hundred years of weariness behind her.

"*Oh God...*" She hesitated, and her hand clenched against his. "I told him that I hated him. I told him he could burn in hell for all I cared. Ten hours later he was dead. I felt his soul leave his body, Michael. I felt it encased in the fires of Hell. I could have stopped it, but I didn't.

Just as I didn't stop my parents" death. They all died because of me."

If she'd seen her parents' death, why hadn't she warned them? Surely not out of hate—she had loved them, that much was clear. "His soul was cursed long before you came along, Nikki. You did nothing more than trust the wrong man."

"But he was good to me. He cared for me."

He was pretty sure the only person Tommy had cared about was himself. But she wasn't ready yet to face that. "He only wanted to make you trust him, make you need him. Where Jasper has tried force and drugs to subvert your will, Tommy used your emotions."

"But I loved him."

Yet even as she whispered the words, there was doubt in her thoughts. For the first time in years, she was looking past her fear and truly seeing the man Tommy had been.

"But he didn't die because of that love, Nikki." He hesitated, the added, "He was a vicious thug who got what he deserved."

"Maybe. But there's still my parents."

Three hours ago she wouldn't have confided this much. And yet he sensed it wasn't so much trust as the need to finally purge her demons. Perhaps she saw the necessity as much as he. "Want to tell me about it?"

"No." She took a deep, somewhat shuddery breath. "They were going away without me, taking a second honeymoon and leaving me in the care of a nanny. I was so furious with them. When I had the dream, I didn't tell them."

"You were a kid, Nikki. All kids do horrible things at one time or another."

"Not all kids watch their parents die. Not all kids feel the caress of their mother's soul as she passes away."

Which was surely punishment enough for her childish rush of spitefulness. "Would your parents have believed you even if you had told them? Would it have stopped them from going?"

She smiled slightly. "No. They would have seen it as a variation on the tantrums I'd been throwing."

"Then you could not have changed what was fated to happen."

"Maybe. Maybe not." There was an odd mix of uncertainty and hope in her eyes.

He smiled and pushed a strand of hair from her eyes. For now, that mix was enough. At least she'd seen beyond her guilt and released some of her pent-up pain.

The deaths in her past would no longer be a weapon for Jasper to use. It might not be much, but it was a start.

She gently touched the silver cross resting against his chest. "Where did you find it?"

"In the tunnel." Fear danced lightly through her thoughts. He placed his hand over hers, pressing her fingers against the flesh above his heart. "Do you want it back?"

She hesitated, then shook his head. "No. Keep it, if you want."

He did want. It was a small piece of her he could take with him when he left. He glanced at the clock. Seven o'clock. Time enough, perhaps, to ease the ache of the past and create a final memory to last a lifetime.

He met her gaze. There was understanding in her eyes, acceptance in her thoughts. Just one more time, he vowed, and reached for her.

Twelve

The morning light washed across her face, painting her pale skin gold. Michael smiled and brushed the stray lock of hair away from her cheek. She looked so much younger in sleep, almost childlike.

Yet the image was a lie. Nikki was an old spirit in a young body. Her parents' death and her brief time with Tommy had forced her to grow up far too early. She'd lived through the nightmare and somehow survived. Maybe now that she'd finally confronted her memories and guilt, she'd be able to do more than that. Maybe now she'd live—and love—without fear.

He eased his arm out from under her head and watched her snuggle into the blankets. Lord, he didn't want to leave her. Not now, not in the future. But he no choice about either. He ran a hand through his hair and looked away. This morning had been a mistake. He should never have touched her a second time, should never have let their minds entwine so strongly. For now he could no longer deny he was human, with human wants and needs.

He'd played with fire and lost his heart.

He rose from the bed and moved across to his clothes. Jasper had to be his first priority, now more than ever. He couldn't risk the fiend capturing her again. Anger washed through him, and he savored its taste. It would help him hunt this morning.

But anger did little to erase Jasper's stain from her mind. While her mind might merge with his and make them one, Michael knew he could never hope to control her.

But neither would Jasper. He'd do whatever it took to prevent her becoming a puppet to Jasper's desires. Even if it meant killing her. At least then Jasper wouldn't be able to call her back from the dead. It was only his own victims he could recall.

The thought sent a chill through his soul. He heard soft steps coming down the hall, and tensed. After a moment, he realized it was only Jake. He finished buttoning his shirt, then moved back to the bed. Bending, he gently kissed her cheek. She stirred and murmured something, but her thoughts were full of warmth and contentment. For the moment, at least, she was free from Jasper's taint.

But how long would it remain that way?

He had no idea, and it worried him. If Jasper called—truly called with the full force of his vampire abilities—what would happen? In three hundred years of existence he'd met no one who could resist such a call. But then, until Nikki, he'd met no mind he could not fully control. Maybe her psychic strength would give her an edge where all others had failed.

Damn it, he *had* to find Jasper first and kill him. And Monica was the key. If he knew his enemy, the teenager would be on her own by now. Jasper very rarely kept his women, turned or not, for more than a week or so.

But she would know where her master was, and one way or another, Michael intended to get that information out of her before she died.

***

After several hours of aimless driving, he finally had to acknowledge their quest was futile. Nikki was right—they needed her help. Lyndhurst was a damn maze; Monica could be anywhere.

Michael rubbed his chin wearily, then winced as the sun caressed his arm. He shifted uncomfortably in the seat, and glanced at the clock on the dash. It was nearly ten.

"Let's call it a day," he said into the silence.

Jake gave him a quick look. "Why?"

Michael shrugged. "I can't take much more of the sun."

"Oh."

Fear washed through the silence. He crossed his arms and controlled the urge to touch Jake's thoughts. For the first time since he'd turned, he wanted someone to accept him without any sort of force. He smiled slightly. Nikki was a bad influence.

After a moment, Jake cleared his throat and gave him another quick look. "Where to, then?"

He glanced at his watch again. It would take them too long to get back to the hotel. He gestured to a small bar just ahead. "Feel like a drink?"

"Anywhere, anytime."

Jake's grin was slightly forced, but at least he was making the effort. And it would be good to sit back and wait out the day's heat with an icy beer. If he couldn't be with Nikki, at least he could sit and enjoy a drink—a normal pastime in his otherwise abnormal life.

Jake stopped close to the entrance, and Michael climbed out. The sunshine raced heat across his unprotected flesh. It was a warning he dare not ignore.

He ran up the steps and ducked inside. The interior of the bar was dark and cool and smelled of sweat and stale smoke. It didn't matter. All he needed was someplace to wait out the worst of the day. He ordered two drinks from the disinterested barman then moved across to a table hidden in deep shadow.

Jake sat opposite him and took a sip of his beer. He smacked his lips in appreciation, then gave Michael a shrewd look. "So," he said, "just what do you plan to do about Nikki?"

He knew Jake wasn't referring to the fact that they'd left without her. The man saw too much. "What's this," he asked lightly. "A little fatherly inquisition?"

Jake shrugged. "I've known her a long time. I don't want to see her hurt."

"Neither do I." He took another mouthful of beer, but its taste had soured. "When did you two meet?"

Jake smiled. "When she was sixteen. She saved my life."

He raised an eyebrow in surprise. "How?"

"I was tracking a runaway for his parents and got cornered by his gang. Nikki came out of nowhere and faced them all down."

It was easy to imagine the skinny little ball of fierceness she must have been. He smiled slightly. Nothing much had changed. "So, she was a hellcat even then."

"But a vulnerable one," Jake said sharply. "Her toughness is just a shell."

"I know."

Like he knew she had problems with trust, that she feared commitment because everyone she'd ever loved had died. The knowledge didn't make things easier, or help him decide how to proceed.

Not that he could proceed.

He met Jake's gaze squarely. "I'm here to do a job, nothing more. Nikki knows that."

"Women are strange folk, buddy. What they know and what they understand are often two very different things."

True. But that wasn't the case with Nikki. She didn't want him close, didn't want anyone close. She might concede to physical attraction, but would definitely allow nothing more. "I don't think that'll be a problem here."

"Until the last few days, I would've agreed with you. But you've cracked her shell, and no matter what either of you might say, I have eyes. I can see what you're both denying."

"I'm not denying I'm attracted to her, just saying that I've been honest with her." Honest where it counted. Up to a point, anyway. "Believe me, I have no desire to hurt her."

Jake nodded. "I just needed to know she's in safe hands. Let's enjoy our drinks, my friend."

Michael picked up his beer and made no comment.

***

Nikki blinked the sleep from her eyes, then flipped the sheets away from her face. Bright sunshine caressed her skin, filling her with warmth. She felt contented and lazy and, for the first time in ages, happy. Like a big, fat cat rolling in the sun.

And this is one fat cat who's not had enough, she thought with a grin, and reached across the bed. Only Michael wasn't there.

Fear leaped through her. The hotel room was silent, empty. She clenched her fists against the sheets. They'd left without her.

"Damn you both," she muttered and flung the blankets aside, climbing out of bed. If they thought they had her beaten, they were wrong. She'd just have to go after Monica alone.

The thought sent a chill down her spine. She ignored it and quickly dressed. Jake and Michael had forgotten one major point—she was still the only person who could accurately pinpoint Monica's whereabouts.

Or was she? Nikki frowned and walked into the kitchen. Last night she'd seen the enormous power behind Michael's gifts. He'd never said he couldn't find Monica. She stopped in sudden horror. Had last night been little more than a convenient way to tire her and make her sleep?

Pain stabbed through her heart. That last time couldn't

have been a lie. Their minds had entwined too closely for any lie to survive.

And yet, with the strength of Michael's gifts, how could she ever be sure? Tommy had been able to make her believe he cared, and he'd only possessed a tenth of Michael's abilities.

She crossed her arms and stared at the smoke-stained wall. Why did it matter so much anyway? One night, that was all she'd asked for, all she'd wanted. One night free from Jasper's taint. Michael had surely given her that.

So why did she suddenly feel so cheated? Especially when she'd been the initiator? She'd only seduced Michael to run Jasper's dark whispering from her mind. But something in his touch had made her feel cherished. Loved, even.

She closed her eyes at the thought. Because it was nothing more than a lie. He'd warned that he couldn't love her and that he couldn't stay. He'd given her last night, but he couldn't give her anything more.

It was totally foolish to even want something more. People died when she cared too much, and she didn't want to see him dead.

The kettle whistled shrilly into the silence. She made a cup of coffee then picked it up and walked back into the living room. The newspaper lay on the sofa, and headlines leaped out at her. *Three more dead in Highgate!*

She took a gulp of coffee, almost scalding her throat in the process. Monica had to be stopped, before she could slake her thirst on more innocents. She put the cup down and shoved a hand into her pockets, dragging out the locket she'd swiped from Trevgard's. Obviously, Jasper hadn't bothered searching her when he'd stripped her.

Dark laughter flickered through her thoughts, and her pulse rate jumped. She swallowed uneasily, but knew she had no choice. Monica had to be found. She wrapped her fingers around the locket. A chill chased horror through her mind. Monica's evil had grown. Images pushed forward, but she held them at bay and sat down.

Only then, after taking a deep breath, did she open her mind to hell.

Darkness flooded her senses. Through it, she heard the faint strains of music...*an organ*. Frowning, she tried to broaden the view. She needed an exact location, not merely the sounds and images of Monica's den.

*A man dressed in black...the cross. Two old cypress trees dusted with snow...*the pictures gradually formed into an area she recognized. Monica hid in the bowels of an old church up in the hills.

She smiled at the absurdity of it. Yet what better hideaway could Monica find? No one expected a vampire to hide in such a place. Not even Michael...

What place?

She jumped. The question sounded so clear he might as well have been standing right next to her. She put her hand on her chest, and took a deep breath to calm the rapid pounding of her heart.

Nikki, what place? Where is Monica?

In a church. An honest answer, but not one that would help him. There were at least twenty churches scattered in and around Lyndhurst. It would take them forever to find the right one.

Where is the church, Nikki?

Annoyance seared her. She smiled grimly. Good. Maybe next time he'd think twice about leaving her behind...But there wasn't going to be a next time, was there?

Nikki?

The sudden wariness behind his question made her wonder if he'd heard her thoughts.

All I know is it's in the northwest, towards the mountains.

Thank you. He sounded surprised, as if he hadn't expected an honest answer. *We'll find her, Nikki.*

Maybe they would. And maybe she would. The bracelet would lead her straight to the teenager's lair.

Stay in the hotel, Nikki. Stay safe.

Yeah, right. She rose and called for a cab. Her car was still parked in front of the agency, and, hopefully, she still had a set of knives hidden under the dash. Even if a knife wasn't an effective weapon against a vampire, she still felt safer with them strapped to her wrist.

She glanced at the time. Two o'clock. She collected her jacket and went outside to wait for the cab.

***

Two hours later, she stopped her car opposite an old

church and climbed out. This was the place. She took off
her sunglasses and leaned against the car to study the
church. A priest puttered around in the front garden,
tending to a few winter flowering plants. Two old cypress
pines dominated the grounds on the right side of the old
building, but the back and left side were bare and open.

She squinted slightly and looked at the sky. It was
after four, and the sun's strength was beginning to wane.
Michael had said any exposure to the sun was dangerous
to the newly turned, but she wanted to be sure of death.
The later it was, the less likely that became.

And it wouldn't wait until Michael arrived. She didn't
question the certainty that he was coming. As he'd warned,
the ties between them had been strengthened by their
lovemaking, and he was using that connection to find her.

Maybe she *should* wait for him...But something drove
her on, told her she couldn't afford to.

She locked the car door then crossed the road. The
priest moved back into the old building.

How could she rid the church of its unknown guest
without raising the priest's suspicions? She frowned and
turned down an old stone path that led through the trees.
There had to be a second entrance around the back of the
church. Maybe she could get in there.

Luck was with her for a change. She climbed over a
small fence and approached the second door. It was locked.
She looked around to ensure no one watched, then quickly
zapped the door with kinetic energy.

It creaked open. The hallway beyond was dark, still.
The murmur of several voices came from a room to her
right, and someone moved around in another room further
down the hall. Below them all, a sense of evil, sleeping.

Thirteen

Swallowing heavily, Nikki stepped inside. She reached into her pocket and dug out Monica's bracelet. It pulsed lightly against her palm, a muted beat that would lead her straight to the teenager.

She moved forward quietly. There were no windows in the small corridor, and the gloom closed in. She resisted the urge to turn on the flashlight, knowing the proximity of the voices meant there was a chance they'd see it.

A cobweb trailed against her face, and she jumped sideways. Her yelp became a squeak as she bit down on it. Heart pounding unevenly, she stopped and listened. The soft murmuring in the other room continued unabated.

Sighing silently, she walked on. The corridor ended at a set of stairs. She hesitated, stomach suddenly churning. She'd climbed a similar set of stairs to escape Jasper's clutches. Oh God, was he here as well?

She couldn't feel his presence, only Monica's, but the fear that she was walking blindly into another trap was a cold weight in the pit of her stomach.

She turned on the flashlight and shone it into the gloom. The dust-caked steps showed no trace of footsteps, yet she could feel Monica's presence in the darkness below.

Could vampire's fly? Bile rose in her throat. She closed her eyes, swallowing heavily. It was ridiculous to think vampires could fly. They didn't have to, when they could move faster than the eye could see.

What if Monica was awake and waiting for her? The rhythmic beat in the bracelet spoke of slumber, but how could she be sure a vampire's heartbeat was in any way the same as a human's?

Sweat beaded her forehead. Biting her lip, she walked slowly down the stairs. Dust stirred, a cloud that stung her eyes and nostrils. She wrinkled her nose, fighting a sneeze. The door at the bottom of the stairs was closed. She touched the handle, then hesitated again. What if Jasper was here? What would she do?

Probably die of heart failure. If she was lucky.

The bracelet told her nothing. Nor could she really expect it to—it was Monica's, not Jasper's. Mouth dry, she turned the handle and opened the door. The air that rolled out to greet her was thick with age and a musty dampness that spoke of leaking pipes. She swept the light across the layers of darkness. It revealed the slimy floor but little else.

A hand came down on her shoulder, and her heart almost stopped.

She screamed and spun, only to find the priest she'd seen earlier in the church grounds.

She swallowed and gave him a somewhat shaky smile. "Father, you gave me a fright."

"It was not my intention, I assure you." His voice was gentle, as if he feared he was talking to someone not quite sane. "I merely wanted to know what you were doing down here."

Should she lie? She eyed him for a moment then decided against it. Something in his green eyes told her he's seen enough of life to know the truth from a lie.

"I'm a private investigator." She pulled her wallet out of her jacket and shone the flashlight on her license. "I got a tip that an escaped criminal was hiding in your cellar."

The priest frowned. "I don't see how. The doors are kept locked, and I've seen no one strange about."

No one but herself, she surmised from his look. "The side door and this one were both open, Father. Have you checked them lately?"

"Not this one."

"Then my informant may be right." She glanced over her shoulder. Something stirred in the darkness—or was it only her imagination?

"Is this criminal dangerous?"

Why wouldn't he just leave? If Monica stirred, the priest was in danger. Nikki doubted if his robes would offer much protection. "Yes, she's dangerous."

"Then I think we should call the police."

She glanced back to the dark cellar. At least the priest would be out of the way if he went to call the police. And maybe it would be better if the cops were the ones to drag Monica into the sunlight and death. As long as they arrived well before sunset, there shouldn't be any sort of danger.

With Monica out of the way, the only nightmare left would be Jasper.

Foreboding pulsed across her skin. "Call them, then.

Tell them Monica Trevgard is trapped in this basement. I'll stay here to ensure she doesn't escape."

His gaze widened at the mention of Monica's name, then he nodded and moved back up the stairs.

Nikki watched his retreat. Did he know Monica? Maybe she should warn him what might happen...She shook her head and leaned against a wall. Priest or not, he wouldn't believe her.

The minutes ticked by, and the silence grew heavier. She glanced at her watch. Perhaps the priest had decided to call the loony bin first, just to ensure she wasn't an escaped nutcase.

She cast her senses into the basement, checking that Monica was still there. The wash of evil was answer enough.

A few minutes later she heard the sirens. Yet she couldn't escape the notion that something was wrong, that *she* was doing something she shouldn't. But they had to get rid of Monica, for everyone's safety.

Didn't they?

Footsteps pounded down the hall. She rubbed her arms, wishing they'd hurry.

MacEwan clomped down the steps and stopped beside her. "This better not be one of your tricks."

His breath washed over her, and she screwed up her nose. Too bad garlic didn't effect vampires. "It's not. She's all yours."

She offered him her flashlight, but he shook his head and produced one of his own. "Jenkins, make sure she stays put. You other two, follow me."

The three men stepped into the basement. The darkness closed around them; only the bobbing light gave away their position. She clenched her fists, half-expecting Monica to wake and try to escape. But no sound broke the silence except for the occasional footstep.

Minutes later, Jenkins' two-way buzzed.

"Call the paramedics in, Jenkins." MacEwan's voice sounded annoyed, even over the two-way. "And get them to bring down a stretcher. The girl isn't looking so good."

"And Miss James?"

"Tell her to stay put, or her ass is mine."

The young officer glanced at her. Nikki smiled sourly. "Message received. My ass ain't moving."

He grinned slightly then headed back up the stairs. Nikki shifted her weight from one foot to the other, waiting uneasily in the darkness. She wanted to go into the cellar and see Monica for herself, but knew MacEwan had meant what he said.

Though with Jasper still on the loose, maybe jail was the safest place to be.

Jenkins returned a few minutes later, but Nikki felt no safer with his large presence next to her. She glanced at her watch. If MacEwan didn't move Monica soon, he might well find himself trying to control a very angry, and very awake, vampire.

Footsteps sounded down the hall. Two paramedics pounded past them and disappeared into the darkness. More minutes ticked by.

Finally, MacEwan reappeared. The two paramedics carried Monica on the stretcher just behind him, with the two police officers following them.

She let the five men pass then followed them up the stairs. The teenager looked more dead than alive. She was limp, boneless, her skin pallid and unhealthy looking. Nikki frowned. Something didn't feel right...

She crossed her arms. However Monica might look, she was still a monster. Like the fiend she called a lover, Monica enjoyed the terror she inflicted on her victims. It had been all too obvious in her eyes when she'd attacked both her and Jake.

But evil's mistress was about to meet her deserving end.

MacEwan glanced over his shoulder. "I don't want you disappearing anywhere. I'd like a word with you first."

She nodded. She had no intention of leaving, anyway. Not until she was certain of Monica's fate. She followed the men down the hall, then stopped as the first paramedic stepped outside. Beams of sunlight touched Monica's still form, washing her skin with warmth. Just for an instant she looked like the Monica of old—a carefree, innocent teenager. Nikki bit her lip and half reached out to stop them. Then she dropped her hand to her side and watched the two men carry her fully into daylight.

Monica screamed—a high, tortured sound that ricocheted through Nikki's mind. *This is wrong. I'm wrong.*

Oh Christ... She took a step forward. Fire leaped through her brain, stopping her. She doubled over, gasping in pain, eyes watering as she struggled to see Monica.

The teenager kicked and twisted against the straps holding her captive. She screamed and cursed and called for her father, over and over and over. The two paramedics swore and struggled to keep hold of the stretcher as the convulsing became more violent. There was a tearing sound, then suddenly she was free and on the ground. Her eyes flew open, revealing a sea of red where there should have been white. Tendrils of smoke began to rise from her flesh. She hissed, a low inhuman sound, and began to crawl towards the doorway and the safety of the church interior.

In Monica's unnatural gaze, Nikki saw past the layers of agony to the child deep within—a lost and lonely child, desperate for hope and love. *Me,* she thought, *if it hadn't been for Jake and MacEwan.*

She stepped forward to help Monica, but the fire in her brain intensified. Gasping, Nikki dropped to her knees. There was nothing she could do—nothing but watch Monica die. Tears ran down her cheeks when she met the teenager's gaze. Deep in the blue depths of her eyes, Nikki saw the sudden flash of understanding—and hate.

"Christ Almighty! Somebody do something." MacEwan's voice rose harshly above the noise surrounding the old church. "Grab a blanket or something."

The priest ran to obey. But they were far too late. Monica burst into flames. Nikki closed her eyes, not wanting to see any more. The pain in her head eased, but there was no way to stop Monica's screams from penetrating every nerve, sickening her soul.

She'd been wrong about one thing. No matter what she'd done, the teenager hadn't deserved a death as horrid as this.

The screams faded into silence. The priest returned with a blanket and a police officer threw it over Monica's body. Yet the fire burned unabated, the flames so fierce they took the blanket with them. A line of dark smoke climbed skyward.

Soon there was nothing left but ashes. Laughter ran through her mind, a distant, taunting evil that crowed at his victory.

Had she been nothing more than Jasper's tool all along? She bit her lip and hugged herself fiercely, hoping, praying it wasn't so. If he could make her do this, he could make her do anything. Even betray Michael.

She took a deep breath and wiped the tears from her cheeks. There was nothing she could do now about Monica, nothing anyone could do, other than mourn a life lost so young.

"I've heard of things like this happening." MacEwan's voice was harsh, full of the pain he would never show. "Never thought I'd see it, though."

She rose and walked over to where he stood. The priest began to murmur over the burned soil and a few scraps of blanket, all that remained of Monica's pyre.

"How in hell am I going to explain it downtown?"

She glanced at him, wondering if he expected an answer. His face showed no sign of emotion, yet she knew the appearance was a lie. MacEwan—the tough, no-nonsense cop—hated losing a kid, no matter how bad that kid had gone. Despite all his years on the streets, he still believed they could be saved, given half a chance.

"You can't." She shoved her hands into her pockets to ward off the chill of the freshening wind. "No one would believe you if you tried."

He lit a cigarette and sucked on it almost greedily. "You knew this would happen, didn't you?" he said, after a moment.

She didn't reply, not trusting him for an instant. Fair cop or not, he was just as likely to march her downtown and interrogate her all night if she admitted too much. Yet her silence was answer enough.

"So," he continued, exhaling a long plume of smoke. "What was she?"

She gave him another uncertain look. How much had he guessed? "What do you mean?"

He gave an exasperated snort. "No games, or I might be inclined to get nasty. Normal people do not explode into flame when the sun touches them. Certainly it's not a problem Monica Trevgard has suffered before."

And wouldn't again, Nikki thought with a shiver. She watched a wisp of blanket turn in the breeze. The intensity of the fire had left the soil under Monica's body a charred mess. She doubted if anything would ever grow there again.

"She was a vampire." It was time MacEwan knew the truth, whether or not he chose to believe it. "They can't stand the sun."

He made no comment. She'd always found MacEwan hard to read and had no idea if he believed her or not.

"And this madman we still have on the loose?"

"Monica's lover. Another vampire."

"I see."

Did he? There was little emotion to be seen on his face, but his eyes were thoughtful.

"And do you intend going after this madman?"

She nodded, half expecting him to warn her off the case. As usual, MacEwan did the unexpected.

"Keep me informed of all developments, then." He dropped the half-finished cigarette on the ground, crushing it under his boot heel. Then he gave her a wintry smile. "I am not as blind as you might think. I've seen things—" He hesitated and shrugged. "Lets just say I'm not unwilling to believe there are some things on this earth that defy explanation. Just be careful. I can do without the extra paperwork."

He gave her a brief nod and walked away. She turned her gaze to the priest, watching him sprinkle water over the soil.

The back of her neck tingled in warning, and she turned. Jake walked across the road and entered the church through the main gate. Michael wasn't with him, but he was near. His anger washed over her, almost smothering in its intensity.

"Heard over the police radio they'd found Monica." Jake stopped and regarded the priest's actions with interest. "This all that's left?"

She nodded. "She went up like a torch."

"One down, one to go." There was little remorse in his voice. Taking her elbow, he pulled her away from the church. "But just what in hell did you think you were doing? You could have gotten yourself killed!"

She wrenched her arm out of his grip and stopped to glare at him. "What in hell did you think you were doing, leaving without me this morning?" If they'd been here with her, Monica might still be alive. And maybe, just maybe, she'd be less worried about Jasper being able to control her.

"We did what we thought best to keep you safe." He shrugged. "I guess it was a mistake."

"I thought we were a team, Jake."

"We are, Nik. But sometimes you scare me. It's almost as if...as if you have no sense of your own well being. You just keep pushing yourself." He looked at her grimly. "Sometimes I think you have a death wish."

She snorted softly. And yet there'd been times in the past when she certainly hadn't cared whether she lived or died. Maybe that was why she had been such an easy target for Tommy. "Even if I did, what business is it of yours?"

"Damn it, do I have to spell it out? You're like a damned daughter to me. I don't want to see you hurt!"

She was an idiot, no doubt about it. She touched his arm gently. "I'm sorry."

He sighed and shook his head. "You've been on your own too long, kiddo. It's about time you let someone in."

He was talking about Michael, not himself. "Father figure or not, does the phrase 'mind your own business' mean anything to you?"

"It's one I have great trouble with." He held a hand out. "Give me your keys. I want you to go talk to Michael. Now, Nikki," he added when she hesitated.

She swore softly but knew better than to argue when he used that tone of voice. She dug the keys out of her pocket. "If I didn't know better, I'd swear you've been drinking."

"One or two. I'm safe to drive."

"My car's parked across the road. I'll see you back at the office."

He nodded. "Trust him, Nik. Let him in."

She scowled and turned away. She had no intention of letting anyone in, especially Michael. It was too damn dangerous. *He* was too damn dangerous.

Jake's Mercedes was parked in the shadows of an old elm. The darkly-tinted windows prevented any view inside, and yet she could feel Michael's anger as if it were her own.

She opened the driver's side door and climbed in. Michael watched her silently, eyes hidden behind dark glasses. He made no comment as she started the engine and drove off.

Though she kept her eyes on the road, she couldn't help being aware of every little move he made. Now that she was here, she feared talking to him. But just what did she fear? Him? Or herself?

"Why?" he asked softly, after several minutes.

It was a question that could have meant anything. She chose to answer the most obvious. "Monica had to be stopped. You know that."

"Yes. But not before she'd led us to Jasper."

Nikki bit her lip. So that was why Jasper had wanted her dead. "You never told me that, Michael. You never trusted me enough, did you?"

He made a sound suspiciously like a deep-throated growl. "No other observations, while you're at it? No other accusations?" His voice was almost mocking, hinting at the anger she couldn't see but could sense.

"There was this morning, when I woke alone." But she'd killed someone since then. Her fingers tightened against the wheel, but she fought the rising fear, not wanting him to sense it. "I've had time to think."

"I just bet you have."

She shot him a quick look, unsure how to take his remark. His face was as remote as ever.

"So what did you come up with?" He shifted slightly in his seat, facing her.

She didn't trust his tone. It was too polite. Too controlled. "One question."

"And that is?"

A quick glance at his face told her little, yet she caught a wisp of uncertainty in his thoughts. And wariness. She unclenched her fingers against the wheel and bit her lip in indecision. She didn't want to voice her doubts, didn't want to hear his answer. And the demons whispering madness in her mind could never force her to do this. She just had to know.

"I want to know what last night meant."

His gaze, though hidden by dark glasses, burned into her soul. "What do you think it was about?"

She couldn't look at him. "Was it only a means to ensure I slept through the night? When our minds merged, did you make me sleep?"

A tide of anger seemed to leap into the car and swirl around her. She kept her eyes on the road, hands tense against the steering wheel. She didn't want to face the fury she could feel building.

"You really aren't capable of trust, are you?"

She wanted to scream that she'd trusted him more than she'd trusted any man in her entire life—except, maybe, for Tommy. Only Michael wasn't just a man.

And this wasn't about trust. It was about deception. Wasn't it?

"I have to know, Michael."

His gaze burned into her. She shivered and tried to ignore the worm of fear in her heart.

"Think about last night, Nikki. Think about what we shared. Look inside your own heart."

No. Never again would she trust what she felt in matters like this. People died when she did. As the lights ahead changed, she slowed the car and risked another quick look. His face was still impassive, giving no indication he'd heard her thoughts. But even if he had, she still needed to know.

"You are a fool, Nikki. A fool who will not listen to her own intuition."

"Intuition has nothing to do with this." Because intuition was telling her to trust him, telling her to grab on tight and never let go, no matter how he fought. But it had told her the same about Tommy, and it had never been more wrong.

"I have to ask, Michael. Surely you can understand that?"

"The only thing I can understand is the fact that I am a fool twice over."

The sudden hint of weariness in his voice frightened her. She glanced at him quickly. What had he meant by that?

"I will not deny there is an element of truth in your fears. I had hoped you might sleep long enough for Jake and me to leave." He took off the sunglasses and rubbed his eyes. "As for what it meant—I warned you before, Nikki. It can never be anything more than just a moment we share."

His words cut through her. While she knew he couldn't

stay, she'd hoped it might have been something more than just a physical release to him. To her, at least, last night had been something of a revelation. She'd never realized that two bodies could become one so completely. That two minds could share a dance so poetic, so full of desire and care.

She blinked and looked away, then shifted the car into gear as the lights changed again, and the traffic flowed on.

"Remember, I was not the initiator last night, nor am I made of stone," he continued softly. "And there's one more question you should ask. Just who was using whom last night?"

Heat crept into her cheeks, and she bit her lip. There was no denying the fact he was right. She *had* used him, used his warmth, the caress of his thoughts, to keep Jasper's nightmares at bay.

But while she regretted her reasons, she didn't regret making love to him. Those memories she would treasure in the long years ahead.

"I'm sorry," she said. "I was wrong. But so were you in leaving me."

He made no comment, and she drove the final few miles to the office in silence. She parked in front of the building and glanced at her watch as she climbed out of the car. It was after five. She frowned. Why wasn't her car here? Jake had left before her...

Her psychic senses sprang to life, and pain ran like fire across her body.

Only it wasn't her pain. It was Jake's.

Jasper's dark laughter whispered through her brain, a teasing gloat, edged with warning.

If she wanted Jake to live, she would have to take his place.

Fourteen

Nikki gripped the edge of the car door and closed her eyes. She couldn't go back to Jasper...Yet she couldn't let Jake die in her place.

"Nikki, listen to me." Michael's voice seemed to come from a great distance. "He won't kill Jake just yet. He'll make sure we have enough time to attempt a rescue. Jasper likes his little games. Break the contact Nikki. Break it, now."

She bit her lip and concentrated on pushing Jasper from her mind. He evaded her grasp, as slippery as an eel, his laughter mocking. She gritted her teeth and pushed, hard. Jasper's poison slid away, but the effort left her trembling.

Michael turned her around and pulled her towards him. She leaned her cheek against the warmth of his chest, and wished she could stay in the safe circle of his arms forever. Why couldn't the rest of the world just go to hell and leave her alone? Better yet, why wasn't there a way to simply turn back the clock to the time before Monica and Jasper had walked into her life? Though that would mean not meeting Michael. Perhaps some good had come out of this whole mess, no matter how brief it was meant to be.

After a moment, she sighed and pulled away. "If Jasper's moved in the daylight, he's stronger than you thought."

Michael shrugged, finally removing his dark glasses as he glanced at the sun. "It's nearly five, and the winter sun is weak. Besides, it was probably the zombies who grabbed him."

"Just how much do you know about Jasper?"

He shrugged a second time. "As I've said before, he and I are old foes. I make it my business to know my enemy."

"Do you make it your business to keep your allies in the dark?"

A wisp of annoyance ran through her, though his face was impassive. "I only tell what needs to be known."

She clenched her fists and tried to ignore the desire to yell in frustration. "Well, right now I need to know everything I can about Jasper."

He nodded, though his dark gaze was suddenly distant. "As I said earlier, he's a twin. He and his brother survived the San Francisco fires of 1906, but the rest of their family did not. We're not sure when they both changed, but we do know it occurred shortly after the fires, when they were fifteen." He hesitated, his face grim. "Even so, Jasper was responsible for the murder of at least five people before his rebirth."

She shifted from one foot to the other and tried to ignore the need to move. Finding Jake would take all the caution and cunning she could muster—and every scrap of information about Jasper and his need for revenge. "You mentioned the royal 'we' again."

Michael sighed, though it was a sound filled with annoyance. "I am a member of an organization known as the Damask Circle."

"Are you all vampires?"

"No. But neither are we all what you'd term human."

Human. The bitter emphasis he placed on that word spoke volumes. He'd heard her thoughts, all right. She bit her lip and glanced away from the accusation of his gaze. "And this circle of yours goes around killing people like Jasper?"

"Yes. So people like you can rest easier at night."

People who fear what cannot easily be explained. People who cannot trust what their hearts know to be true. She closed her heart to his thoughts. This wasn't the time to argue about her refusal to trust. "Is that why you killed Jasper's brother?"

Again Michael hesitated. Pain rose briefly through his soul. She wanted to reach out and tell him she understood. Instead, she clenched her fingers and waited for him to continue.

"No. I killed Jasper's brother because he murdered my brother, Patrick."

Revenge. Everything was based on revenge, and it could end up killing them all. "How often have you and Jasper met in the past?"

Then she frowned. "If you're three-hundred-years-old and Jasper is only one hundred, wouldn't your brother have been well and truly dead before Jasper and his brother were even born?"

The pain in Michael's soul became sharper. "Patrick was a vampire."

And Michael had turned him. Nikki wondered why. "How often have you and Jasper met in the past?"

"Three times."

And each time Jasper had somehow slipped from Michael's noose. But it wouldn't happen again, she thought, staring at him. Deep in the dark depths of his eyes she could see the promise of death. One way or another, Michael was determined to finish it here in Lyndhurst.

Foreboding pounded through her. Shivering, she turned away and locked the car door. Dark laughter ran through her mind, taunting her. She closed her eyes briefly and took a deep breath. Jasper wouldn't win this battle, either.

"Let's go inside," she said, avoiding Michael's gaze and walking around to the front of the car. "I should be able to find something to trace Jake with."

She climbed the steps and unlocked the door. The office was as cold as the ice forming in the pit of her stomach. Dark laughter again scurried past the edges of her mind.

"Nikki." Michael touched her arm and swung her around to face him. "Jasper's only teasing you, trying to make you fear every step."

"He's doing a damn good job of it," she muttered, wishing Michael would wrap his arms around her and hold her until the scent of evil left her skin. But it was no use wishing for things that could not be. He couldn't stay. She didn't want him to stay.

So why did the thought of him leaving cut pain through her heart?

He placed a finger under her chin, raising it until her gaze met his. "He can't control you, Nikki, only undermine your confidence."

It was a lie. He knew, as she did, that Jasper only had to call, and she'd probably go running. "Why is he bothering? I'm no threat to him."

Michael's smile was edged with anger, his eyes layered with a darkness that chilled her soul.

"He fears you, Nikki." He raised a hand, pushing a wisp of hair away from her eyes. His touch trailed heat against the ice of her skin. "Fears the strength of your abilities."

His touch felt so good...She shivered, fighting the need to fall into his arms. Fighting the desire to jerk away from it. "Why? My psychic talents can't hurt him."

"Can't they?" His voice was distant, distracted, as he ran a finger lightly down her cheek and neck.

She licked her lips. It was hard to concentrate with him touching her so gently. Lord, all she wanted to do was fall into bed with this man—but she couldn't. The time and the place were all wrong. Damn it, *they* were wrong. A man who couldn't love and a woman afraid to love—what hope would there ever be for them?

Michael's hand stilled near her breast. She glanced up quickly, but he avoided her gaze and stepped away. It didn't matter. She knew his thoughts. Knew he wouldn't touch her like that again.

"I'm sorry," he said softly.

She nodded. It was as much her fault as his. She should have pulled away the minute he'd touched her.

She walked across to Jake's desk and raised a hand. There had to be something here that held enough of Jake's vibes to enable her to track him.

She found it within a few minutes—an old fob watch lost among the junk in his bottom draw.

"It has his imprint?" Michael asked, sitting on the edge of the desk.

She nodded and tried to ignore the sensations running through her fingers. "How do you want to go about this?"

"That would depend on how much you really trust me."

She gave him a sharp look. He was sitting on the edge of the desk, swinging one leg slightly. So very casual in appearance, but she could feel his tension. See it around the edges of his dark eyes.

"What do you mean?"

"Jasper knows you will attempt to find Jake, so he will have set some sort of trap again."

She nodded. That much she'd guessed. But she had to find Jake, and this was her best option. Probably the only option, if they wanted to find him alive.

"You have a plan to stop him?"

"Yes. But it would involve my mind joining yours," he hesitated and shrugged lightly. "Completely."

She stared at him. Merge minds? To know each other's thoughts and desires?

"We already know each others thoughts, Nikki."

"But I can't—"

"You can." He studied her, face grim. "And all too often you have. It's something neither of us can really control, something that gets stronger every time we..." He hesitated, then shrugged again. "The point is, do you trust me enough to allow our minds to merge?"

"How deep a merging would it be?" The prospect made her stomach turn. Did she really want Michael to know all her wants, all her secrets and fears?

"It would have to be complete enough to allow me some kind of control if I need it. But I promise not to delve, not to open any doors you wish kept closed. And you must promise the same."

She nodded and wondered if it mattered. Michael's abilities far outstripped hers. There was no way on earth she'd be able to control him. "But how will this merging screw up the kind of trap Jasper had waiting last time?"

"I intend to direct your abilities along a slightly different path."

She licked her lips. For all intents and purposes, he'd have control of her. Her willingness to go along with this would allow Michael to succeed where Jasper had so far failed—would give him the access Tommy had wanted but couldn't fully control.

"Damn it, Nikki, I'm not Jasper. Or Tommy."

He rose and moved around the desk, stopping only a foot away from her. She bit her lip and backed away a step. Her back hit the wall. The wood paneling felt cool against her palms when compared to the fire of his gaze.

"I don't want control of your mind—or your body—or anything else, for that matter. When will you get that through your head? I just want you to trust me."

She stared at him. Deep in his eyes she saw a flicker of longing and knew in that instant he wanted something more than he'd ever admit or allow.

"Just tell me what you intend to do."

He sighed and turned to the window, staring out through the lace. "Instead of merely tracking Jake's whereabouts, I intend to join his mind. That will prevent Jasper from detecting us, and it will give us a better idea of what is going on."

So Michael would have control of two minds. She remembered how easily he had made the waiter do as he asked, and shivered. But that had only been surface control. This would be so much deeper. "Won't it be dangerous?"

"Anything that deals with this kind of mental intrusion can be dangerous."

"For us or for Jake?"

"For everyone. But we should have no trouble linking with Jake. I've already done it."

She gave him a long look. He ignored it, though she knew by the taut muscles in his crossed arms that he was well aware of her gaze. "When was this?"

He shrugged. "The night before I met you. I needed to know Lyndhurst's background in a hurry, and who would know more than a private investigator?"

Who indeed? And Jake had been an investigator long enough to know his fair share of secrets. She just had to hope he'd be around long enough to learn a few more.

She swallowed to ease the sudden dryness in her throat. "Will we be able to feel what he feels?"

"Yes. But I will protect you from it as much as I can."

"I don't know—" —*if I can cope with Jake's fear on top of my own.*

"You must," Michael said gently. "If you want him to survive."

She took a deep breath then nodded. Jake was the closest thing she had left to family. She didn't want to lose him. "What do I do?"

"Sit in his chair and relax."

She did. Michael held her hand. Heat burned through her flesh, warming the ice formed by her apprehension.

"Now relax and close your eyes."

She listened to the rhythmic flow of his breathing and tried to match it. Gradually, she felt the tension begin to leave her limbs.

"Relax, relax." Michael's voice was a whisper that soothed her soul. "Allow our thoughts to touch, become one."

Heat danced through her, warmth that burst like an explosion through every fiber of her being. It was a caress, a lover's kiss, and nothing like the invasion she'd imagined. The fire that burned when they touched was nothing when compared to the inferno they raised as their minds became one.

Concentrate, Nikki

The cool breeze of his thoughts whispered through her. His mind ran like a wave before hers, separate yet united with her own. She could see his thoughts before he spoke them. See his emotions, a blaze of color that almost left her blind. Could see the areas he wished kept hidden, vast tracts of forbidding darkness.

Find Jake, Nikki.

She reached for the watch. The metal was cold against her skin, but her hands twitched, burned by the images rushing from the fob. Her senses leaped away, following the trail that led to Jake. Shapes began to form. She felt a tremor of fear, only to have Michael chase it away.

Concentrate on Jake, Nikki. See him. Feel him. Become one with him. . .

. . .Pain throbbed through his temples. Jake cursed and ran a hand through his hair, only to stop when he felt the sticky dampness matting it all.

What the hell? He struggled into a sitting position and tried to remember what had happened. Cold stone nudged his butt, and a breeze pulled at his wet clothes. Where on earth was he? The air was heavy with age and the scent of decay. Somewhere ahead in the darkness he could hear the steady drip of water.

It had to be a cave of some kind. But how in hell had he gotten here—wherever here was?

"Hell is an apt enough description of this place, my friend."

The words came out of nowhere, reverberating around the walls. Jake tensed, studying the darkness.

"Who are you? What do you want?"

"Questions." The stranger's voice dripped cold sarcasm. "Always questions from my captives."

Jake swallowed. He knew who had him. Knew why.

"Nikki won't be fool enough to fall into your trap a second time."

"We shall see." The darkness moved, forming shape. Became a man with the eyes of a demon.

It was easy to understand Nikki's fear, Jake thought, studying the muscular form warily. He wasn't psychic, but he could feel the power that oozed from the man. And those eyes...they were almost hypnotic.

Don't look, he thought with a frown.

"Interesting," Jasper murmured. "You have a certain...strength I did not expect."

Jake made no comment and studied the darkness beyond Jasper. There had to be some clue as to his whereabouts—some way to warn Nikki not to come after him.

"You will find no escape."

His gaze darted back to Jasper. He noted the insanity entrenched in the blue depths of his eyes, saw the gloating. Knew he was a man who enjoyed toying with his victims. *No, not a man. A vampire.*

Jake cleared his throat. "Where are we?"

"Underground. Deep underground." As Jasper spoke, a tremor ran through the ground, a vibration that shook the air and rushed wind through the darkness.

Were they in a tunnel? Did some sort of vehicle passing through cause the vibration? Maybe a train?

"Not even close," Jasper mused. "I could, of course, tell you, but I doubt it would do you any good."

"Nikki won't look for me," Jake replied, trying to sound casual, though tension knotted his gut and constricted his throat. "She won't run the risk of falling into your trap a second time."

"You lie, little man. I know her mind. I know how much she values your friendship."

Jake closed his eyes. "They will stop you," he whispered. "No matter what it takes."

"I like a man with confidence." Jasper smiled sharply. "What if the cost is your own life?"

Jake shrugged. He would die no matter what happened. He could see it in the monster's eyes. But he wasn't about to give Jasper the pleasure of his fear.

"I can read your mind, little man. I know what you feel."

"Then you know I loathe you more than I fear you."

The chill in the mad blue depths sent ice splintering down his spine. For an instant he regretted his rash words.

"Bravery must run in your profession," Jasper said. "As much as I'd love to stay and chat, I must go tend to my traps. But first, a drink is called for, I think."

The fiend lunged at him. Jake scrambled backwards, but talon-like fingers caught his arm, tearing into skin.

Jake swore and kicked out. Jasper only laughed. Fear slammed through Jake's entire being, and no amount of fighting against Jasper's hold could stop the journey towards the gleaming white teeth and death.

"Struggle little man. Struggle as hard as you can. I like my meal accompanied by fear."

Teeth tore into his neck. Jake screamed as the warm gush of horror plunged him into darkness. . .

Nikki's scream echoed through Michael's soul. He tore her from Jake's mind and lurched forward, catching her as she fell sideways out of the chair.

"Easy, little one. We're safe. You're safe," he whispered and held her gently, one hand caressing the silky length of her hair.

She shuddered and wrapped her arms around him, holding on as if she'd never let him go.

Which was about as far from the truth as you could get. "I'm sorry, Nikki. I should have pulled us out earlier."

"Yes," she agreed softly.

Lightly linked as they were, he could see the visions running riot in her mind, felt her shudder as she remembered Jasper's teeth tearing into her flesh...

"Jake's memory. Not yours." *It will not happen to you, Nikki. I won't allow it.*

"My memories because we were there."

"Hush. It's over."

She sighed into his chest, her breath warm against his skin. "For us. Not for Jake."

True. He pulled away from her, though it was the last thing in the world he wanted to do, and held her at arm's length. "If we want to save him, we'll have to move quickly."

She sniffed then turned and sifted quickly through the papers of Jake's desk. "There's a map of the area...here it is."

"Right." He stood, giving her no time to dwell, no time to fear. "Where are all the tunnels situated?"

She frowned, studying the map. "If it was a rail tunnel, there are three." She pointed them out with a trembling hand.

He ignored the sudden desire to comfort her again. They had no time, nor was it right for him to keep touching her like he cared. "What about old caves? Mine shafts?"

"This section of the mountains is literally littered with old mines. I know a lot of them were filled to stop people falling down them, but there are about a dozen that still remain. Jake could be in any one of them."

But Jasper couldn't. The shaft would have to be deep and long to provide the protection he needed. "The tunnel was wet. We heard drips, remember?

She nodded, chewing her lip thoughtfully. "There are two old mines near the new dam they're building here." She pointed to an area on the western edge of the map. "I'm pretty sure one of them goes into the mountain rather than down."

He saw her glance at the watch in her hand, saw her fingers twitch against it.

"Is he there, Nikki?"

"I think so," she whispered. "But I've been wrong before."

And it had resulted in death, Michael thought. Too much of her young life had been affected by death, and there wasn't a damn thing he could do about it. But he'd do everything it took to stop Jake dying on her as well.

"We'll need some supplies," he said.

"Out back."

She stood, but rather than brush past him, took the long way around the desk and walked across to the storeroom. He shook his head and followed her. She'd trusted him with her soul, but still wouldn't trust him with her heart. He wondered if she ever would.

But what in hell would he do if she ever did?

He leaned against the doorway and watched her collect some chocolate and a few cans of soda and throw them in a backpack. She pulled on a heavy coat and turned to face him. Fear was everywhere, in her thoughts and in her eyes.

"Ready?" he said softly.

Ready to dance with the devil himself? Never. Her thought ran through his mind like a frightened gazelle. Her gaze was grim when it met his

"But for Jake I must," she said softly. "Let's go."

Fifteen

Nikki leaned against the trunk of a scrawny old pine, her breath ragged gasps that tore at her throat. She'd thought she was reasonably fit, but climbing this mountain had quickly put that notion to rest. She eyed the darkness ahead and wondered how much more they had to climb. And how in hell she was going to make it? The muscles in her legs were on fire. She couldn't possibly walk another step.

"Have a drink." Michael took a soda from the backpack he carried and handed it to her.

"Thanks," she replied and popped the top.

He nodded, his gaze sweeping the still night.

"Anything?" she asked, after a long drink of the lukewarm cola.

"Nothing. You?"

Her gaze skimmed the darkness. Ice crawled across her skin. There wasn't anything she could pin down, just instinct, warning her. "He's here, somewhere."

Michael nodded. "He'd hang around to watch the fun."

She looked at him in irritation. "Attempted murder cannot be classed as fun."

"To a man like Jasper, it can be." His gaze when it met hers was assessing. "Ready?"

No. She quickly drank the remains of the cola, and handed him the can. As she followed him up the slope, she couldn't help noticing his free and easy walk. He looked like he didn't have a care in the world. Yet tension and worry washed down the link. She still couldn't fully read his thoughts, but then, she didn't really want to. Not if it meant knowing how small their chances were of pulling this rescue off.

She wrapped her fingers around the fob watch in her pocket. Its warmth comforted her, as did the slow but steady beat that told her Jake was still alive.

The entrance soon loomed before them, a cavernous hole framed by timber that looked older than Lyndhurst. Older than Michael.

"The timber's not *that* old," he said, half smiling as he handed her the flashlight. "Here, hold this."

She shined the beam at the entrance. The light penetrated only a few feet of darkness before being swallowed. But it was enough to see the footprints. Michael squatted on his heels and ran his fingers around the outline of the prints.

"Zombies," he said, indicating a scuffed section on one print. "See? Their step is heavy, and they drag their feet. Jasper would leave no prints, and he would have carried Jake in."

"We knew he'd have traps waiting." So why hadn't her psychic senses kicked in and warned her?

"They won't." Michael stood and brushed the dirt off his hands. "Jasper's using the psychic net again—I can feel it pulsing. It's shielding this entire area, and probably interfering with your abilities."

Yet the watch still beat between her fingers. "I can still feel Jake."

"Only because Jasper wants you to find him."

She shivered. "Then the rest of my abilities will be useless?"

"Probably. You can't find out without trying, and the net will catch you if you do."

Her stomach twisted. While she'd often wished to be normal, to be free of the gifts that had somehow always set her apart, she'd known deep down that she relied on them too much to ever let them go. And her brief time with Jasper had proven just how useless she was without them.

Michael wrapped his fingers around hers. "You're not alone, Nikki."

She closed her eyes, fighting the warmth that sprang through her body. It wasn't right to want someone as much as she wanted Michael. Wasn't right to need his touch, the comfort of his arms to chase the demons away.

"I'll always be alone," she said, and stepped away from him. It couldn't be any other way. Not when her love was a curse of death. Michael might be a vampire, but that didn't make him invincible. Monica had proven that vampires could die as fast as any human. "Let's go."

He made no comment and turned away. She followed him into the darkness, her shaking hands making the flashlight's beam dance erratically.

The steady drip of water was all she could hear above

the sound of her footsteps. Michael made no noise, as silent as a ghost. The chill in the air crept past the layers of her clothing and touched her skin with icy fingers.

She shivered and inched closer to Michael's broad back. Her psychic senses might be useless at this point, but she could still feel Jasper's evil all around her. Even the air they breathed seemed tainted by it.

She swept the flashlight's beam across walls slick with slime. Rivulets of water ran down the slope past their feet, but to where? She remembered how damp Jake's clothes had been and guessed somewhere along the line they'd hit water. Hopefully it wouldn't be too deep. She was not a swimmer.

Michael stopped abruptly, and she plowed into his back. "Give a girl some warning next time," she muttered, rubbing her nose as she stepped around him.

The path led into a wide, still lake. She groaned. The path didn't seem to resurface anywhere near, if at all.

"How well do you swim?" Michael knelt and dipped his fingers in the water.

"Like a rock." She shined the flashlight down onto the water. There was no telling how deep it was. It was too dark to see the bottom.

Michael sniffed the water on his fingers, then carefully tasted it. "Putrid," he muttered, and spat the taste away. "Whatever you do, don't swallow it."

"I don't even want to go in it, let alone drink it." She backed away from the edge. The more she stared at the water, the more certain she became that it was a trap. *She had to get out of this tunnel and away from the death closing in on her...*

And if she did, Jake would die.

Michael touched her hand. This time she didn't pull away.

"Keep close and hang on to my hand, no matter what happens."

His concern ran down the link, a fire that warmed her soul. She squeezed his hand lightly. "I intend to, believe me. Whether I'm *allowed* to is another matter entirely."

He brushed his fingertips along her cheek. "Just hold on to me. They can't drown me, but you're vulnerable."

As if she needed reminding. He tugged her forward.

Black waves rippled across the lake's surface and raced away into the darkness. The water crept up her leg, then past her hips, and every step forward became more difficult. She kept her arm raised well above the lake, allowing the flashlight's beam to wash across the darkness. But she kept an eye on the water—just in case something jumped out and tried to grab the light. What she didn't need right now was utter darkness.

The link flared to life, and Michael touched her thoughts. Warmth wrapped around her, a cocoon of comfort and strength. A girl could get used to this, she thought, and alarm stabbed through her heart. Because she *was* getting used to it, and it would only make his leaving all that much harder to bear.

They plowed on through the icy water, but each step felt as if they were forcing their way through molasses.

Michael squeezed her hand gently. "Halfway there. Don't worry, we'll make it."

"You mean there is an end to this lake?" If there was, the flashlight couldn't pick it out.

"Yes. And the path's beginning to slope upwards again."

They'd been following a path? She stepped on something slimy and slipped sideways, yelping in fright. The flashlight dipped under the water and darkness closed in, thick and heavy. *Oh no...*

Michael yanked her upright, almost pulling her arm out of its socket.

"Great," she muttered, hoping she didn't sound as scared as she felt. "Now I'm completely wet."

Amusement and concern ran down the link. "Are you okay?"

She gave the flashlight a shake. Droplets of water sprayed across her face, lightly burning. The bright beam flickered then stayed on. "Now I am."

"Good. Don't slip again. You'll give me heart failure."

She glanced up sharply. The seriousness behind his light remark shook her. It sounded like he cared—really cared. He'd told her vampires didn't have feelings—that they couldn't love. Was that a lie? Every now and then he said or did something that made her think it was.

"Ready to move?"

She touched the fob watch. Its beat was shallow. "Let's

go," she said.

Besides, moving was definitely better than standing. Moving made them harder targets. Shivering, she shined the light across the water. Tiny waves continued to roll away from them, fanning out across the darkness. In the distance water dipped steadily, but the lake seemed to swallow all other noise.

But someone was out there, watching them. She licked her lips. It was getting harder and harder to ignore the urge to run. "Michael-"

"I know." His voice was terse. "Just keep moving. There's nothing we can do here, anyway."

The water level began to drop, inching down from their chests to their hips. But it still held the consistency of glue, making every step difficult.

Something pushed at her wet jeans. Biting her lip, she battled the desire to run. The soupy water made any sort of quickness impossible, anyway. She'd only fall...and that was probably what Jasper had in mind.

But she wished she knew what was touching her ankle.

Again it trailed past, more solidly this time.

"He's playing games."

Though Michael's voice was calm, anger burned along the link. "Then you don't think we'll be attacked?"

"Not here. Not yet."

She wished she could share his certainty. The dark water receded further, and walking became easier. She swept the flashlight's beam across the darkness ahead, noting the tunnel was beginning to close in around them. The roof was only inches above their heads.

"Hope we don't have to crawl," she muttered. The thought of getting down on her hands and knees to wade made her stomach churn.

"I can't imagine Jasper doing it, so I doubt we will."

"You really do know him well, don't you?"

"It pays to. As I've said, he's eluded our circle for years."

"And was your circle after him before or after he killed your brother?"

"Before."

But it became personal when Jasper killed Patrick. "Does the circle attempt to kill every vampire who has a thirst for human blood?"

He shrugged, a movement she caught in the edge of the light. "Not all. There are some who can restrain the urge to kill and live long lives."

Some, but not many, she deduced from his tone. She wondered how he'd managed it, how long it had taken him to curb the lust all too evident in Jasper.

"Jasper is a killer," Michael continued grimly. "Always was. Even before the change, he feasted on the suffering of his victims."

And now he feasted on Jake. Her stomach turned. She swallowed and forced a little lightness into her voice. "And his sort gives the vampire world a bad rep, huh?"

He squeezed her hand. "Something like that."

They continued on in silence. She swept the light across the layers of darkness. Nothing moved, yet something was out there, stirring the darkness ahead.

Michael stopped abruptly. "Movement ahead."

"Where?"

"The tunnel rounds a corner just ahead. Something moved in the shadows."

She shivered. It had to be the zombies. It wouldn't be Jasper, not this soon. He'd play with them a little longer.

"We could go back." But that would mean leaving Jake to die.

"No. I doubt if Jasper would allow a retreat, anyway." His answer was absent, as if his attention was elsewhere.

Power washed through the link. He was using his abilities to study the threat ahead. Why didn't Jasper's net affect him?

"It's not aimed at me. And there are two of them up ahead. A tease, nothing more."

Some tease. "What do we do?"

"*We* do nothing. I'll take care of them." He brushed a kiss across the top of her head then faded into the darkness.

"Michael?" she hissed as his hand left hers. "Michael!"

No answer. Wonderful. What if the zombies were just a diversion to separate them?

Movement whisked around her legs. Biting back a yelp of fright, she shone the light down at her feet. The water stirred, and something slick, brown and long rose briefly to the oily surface before slithering back underneath.

Her mouth went dry. Snakes. There were snakes in

the water with her...

Sweat broke out across her brow. The dark waters began to churn, the snakes bumping and entwining their sleek bodies around her legs. Were they real, or some form of illusion?

They sure *felt* real. One entwined around her legs, and she kicked out. A sleek brown head rose from the water, hissing. She screamed and swiped at it with the torch. It sank back down and joined the circling pack. She leaped over them and ran forward, heading for the zombies and Michael.

The beam of the flashlight jumped erratically, creating crazy shadows on the slick dark walls. The darkness beyond the light seemed oppressive, a monster waiting to pounce. She splashed on, cursing Michael for leaving her.

The snakes pursued. Real or not, they were coming after her. She gripped the flashlight tightly and tried to run faster.

Michael! Frantically, she reached for the connection between them. There was no answer, just a sense of absence. Could he hear her when he was little more than a shadow?

It was just one more thing she didn't know. Heart pounding as fast as her feet, she listened to the sounds of pursuit above the noise of her own panicked flight. She was tempted to use her psychic abilities, but knew this might be what Jasper wanted. He'd snare her the minute she tried.

Damn it, she *wasn't* helpless without her abilities. She had her knives. She could use them to defend herself. Why play Jasper's games any more than she had to? She stopped and swung around. The water was still, silent. The snakes, if they'd ever been real, were gone.

Almost with you, Nikki.

She closed her eyes and took a deep breath, trying to calm her churning stomach. It had been nothing more than a game. Once she'd stood her ground, Jasper had backed away. Maybe Michael was right. Maybe Jasper did fear her abilities.

The thought did little to ease the sick tension in her stomach. She turned and shined the light across the waters ahead. Ripples of movement stirred the surface, but she couldn't see Michael. Only when he was near her did he shake himself free of the shadows.

"Are you all right?"

He brushed his knuckles lightly against her cheek. She wished he'd just take her in his arms and hold her until the chill and the fear left her. But they had no time—Jake was dying. They had to get to him quickly.

"Yeah, sure." She ran a hand through her damp hair. What would he think if he realized she'd been running from nonexistent snakes? "This place is just starting to get to me. What about the zombies?"

"They've disappeared."

She raised an eyebrow. "How can zombies just disappear?"

He shrugged, his gaze on the darkness ahead. "I don't know. As soon as I neared them, I lost all scent of them."

She studied the darkness uneasily. If Jasper could fool Michael's keen senses, they might be in big trouble.

"Come on." He ran his hand down her arm and clasped her fingers gently. "There's nothing we can do but move forward."

The warmth of his touch made her feel more secure as they walked on. But after a few minutes, they stopped again.

"Fork in the tunnels. Which way, Nikki?"

She closed her fingers around the watch fob. It pulsed lightly, but its rhythm was slower, more erratic. They had so little time left.

"Left." She swung in that direction, but Michael jerked her back, again almost dislocating her shoulder in the process. She swore softly. "What's wrong?"

"The zombies are back."

She shined the light into the tunnel but could see no movement. "We can't just stand here, Michael. We have to get to Jake."

He hesitated, then shrugged. "Let's go, then."

The walls began to close in, threatening to smother them. Ghostly tendrils of slime brushed against her clothes and felt like long green fingers of the dead.

Twenty feet on, they came out of the ankle deep water and into a cavern. She blinked and stopped, taken by surprise. The flashlight filled the cavern with dancing shadows, dark demons that teased her imagination. Something about the air gave a feeling of vast emptiness.

Then she saw the figure huddled against an outcrop of rock. With a small cry, she ran across. Squatting next to Jake, she frantically felt for a pulse. It was there, slow, erratic and weak.

"He's dying," Michael said softly, stopping just behind her.

She swallowed the lump in her throat and blinked back sudden tears. "No. I won't let him die."

He couldn't die and leave her alone. She couldn't cope with it.

"Jasper has fed on him. There's barely enough blood left to pump his heart..."

Michael's voice faded, and she glanced up quickly. He was listening to the silence, his face as still as his thoughts, giving nothing away. Evil closed the air around them, and her heart lurched in sudden fear. Jasper's plans were about to be revealed. She reached out and touched Jake's pallid cheek. His skin was colder than her fingers.

"Jake? Please, wake up."

No response, nor did she really expect any. They had to get him to hospital if they were to have any hope of saving him.

"We can't stay here—"

"And I won't leave him!"

"Nikki—"

"I don't want to hear it, Michael." She clenched her fists and glared at him. She wasn't about to leave Jake here to die, as she'd left everyone else in her life she'd cared about to die.

"I was only going to say we have to get going. Now, move aside, so I can pick him up."

She rose and stepped to one side, watching him haul Jake's unconscious figure upright. Something quivered in the air between them. She spun—too late to see what it was. She bit her lip, and clenched her fists. Jasper was playing games, again. Damn it, she had to ignore him, had to...

An explosion ripped across the silence. The ground bucked, and she screamed, staggering sideways as the darkness filled with fire and imminent death.

Michael grabbed her arm and held her upright. An ominous rumble ran through the darkness. Jasper hadn't finished with them yet.

"Go," Michael shouted, and thrust her forward.

She ran, dodging falling dirt and stone, the flashlight's beam barely picking out the ground a foot away. Dust filled the darkness, a thick cloud that tore at her throat, making it difficult to breathe. She had no idea where she was going. She just ran, staggering from side to side in rhythm to the earth's contortions.

Michael was at her back, his breathing labored. She didn't want him to die, and knew they all would if they didn't get out of this tunnel soon. The thought sent fresh energy though her legs.

"Swing left."

Her foot slithered on the slick footing. She threw out an arm for balance and struggled to keep upright. Hopefully, Michael had a far better sense of direction than she did. The falling debris made the darkness an alien world. It was difficult enough to breathe, let alone remember which tunnel was where.

Another explosion ripped across the darkness. Rocks rained down from the ceiling. She threw up her arms, trying to protect her head. Debris hit her, bruising her hands and shoulders. She stumbled, falling, and jarred her knee. Michael's arm went around her waist. With a grunt, he lifted her up and ran them all out of immediate danger.

After several minutes, he released her and pushed forward once more. "Move, move," he said.

His fear was tangible, filling the darkness. Not fear for him but for her. The knowledge lent her feet wings.

"Turn right now!"

She swung, dodging rubble, her breathing sharp and labored under the thickening cloud of dust.

"Watch it—"

Michael's shout echoed as her instincts cut in. She twisted sideways, barely avoiding the foul gasp of a zombie. She slipped, and cursed, then twisted around and shone the light into the creature's eyes. It leapt at her anyway. She dodged and flicked her knife into her palm.

Michael grabbed her arm and pulled her back.

"Let me," he said, and thrust Jake at her.

Jake's weight hit her, and she grunted, staggering backwards until she hit a wall. Rock dug sharply into her back and pain ran hot down her legs. She cursed but wrapped an arm around Jake's chest, holding him upright.

Another rumble ran through the darkness. She glanced upwards, wondering uneasily if Jasper's plans included bringing the entire mine down on top of them. Maybe it was just a neat extra.

A chill ran through her. Jasper was close, so very close. She sensed his evil, felt his gloating...

A figure loomed out of the darkness. Nikki swallowed, fingers clenched around the knife. Michael, not Jasper. Relief shot through her, its intensity shocking.

"Go," he said, and took Jake from her.

The water grew deeper, inching back towards her chest. She remembered the snakes she'd encountered earlier. Real or not, it wasn't an experience she wanted to relive. She faltered, not certain what to do next.

Another explosion ripped across the darkness. The roof above her collapsed, and a rush of rubble and dirt swept her off her feet.

"Nikki!"

Michael's cry was cut off as she was swept under the water. Dirt and stone fell around her, encasing her, trapping her under the foul waters. Panic swelled. She kicked her legs, desperate to get free, to get back to the surface. Fire burned in her chest, and she fought the desire to breathe. More rocks fell, churning the water, confusing her senses. Pain exploded through her body, and the need to open her mouth, to suck in air, grew desperate.

She thrashed sideways as rock smashed against her shoulder, and her head hit something solid. Red fire spread through her brain. She gasped in agony, swallowing water, crying a denial as darkness engulfed her.

*****

Nikki, Nikki! Hear me!

The frantic call pulled at her consciousness. She frowned, unable to move, unable to see, her body a motionless weight tying her down.

Nikki! Listen to me!

Golden light surrounded the stillness around her, freeing her from fear, filling her with peace and an intense need to be one with the light.

NO!

Gentle music washed across her senses. It flooded her cold body with warmth, releasing her from the dark weight of pain holding her captive. Suddenly free, her spirit rejoiced, dancing in radiance as she drifted towards the long golden tunnel.

Stay with me!

Something in that urgent plea made her hesitate, and the call of the golden light muted. Yet she didn't have the strength to go back, didn't have the courage to face the fear and the pain. The honeyed light pulsed, welcoming her, calling...

Nikki, I need you. Don't leave me.

The cry made her heart weep bitter tears. She wasn't worthy of the urgency in that entreaty, wasn't sure she was even capable of understanding it. And it was too late. Far too late. Dancing in brightness, she drifted closer to the light.

Nikki, do you want to live?

Did she? The question echoed through the soft warmth surrounding her. Did she want to live? Images of Michael ran through her mind. Oh yes, she wanted to live. But only with Michael. And that was an impossible dream.

It was too late anyway. The choice had gone.

No! If you trust me, there is a way.

No! Not as a vampire! Better death than a vampire.

Cold steel filled his thoughts. *Do you trust me?*

Trust was a flickering fire, so easily put out. So few people had earned its warmth after her parents' death. Only Jake, and he too was dying.

Jake needs you Nikki. I need you.

She closed her eyes against the pain in his entreaty. Michael didn't need her. He didn't need anyone. Maybe that was half her problem. He could walk away, and it wouldn't matter to him.

But Jake had to live. He couldn't die because of her.

Come to me Nikki. Let me save you. For Jake's sake, if not for mine.

She spun in confusion, afraid to go forward and afraid to go back. The warm light pulsed, healing and calming. She sighed. Here at last was the peace she had searched so long for. It would be so easy to give in to its warmth. Easy, but was it right? She didn't know, and that scared her more than the thought of dying.

Forgive me, Nikki. I can't let you do this.

Something grabbed her soul and yanked her down into darkness. The golden light began to recede. She wept and reached out towards it, a desperate swimmer fighting the tide pulling her away. Her efforts were ignored. The light disappeared, and she was thrust through layers of darkness and gathering pain.

Then the red mist enclosed her brain and swept her away.

Sixteen

Michael?

The harsh whisper ran through his mind. He closed his eyes and leaned back in the armchair. He didn't feel like talking to anyone right now, particularly Seline. Yet she was the one person who might understand. He sighed and silently acknowledged her probe.

Michael, what have you done?

He smiled grimly. What had he done? Even now, he wasn't entirely sure. He'd risked his life and cheated death, but until Nikki regained consciousness, he wouldn't know if it were all worth it. There could be aftereffects, either from her drowning or his own intervention. There was a very real possibility he might have destroyed the fire he was trying to save.

He raised the beer, taking a long drink. It didn't ease the burning in his throat.

Michael?

Worry shot through Seline's mental tones. He sighed again. She'd be out to Lyndhurst in a flash if he didn't start answering. The last thing he needed was a face-to-face confrontation with the old witch.

Here.

Michael, what on earth have you done? Half the circle has had visions of you in trouble.

And it was unusual enough for Seline to worry. No doubt his ice cool reputation had been shot all to hell, as well.

I think I've fallen in love, Seline.

Heavens, boy, I knew that ages ago. Just answer the question, or I'll come over in person and box your ears.

The threat made him smile, as she no doubt intended. Seline barely reached his shoulders, and was a thin, frail-looking woman. But she didn't look the one hundred and eighty years Michael knew her to be, and she certainly didn't act it.

We've known each other a long time, Michael. I thought trust was part of what we shared.

Trust wasn't his problem. Would she understand the sheer desperation that had made him act as he had? Would she accept his need to break a vow? Understand that he might lose Nikki anyway, because of his actions?

She was dying, Seline. I shared my psyche with her.

Made her live, against her will. He closed his eyes and took another long gulp of beer.

The sudden tension down the mental lines told him Seline understood the risk he'd taken.

Dear heavens, Michael, are you all right?

Exhausted. Weak. But alive. Obviously.

Can you cope with Jasper? Will you have the strength?

I'll cope. And Jasper would pay for every ounce of pain he'd put Nikki through.

Is she...all right?

Michael opened his eyes and studied Nikki's still features. She lay unmoving on the bed, her skin almost translucent, as if still held by the specter of death. He couldn't reach her mind, couldn't open the link between them, and it worried him.

I don't know.

How did all this happen?

Jasper set a trap, using Nikki's boss as bait.

That Jake still lived was a miracle. With the injuries he'd sustained, he'd have to be surviving on sheer force of will alone. But such courage deserved respect. Michael hoped the hospital could work a miracle. Not just for Nikki's sake, but his own. Jake was a rare find in this day and age—someone who looked beyond fear, beyond humanity, to see the person that lay beneath.

Do you need a hand? Gail's available.

I'll handle it.

But—

I said I'll handle it.

Concern ran down the link. *Are you sure? Gail's ready to go.*

The bastard's mine!

Her thoughts recoiled from the force of his anger, and he cursed. Lashing out at his friends would help no one, least of all Nikki.

Sorry.

I understand, Michael. Just be careful. You're no good to your Nikki if you make yourself so damn weak you can barely stand.

I know. He took another gulp of beer. *What the hell am I going to do once all this is over?*

What do you think you should so? What do you want to do?

What he should do and what he wanted to do were two very different things.

They don't have to be, Michael. She's a very resilient young woman. She'd fit nicely into our circle.

And have her share his world of darkness? As much as he ached to do just that, to finally have someone to walk by his side, it wasn't right or fair to ask her to do so. Darkness had been too much a part of her life already.

You should at least give her the opportunity to refuse, Michael.

She doesn't want me in her life. She doesn't want anyone in her life.

Amusement filtered down the line. *That sounds terribly familiar. Wonder where I've heard that before?*

He smiled. *I have to leave her. I have no real choice.*

Believe an old witch when she says the future is clouded when it comes to the two of you. There is no clear-cut choice here, no right or wrong.

He ran a hand through his hair. *Fat lot of good that advice does me.*

Then listen to your heart Michael. It may be buried deep, but I know it's there somewhere. Now get something to eat before you fade into shadow.

She broke the contact. He sighed and finished the rest of his beer. Seline was right. If he couldn't touch Nikki's mind now, after all they'd shared, what hope did Jasper have?

He pushed out of the chair that had been his home for the last thirty-six hours and walked across to the window. The late afternoon light washed through the lace curtains. Even in his weakened state, the sun held no threat.

But fatigue did.

He had to eat, had to regain strength as quickly as he could. When he finally caught Jasper, he had to be fit enough to take him.

The bastard had to pay.

***

She floated in a soothing sea of darkness, a world

without sound, without worry. At peace. Yet something within was restless, needing to be gone from this place.

A voice called, but she turned away, not wanting to confront the pain it represented. The voice would not be ignored. It filled her mind, demanding her return, relentless in its pursuit. Stirred to life, she finally woke and opened her eyes.

She was in her own room. Nikki blinked, confused. How did she get here?

Michael, obviously. Somehow he'd passed the barrier threshold of her home.

Somehow, he'd forced her to live.

She bit her lip and looked around the room. Nothing had changed. But she was alone and had been for some time. Michael was nowhere near—he was several miles away, gaining nourishment from a herd of dairy cows.

She blinked. How could she possibly know that without reaching for the link? *What has he done to me?*

She clenched her fists and closed her eyes, trying to recall the last moments in the mine. She remembered the golden light and its comforting warmth—remembered Michael's desperate plea. Then something had yanked her back into darkness.

Michael. Breaking his vow.

He'd saved her life, but at what cost? Was she even human anymore?

She threw the covers aside and scrambled out of bed, running across to the window. The sun peeped brightly around the edges of the curtains, and she flung them open, allowing the late afternoon sunshine to wash over her. Better a death like Monica's than life as a vampire.

Nothing happened.

The sunlight caressed her skin, warming but not burning. She leaned her forehead against the windowpane and closed her eyes. So she wasn't a vampire. At least Michael had heeded her wishes in that regard. But how had he saved her? Why did she feel no pain, no aches, after being trapped in the water under rocks and debris? How had he saved her, and at what cost to them both?

Her senses danced with the knowledge of change, yet blurred into confusion when she tried to understand how. And though she needed answers, she didn't want to reach for the link and Michael. A line had been crossed. Nothing would ever be the same—not with her life, and not with Michael.

She opened her eyes, and stared at the traffic running past her window. One thing hadn't changed, at least. He had to leave.

Jasper was still loose. And despite what Michael might say, Jasper's grip on her was growing stronger. His darkness stained the far corners of her mind, and it was becoming harder and harder to ignore.

She turned and made her way into the kitchen. Opening the refrigerator door, she was shocked to see it brimming with fresh food.

Make use of it.

Michael's comment came through like an order. A compulsion to obey leapt through her. She gripped the edge of the refrigerator, fighting it. Taking a deep breath, she slammed the door closed and leaned back against the bench.

He only had to make an order, and she wanted to leap up and obey. Why? What had happened in the dark hours lost to her memory? Had Michael succeeded where Jasper had failed?

A sigh of frustration ran through her mind. She tried to shut him out, needing to be alone, needing time to simply think.

Yet she knew time was the one thing they had precious little of.

She made herself a cup of coffee and grabbed an apple from the fruit basket, alternating between the two as she wandered aimlessly around the living room. Waiting—but for what she wasn't sure.

The phone rang shrilly into the silence. Her heart accelerated as she reached for the receiver. She knew who called. Knew why.

"Mary," she said softly, blinking back a sudden rush of tears.

"Nikki, you're awake. I was hoping you might be." Her voice sounded weary, old. "Though the last time I saw you, you looked like death."

She had a sudden vision of Jake, pale and dying, and felt a rush of despair. *Don't let me lose him, too. I couldn't bear it.*

"Nikki?"

She swallowed the lump in her throat. "How's...How's Jake?"

"That's why I'm calling. He's alive, Nikki. It was touch and go for a while, but the doctors think he'll pull through."

She closed her eyes and sent a prayer of thanks to the heavens. Then the rest of Mary's words hit her. How long had she been out?

Three days. Michael's thought winged lightly into her mind.

I need to be alone, Michael. Please, just leave me be for a while.

At least until she figured out how to get him out of her life—or if she even could, anymore.

"Jake wants to see you, Nikki. He won't settle down until he does," Mary said into the silence.

She glanced across to the window. Twilight was settling in. She had, at best, an hour's light left.

Jasper would be up and about.

She closed her eyes, weighing her fear of him against her need to see Jake. It wasn't even close. "I'll be there in twenty minutes."

Hanging up the phone, she returned to her bedroom and got dressed. She strapped on her wrist knives, then hesitated, staring at the floor. If she was going to do this, she had better make sure she could protect herself. And that meant getting something that might deter a vampire.

She walked across the room and opened the closet door. Squatting, she dragged out the old cutlery set and took out two knives. They were badly tarnished, but hopefully it wouldn't matter. It was still silver underneath—just how much silver though, she couldn't say. She pushed a knife down each boot, then rose and stamped her feet lightly. The knives might make walking slightly uncomfortable, but she felt better for their presence.

Wait for me.

She ignored Michael's request. Grabbing her coat and car keys, she headed out the door. Jake wanted to see her right now, and that was all that mattered.

The hospital was only a ten-minute drive away, but shadows were crowding the parking lot by the time she stopped the car and climbed out. Jasper wasn't anywhere near, yet something watched her. Something not quite human.

She shivered. It might have been wiser to wait for Michael, but he was on his way here, anyway. She could feel him getting closer.

She quickly locked the car, then fell in behind a family of four, following them through the parking lot and into the hospital foyer. A nurse directed her to the eighth floor. Mary waited near the elevators.

"He sent me," she explained. "Come on. He won't rest until he sees you."

"Do you know why?" Nikki asked, following the older woman up the corridor.

Mary shook her head. "No. All he tells me is that it's urgent." She shrugged and stopped near a door. "In you go. I'll wait here."

Nikki gave her a forced smile and stepped into the small, bright room. Jake's broad body was almost lost amongst the machines and tubes surrounding him. She stepped closer, smiling when he opened his eyes.

"Nikki." His voice was harsh and forced through thin, pale lips.

"You're looking good, Jake." She didn't care about his ghostlike color, the tubes, or the huge bandage around his neck. He was alive. That was all that mattered, all she cared about.

"Liar." His gaze pinned her, shrewd despite the pain haunting his pale features. "How are you?"

She shrugged. " I'll live."

He reached out and took her hand. His grip was weak, yet oddly reassuring.

"I'm not going to die on you, Nik. I'm far too stubborn to let the likes of Jasper win so easily."

Tear stung her eyes, but she blinked them back. Jake didn't need her tears—it would only make him worry. "I'm glad."

He squeezed her hand. "I just needed you to know. I don't want..." he hesitated, looking uncomfortable. "Nik, not everyone in your life has to die. Don't be afraid to live because you're so afraid of death. Don't let fear close your heart."

His words cut through her. She stared at him, wondering how he'd known, how he'd guessed.

"I'm no fool, Nikki. I've watched you grow from an untamed urchin to a warm but distant woman. Let someone break the ice, kid. If not Michael, then someone else. You can't go on as you are."

Why not? Why was everyone so intent on changing her life when she was happy?

But am I really? She remembered the long nights of loneliness and wasn't so sure.

Awareness raced like fire across her skin. She knew without looking that Michael had stepped into the room. Still holding Jake's hand, she turned and watched him walk to the opposite side of the bed.

She wondered if it were a deliberate choice. His gaze, when it met hers, was dark, emotionless, and there was a similar stillness in the link. He was keeping his distance as she asked. So why did she feel so uneasy?

"Good to see you're alive," Michael said softly. Though his gaze had turned to Jake, she knew all his attention was on her—waiting, assessing.

She shivered, biting her lip. She didn't want the confrontation she sensed coming. She wasn't ready for it. How could she be? Her whole life had changed in some unfathomable way, and the man standing so calmly on the opposite side of the bed had worked that change.

"As I was just explaining to Nikki, I'm too bloody stubborn to die." Jake's smile was a pale imitation of its usual self.

His eyes closed. She lightly squeezed his hand, then placed it back on the bed. He needed to rest. And she needed to get out of this hospital.

"We should go," she said softly, glancing at Michael.

He nodded and stepped away from the bed.

"Get the bastard for me, Michael," Jake murmured as they left.

Michael's gaze was bleak as it met hers. "I will."

There was a promise of death in his voice. Nikki gave Mary a brief hug, then followed Michael down the corridor.

"He'll live," Michael commented as they waited for an elevator.

"I know." She glanced at him, studying his still features.

"Thank you for not leaving him in the tunnel."

He shrugged. The elevator doors opened, and several people got out. Nikki stepped inside and pressed the lobby button. In silence, they walked out to the car and drove home.

Her nerves were stretched to the breaking point by the time she walked into the kitchen. Michael followed her inside and watched her make coffee. The time for confrontation had come. She feared it, and sensed she wasn't the only one.

Apprehension stole through her heart. She ignored it, finally turning to face him. His body was as shadowed as his thoughts, lost to the darkness filling the kitchen.

"What did you do to me, Michael?"

He didn't answer her right away. She gripped her coffee cup tightly, watching his shadow, waiting.

"I saved your life."

His answer was little more than a whisper across the darkness. She couldn't see him—but did she really need to? All she had to do was reach out and listen to the color of his thoughts...

She shuddered and resisted the temptation. It wasn't natural to be linked so intimately. And the link was stronger now than it ever had been.

"At what cost? Why do I feel so different?"

"You were dying, Nikki. I had to save you."

"And in the process you broke your vow never to make me do something against my will."

He made no answer, a still, silent presence she could feel but not see.

"What did you do?" she repeated, her voice a harsh whisper.

"What I had to do."

"Answer me, damn it! I have the right to know."

"But have you the courage to look beyond it?" A trace of bitterness haunted his words.

She glared at the shadows that hid him so well. He sighed.

"What I have done cannot be undone."

"What can't be undone, Michael? What the hell did you do to me?"

"I gave you part of what I am."

Horror rose anew. Did that mean she *was* a vampire?

"No, it does not." He moved, though it was something she felt rather than saw. "All I've ever asked of you is trust. I wonder now if you are even capable of it."

His contempt lashed at her. She flinched but made no comment, waiting for him to continue.

"What I did was give you part of my...psyche, part of my strength, part of my life force, I suppose. It gave you life."

And linked us together forever.

She took a step back. Linked for the rest of her life, never to be separated. The one thing she'd been fighting desperately to avoid.

"Not your life. My life."

Her heart skipped several beats. She clenched her fists against the fear pounding through her heart. "What do you mean?"

"Your life force is linked to mine. As long as I live, you cannot die."

She groped for the edge of the bench, her knees suddenly weak. "Oh God, Michael, you're kidding... right?"

"No. Unless you're beheaded, or have your neck broken, you cannot die." There was no remorse in his voice, only an odd harshness that somehow spoke of pain.

She ignored it. She was immortal? As eternal as the moon and the stars... and Michael?

"I am not immortal, Nikki. You noted that yourself some days ago."

"Damn it, Michael, that's not the point."

"Then what is?" he asked wearily.

"I don't want to spend eternity with a man who lives his life in shadow, a man who could rule my every thought and desire!"

He made no comment, but his anger rolled across the darkness towards her.

Energy burned at her fingertips. She clenched her fists against it. "Could you control me now, if you tried?"

He seemed to hesitate. "I don't know."

She closed her eyes, fighting terror. Michael wasn't Jasper. He wouldn't want to control every aspect of her life. At least not now. But what about one hundred, two hundred years from now? What would happen when he tired of her?

"Questions that mean nothing, because nothing will ever evolve from this. You do not want me in your life, Nikki, and I...?" He hesitated. "...cannot have you in mine."

Cannot, or would not have? Either way, it made little difference. "Then why save me? Why not let me die?"

Again he hesitated. "Had you died in Jasper's trap, he could have raised you as one of the undead. I couldn't have stood that."

She rubbed her arms. What a choice. Life as the undead, or life everlasting. Both had their drawbacks, though in far different ways. "How could you possibly share a life force, Michael? How is something like that even conceivable?"

"I'm not sure of the mechanics of it myself. I only know it is possible when two people are...compatible."

What had he meant to say? She shook her head, not sure if it even really mattered. "Is this the first time you've attempted something like this?"

"Yes." And the last, if the acidity in his voice was anything to go by. "Do you think it was easy, Nikki, to tear part of what I am away to give you life?"

She winced at his anger. She wasn't a complete fool. Life was a miracle she surely didn't deserve. She was just trying to understand the ramifications.

"Do all vampires do this?"

He hesitated, and doubt ran through the color of his emotions.

"Very few. There are problems. I know of only one other, and he found himself in need of an...assistant."

"A servant," she corrected tightly.

He sighed. "There were reasons, Nikki, and his friend was very willing."

"Well, at least the friend was given a damn choice!"

A short, sharp movement stirred the air. Light filled the room with brightness, then she was spun around. His eyes glittered with fury and some deeper, darker emotion she couldn't define.

"What is your problem, Nikki? Why do you refuse to trust me? Why can't you just accept the gift I gave you?"

I can't trust you because I might find I love you. And I don't want you to die. "I don't want eternity, Michael. I don't want to live with the fear that one day you will turn on me."

His breath hissed through clenched teeth. "If you think me such a monster, then kill me. Take the knife from your boot and stab it through my heart. It will end my life and revert yours back to normal."

She stared at him, appalled he could think her capable of such a brutal act.

"Why not? You're doing a damn fine job of it as it is. Why not finish it?" His grip on her arms tightened, bruising her. "But maybe you're happier wrapped in a cocoon of ice. Maybe I was a fool to think otherwise."

"Maybe you are," she muttered.

He let her go suddenly and thrust a hand through his hair. "Christ, I don't even know why I'm bothering."

He turned and walked to the other side of the room. It was a distancing that was mental as much as it was physical. And though this was what she had wanted, it still tore at her.

"What are we going to do then?" he asked after a moment. Arms crossed, he leaned against the wall, his face impassive, distant. As cold as when they'd first met.

She studied him. Anger she could cope with. Frustration and bitterness she could understand. But this? "About what?"

"You and me, Nikki. What else are we talking about?" His voice was lifeless, his thoughts a vast desert.

She met his gaze, uncertain what he wanted from her. He'd stated his intention of leaving so very clearly, and so often, she had no doubt that he would. And yet he obviously needed—or wanted—something from her. "There is no you and me. You said that yourself."

He simply stared at her. She shuffled her feet like some errant child and finally looked away. Because, deep down, she knew. He wanted her to confront what she felt, and that was the one course she could not take. Because she was a coward, and because her love had always signaled death. Vampire or not, he could die.

Better to live a lifetime alone than face the weight of one more death on her conscience.

Only now, it wasn't just one lifetime she had to face, was it?

"I don't know what else you want me to say, Michael."

"And therein lies our problem." He pushed away from the wall. "Perhaps the fault is mine. Perhaps I simply expect too much."

She stared at him. Did he want a lie? How could she admit to loving him when she wasn't sure?

And what good would it do, when he intended to leave anyway?

She blinked back sudden tears. Once she had told such a lie. It had led her and Tommy down a path to destruction. His life had slipped as quickly through her fingers as his blood, and she'd vowed never, ever to again admit to feelings she wasn't sure about.

"I'm not Tommy, Nikki. I'm not your damn parents or anyone else. I'm me. And I just want you to admit the truth, if only to yourself."

I can't. Don't you understand that? I can't!

"Then I truly must go."

She was losing him. Fear squeezed her heart tight, almost suffocating her. Afraid to love him, yet afraid to lose him. What a laugh.

"Perhaps this time is wrong for us," he said, dark eyes gentle. "Perhaps this was a fire always destined to flare brightly and die."

No, she wanted to say, no. But she held the words in check. He has to leave. He can't stay. The statement ran through her mind, over and over, as he turned and walked to the door.

"Don't," she whispered, as he reached out to grab the door handle.

He glanced back at her. "Jasper won't come near you again. I vowed that, and I meant it."

She wasn't afraid of Jasper right now. She was afraid that Michael would walk out the door and she'd never see him again.

Wasn't that what she wanted?

"Bye, Nikki." He turned and left. The door slammed shut behind him, rattling the display case in the living room. A crystal vase rocked and fell to the floor.

The sound of it smashing was the sound of her heart.

Seventeen

The silence drove her crazy. Nikki prowled through the house, trying to find something, anything, to do. Now that she had the time to think, it was the one thing she was desperate to avoid. Michael had walked out the door, probably forever. And she couldn't help the notion that, in a lifetime filled with mistakes, she'd just made her biggest.

But I want to be alone. I don't want to share my life with anyone, don't want to share my heart...

But did she really want to spend eternity alone?

The answer to that was simple. She didn't really want to spend *this* lifetime alone, not to mention the next three or four.

But what other choice did she have?

She stopped in front of the window and stared out blindly. Jasper's whispers ran laughingly through her mind, touching her soul with his darkness. His presence grew stronger. One day soon he would call to her, and she would have no choice but to obey.

She crossed her arms, rubbing them lightly. She'd done the right thing in telling Michael to go. At least now she didn't have to worry about betraying him. But what would she have done if Jasper wasn't a problem? What if there'd been only Michael and her and an endless eternity to share together?

Outside, a young couple strolled hand in hand across the road. She didn't have their courage. It was simple fact. Jasper only gave her a more believable excuse to push Michael away.

She turned from the window and walked across the room. Maybe she needed to work. Maybe if she buried herself in mundane office tasks, she wouldn't have to think about Michael or Jasper or long years of loneliness left ahead.

She walked into the bedroom to collect her coat and keys, and brushed past the bed. Memories rose to haunt her—being in Michael's arms, his bed, his throaty laughter as she'd whisked his pants away, the fire of their minds, touching and loving.

How could she have given it all away? How could she

have thrown away her one chance of lasting love?

She froze. There, she'd finally admitted it. She loved him. But it didn't matter a damn. She didn't want him to die, so they simply couldn't be together.

She spun away from the bed and its memories and retreated to the front door. After a quick glance around to check that all the lights were off, she opened the door and went outside.

The night was clear and held the promise of being cold. A chill ran up her spine as she unlocked the car door. It had nothing to do with the wind's icy fingers teasing the back of her neck. Someone was watching her.

She ignored the sensation and got into the car. There was little else she could do. It wasn't Michael or Jasper, so more than likely it was one of the zombies. And she sure as hell wasn't going to confront one of them.

But if only one zombie was watching her, what were the other two up to? Foreboding pulsed, a warning of trouble ahead. She grimaced and drove out of the driveway. It would be a nice change if the warnings were a little more specific.

The first thing she saw as she walked into the office was the madly flashing light on the answering machine. Throwing her keys on her desk, she grabbed a pen and paper and sat to answer some calls.

It was nearing midnight when she stopped. She rubbed at the crick in her neck and closed her eyes in sudden weariness. *I need a drink*, she thought, *something strong*. But Jake kept the whiskey under the cupboard near his desk, and she just couldn't be bothered with getting up. It was probably just as well. The mood she was in, she'd probably get drunk and end up feeling sorry for herself.

She leaned back in the chair and rested her feet on top of the desk. For some reason, she felt safe in the office. All the doors and windows were locked and barred, so if anyone tried getting in she'd hear them. A few hours' sleep would not go astray. She closed her eyes and drifted.

Images formed in her mind. Images that were indistinct and blurred, but full of panic. Figures lurched and spun in a gentle and terrifying dance. Death laughed, white teeth flashing across the darkness.

She jerked upright, her feet crashing to the floor. Now

she knew what the other two zombies were up to. Jake was in danger.

She reached for the link, then stopped. It wasn't fair to call Michael every time she or Jake was in trouble. He was here to find Jasper, and she shouldn't keep distracting him from that.

It left her with only one other option. Picking up the phone, she quickly dialed MacEwan's number. He answered on the second ring.

"It's Nikki James. I need help," she said.

"To do what?" His voice was terse, annoyed.

She wondered if she'd woken him. "It's one of those situations that can't rationally be explained."

Silence met her reply. She waited, her knuckles white with the intensity of her grip on the receiver.

"Tell me what's going on," he said, after a long moment.

She sighed in relief. At least he hadn't dismissed her outright, as many others would have. "The man responsible for the recent spate of murders is going after Jake. Only he's sending his people to do it."

"I see no problem. Jake's still in the hospital?"

"He is, but it's not that simple." She hesitated, then softly cleared her throat. "The people being sent are... well, they're zombies."

MacEwan made no sound. Even the soft rasp of his breathing had disappeared.

"They're two of the four women who went missing in Highgate Park."

MacEwan swore softly. It was hard to tell whether he believed her or not, and all she could do was wait. Jake was in danger and needed help. If MacEwan wouldn't assist her then she'd have no choice but to turn to Michael. She couldn't cope with two zombies on her own, and she wasn't going to let Jake die now.

"And I was worried about explaining Monica Trevgard's sudden crisping. Jeez..."

If he had any doubts as to her sanity, she couldn't hear it in his voice. Maybe he had seen too much on the streets to be fazed by anything life threw at him now. Or maybe he was just humoring her while he called the men with the white coats on the spare line.

"How do we deal with these people?"

"I'm told the only way to stop them is to break their necks."

"So I'm supposed to order my men to break the necks of a couple of dead women?" His voice was scratchy with either disbelief or amusement. Maybe both.

"There's no other way to stop them." She glanced anxiously at her watch. Three o'clock. Time was running out for Jake. She had to move.

"Maybe." Disbelief was stronger in his voice this time. "We'd better meet at the hospital. Ten minutes?"

"Ten minutes," she confirmed and hung up.

She stood and looked around the room. While she still had the silver knives down her boots, she wasn't so sure they'd be a deterrent against the zombies. And her wrist knives certainly didn't worry them. Jake had a gun locked in the safe, but would that work any better than a knife? Could a dead person be killed by a gunshot? What was that old rhyme? *One fine day in the middle of the night, two dead men got up to fight...*

What about salt? Michael had said it was useless against zombies, but thrown into their eyes, it *would* stop them, if only briefly.

She walked across the room and opened the small cupboard under the sink. Jake had a fetish for extra salt on his chips, so there had to be some in here somewhere. She moved several jars around, eventually finding a large shaker. For good measure, she grabbed the pepper and shoved both in her pocket.

Then she retrieved her keys from her desk and ran out to the car.

MacEwan was waiting for her at the hospital, leaning against the side of a car almost as battered as her own. Two other officers waited near the hospital's main entrance. She knew there would be others guarding the remaining exits. When MacEwan did something, he did it properly.

She stopped her car beside his and got out. "How many men do you have?"

He exhaled a long plume of smoke, then dropped the rest of his cigarette, crushing it under his heel. "Six, two men guarding each of the exits."

Six men, plus the two of them. Surely it was enough? "Have you been inside?"

He nodded. "Just to let the staff know what's going on."

She stared at him. "You told them about the zombies?"

He snorted. "I'm not a fool."

"And your men?"

"They've seen pictures of the missing women. I've told them to expect the unexpected." He shrugged. She knew then that he didn't really believe he'd be confronting zombies. "You ready to go in?" he continued.

She looked around, then nodded. There was no one watching her. Maybe she'd lost the zombie. And maybe it had somehow beaten her here and joined its brethren.

Seven men might not be enough to cope with the inhuman strength and speed of three zombies.

God, she missed Michael. She missed his strength, his ability to make her feel safe. Missed all his secrets and irritating ways. *Admit it*, she thought, *you simply miss him.* But there wasn't a hope in Hades she'd reach for him. Jasper's last two traps had almost killed her. If he succeeded with the third, she didn't want to take Michael with her.

She stopped suddenly. She couldn't die. Michael's gift of life meant she couldn't be raised as one of the dead, simply because Jasper couldn't kill her—not unless he severed her head. And even if he did that, he couldn't raise her.

The implications were more than a little mind-boggling.

MacEwan opened the door and frowned back at her. She hurried forward. The nurse stationed at the front desk looked up, and Nikki gave her a brief smile then led the way to the elevators.

MacEwan spoke into a handset as they got into the elevator, ordering his men to keep sharp. She watched the floor numbers roll sedately by and hoped the men listened to him. Their lives might depend on it.

The doors opened on the eighth floor. MacEwan held her back and looked out, then made her follow him as he led the way down the silent hall. When they reached Jake's room, he motioned her to one side of the door, then stood on the opposite side and slowly pushed it open. Nothing happened. After a few seconds, she peered around the corner of the door. The room was dark.

Foreboding pulsed in her brain. MacEwan reached out and turned on the lights. She blinked at the sudden brightness. The room was empty. Jake was gone.

MacEwan swore and spoke quickly into the handset. Nikki ran forward, hand outstretched as she neared the bed, desperate to find something...there! She lunged forward and grabbed his reading glasses. Her palm burned as images rose. Jake was alive.

"The stairs!" She pushed past MacEwan and ran from the room.

He cursed and spoke quickly into the handset as he pounded after her. He grabbed her arm as she reached the stairwell and wrenched her backwards.

"Don't be a fool," he said. "You're unarmed. Let me go first."

He drew his gun and cautiously opened the door. It was useless protesting, especially when he refused to believe what she was up against.

It was also a damn good reason for contacting Michael. But maybe that was what Jasper really wanted—her calling Michael here to help when the odds were on Jasper's side.

The stairwell was silent, dark. Warmth pulsed through her fingers. She glanced at the glasses in her hand.

"They're on the roof," she whispered.

MacEwan gave her a curious look, but didn't refute her statement. She followed him into the stairwell, squinting up into the darkness, straining to see something, anything that might indicate Jake was near.

The sound of a dragged footstep rasped across the silence. The handset squawked.

"Heading to the roof," MacEwan answered.

Though he spoke softly, his voice echoed. The zombies would know they were coming, if they didn't know already. She licked her lips and followed MacEwan up the stairs. Somewhere above them, a door opened, then slammed shut. She gripped the handrail tightly. They didn't have much time left.

"Quickly," she whispered.

"It's a black hole in here. I'm going as fast as I damn well can."

Tension edged his whisper. She smiled grimly. Maybe MacEwan wasn't the cool, calm and collected type he liked to appear. They reached the exit to the roof. MacEwan opened the door and peered out. A cold wind ran in, whipping around her ankles. She shivered and peered over his shoulder, trying to see Jake.

MacEwan nudged her back. "I see them. Wait here."

He disappeared out the door. Nikki snorted softly. *Stay here indeed.* Slipping out the door, she ran in the opposite direction. The warning pulse grew more urgent. The zombies were dragging Jake to the edge of the building.

She raced around a crumbling chimney, then stopped. The wind slapped against her face, as cold as ice. The zombies were heading for the building's edge, Jake's unconscious figure held between them. MacEwan stood twenty feet away, gun drawn but by his side.

"Police! Stop or I'll shoot," MacEwan warned.

The zombies paid no notice, ambling on towards the edge. Again MacEwan shouted a warning, this time aiming his gun. The zombies continued to ignore him.

The gunshot reverberated through the night. One zombie stopped, then dropped his hold on Jake and ponderously turned to face MacEwan. The other limped on, dragging Jake's still body by an arm.

Nikki broke into a run. Out of the corner of her eye she saw MacEwan take a step, saw him raise the gun.

"Stop or I'll shoot!"

The creature continued to ignore him. Another shot reverberated. The zombie staggered sideways as the bullet hit, but it wasn't stopped. She didn't know if MacEwan had aimed to wound or kill, but it didn't really matter. Bullets wouldn't stop them, as she'd feared.

The second zombie had almost reached the building's edge, and she wasn't close enough to do a damn thing. Desperately, she kinetically wrenched Jake's unconscious body away from the creature, hauling him across the darkness into her arms.

She staggered under the impact of his weight, her mind reeling with pain. She'd never attempted to move anything as heavy as a man before, and it was harder than she'd ever imagined it could be. Sweat broke out across her brow, quickly chilled by the cold wind. Licking her lips and tasting fear, she thrust her shoulder under Jake's arm. Holding him tight, she walked away as quickly as she could.

The zombie howled in frustration. Heavy steps followed.
"How the hell do you stop these things?"
MacEwan's sharp question jarred the silence.
"I told you. Break their necks." She barely glanced at
him, all her attention on the exit across the far side of the
roof. A warning pulsed through her, and she checked.
The door opened, and two of MacEwan's men stepped
out. They looked around, then ran towards the detective.
Behind them, the door opened again. The third zombie
stepped out.
She swore and stopped. The creature had the exit
blocked, and there was no other way off the roof.
They were trapped.

***

The plaza pulsed with music and light. People danced
and drank, filling the night with heat and music.
Michael kept a close watch on the partygoers from his
vantage point above the square. Jasper wove his way
through the unsuspecting crowd, a red haze in the
darkness, easy to follow. Michael sensed the other vampire's
hunger, felt his need. Knew he would attempt to feed
tonight. He watched him move from figure to figure,
searching for easy prey, someone to lead off into the night
and feed upon.
Only Michael had already made sure there were no
loners in the immediate area, forcing the drunks and lone
partygoers to move on. Jasper would have to extend his
search to a less populated section of the city.
And there he would die. Nikki would be safe.
He stirred, shifting from one foot to the other. He
wouldn't—couldn't—think about her. Not when he had a
murderer to catch. Maybe not even after.
But the memory of her smoky amber eyes, clouded in
confusion and fear, kept running through his mind,
haunting him.
He sighed and leaned wearily against the wall. He had
never wanted to fall in love. Not with Nikki. Not with anyone.
His life was too dangerous and human life too tenuous,
too short. But right from the beginning he'd had no choice.
He might have told himself he was only using her as bait,
but the truth was, he had simply used it as an excuse to
stay near her. She was a flame, a bright torch that had

pierced the darkness surrounding him. He needed the touch of that fire. Needed her.

He didn't want to return to the emptiness of an eternity alone. Better death, if it came to a choice.

He frowned and watched Jasper move back to the center of the square. What was the fiend up to now?

The younger vampire found shape, intercepting the attentions of a pretty young woman, spinning her away from her partner in a dance both erotic and sensual.

Why the hell was Jasper dancing? Why was he risking exposure like this? Michael stood up straight. Something was going on, though he wasn't sure what.

The younger vampire turned. Their gazes locked in a battle Michael knew neither could win. Then Jasper sneered and mouthed a word.

Jake.

Michael clenched his fists. Somehow, Jasper was going after Jake. Probably the zombies again, he thought, and wished he'd killed them when he'd had the chance. Though what was the point when Jasper could so easily call more of his victims from the dead? He jumped to the ground and moved forward, slipping quickly through the crowd. There was nothing he could do for Jake right now. As much as he liked the man, as much as his death might hurt Nikki, he wasn't going to let Jasper slip through his fingers now that he almost had him...

Jasper's laughter stopped. His eyes widened as he suddenly realized his plan wasn't working. The fiend turned and ran, pushing his way through the crowd.

Michael smiled grimly. Jasper could never escape, no matter how fast he ran. Not when the air recoiled against his evil.

He walked quickly through the crowd, following Jasper's trail. They moved out of the square and into the main street. Jasper crossed the road, then ran into an alley. Michael hesitated as a car drove by, and picked up an old steel bar from a bin before he entered the alley.

Jasper's life force shimmered ahead. He tossed the bar in his hand a couple of times, then glanced towards Jasper. Hefting the bar a third time, he threw it as hard as he could.

It hit with a satisfying thump. Jasper staggered forward,

then regained his momentum and kept on running. But for the first time, Michael felt fear rather than gloating in the younger vampire's thoughts.

Jasper crossed another street. He was heading for the docks, perhaps hoping to lose Michael amongst all the old warehouses.

The tang of salt air grew heavier on the wind. Michael listened to the waves breaking across the wharf supports, an angry sound that matched his mood. Jasper ran down a wooden walkway and into a building.

Michael studied it. The warehouse appeared deserted. There was no one about, either inside or in the nearby buildings.

A trap waiting to be sprung.

He stopped near the door, then moved around to the left. Turning a corner, he saw a small building in the shadows of the next warehouse. He walked across, keeping watch on the building to make sure Jasper made no attempt to escape.

The door was padlocked. But from inside came the smell of gasoline. Michael wrenched the door open. How fortunate, he thought, seeing a dozen or so cans.

Picking up two, he moved back to the warehouse. Jasper hadn't moved. He could see his red haze hunkered down in one corner.

Michael opened the can and splashed the gas across the building's wooden wall. Then he stepped back, reaching into his pocket for the matches he'd picked up earlier.

The fire wouldn't kill Jasper, but it would make him sweat. Make him relive the horror of his childhood. Make him fear, as he'd made Nikki fear.

Lighting a match, Michael flicked it at the wall, then stepped back quickly as the wall exploded into flame.

Fear hit him, almost suffocating his senses. Only it wasn't Jasper's fear. It was Nikki's.

He immediately opened the link and reached out, demanding to know what was wrong. Her mind was closed to him, refusing to acknowledge his call. He cursed softly. When he'd shared his psyche with her, he'd not only strengthened the link between them, but he'd also strengthened her ability to ignore him as well.

He glanced back at the fire. Hungry fingers of flame

were beginning to spread along the roof. It wouldn't be long before the whole building was ablaze. Jasper hadn't yet moved. He would wait until the last possible moment. But Michael couldn't.

Nikki was in danger. He had to leave.

At least dawn wasn't far off. With a bit of luck, Jasper wouldn't have the courage to do any hunting tonight.

And that, in turn, would weaken him, make them a more even match. When Michael had shared his psyche with Nikki, he'd lost a lot of his strength. If Jasper fed, he would be hard to beat. Not that it mattered. If Michael had to die, then so be it.

As long as he took Jasper with him.

He turned and broke into a run, heading for the hospital and Nikki.

***

The zombie charged her. Nikki leaped away, but not fast enough. The creature's fist clipped her jaw and sent her flying. She hit the concrete hard, her breath whooshing from her lungs. The zombie turned, its movements ponderous yet not slow. A sick grin marred the features that had once been pretty.

Rolling over, Nikki scrambled to her feet. The zombie rushed again. She dodged sideways, barely avoiding the creature's fist, then glanced at the shadows at the chimney's base. Slowly, foot by foot, she was leading the creature away from Jake.

A shot rang out through the silence, then a string of curses and the sound of running footsteps. MacEwan and his men were trying to deal with the second of the creatures. The third still held guard near the door.

The zombie rushed Nikki again. She ducked, but not fast enough. The creature's hand smashed into the back of her skull and sent her flying. Her knees skinned against the concrete, and she shook her head, fighting tears and the stars dancing before her eyes.

From behind her came the sound of a scraped footstep. Panic surged. She twisted away, but the zombie hit her hard, knocking her sideways, back onto the concrete. It laughed, an oddly vacant sound that chilled her soul. She blinked back tears of pain and tried to roll to one side. The zombie reached down and stopped her, then put its hands round her neck and hauled her upright. She might not be able to die, but right at this moment, it sure as hell felt as if she could.

The creature's grip tightened. Gritting her teeth against the pain, gasping for breath and trying not to panic, she reached into her pocket.

The edge of darkness was closing in fast. She quickly loosened the top of the salt container, then took it out of her pocket and flung it into the zombie's face.

The creature roared and let go, tearing at its eyes as it staggered away. Nikki pushed upright. She could barely see through tears, and her throat felt raw, as if it were on fire. It hurt to breathe, let alone move. But she had to move, before the creature came back.

A warning pulsed through her mind. She scrubbed the tears away and turned. The zombie sniffed the breeze, using scent instead of vision.

It spun and charged. Nikki didn't move. The creature was too fast to outrun, too strong to fight by normal means. All she had left were her abilities. But she needed time to use them again, time to recover from the stress of lifting Jake. Time she didn't have.

She took a deep breath and prayed for a miracle.

Thrusting a tight beam of energy at the creature, she halted its charge. It screamed in fury, struggling against the invisible cords holding it immobile.

Sweat broke out across Nikki's brow, running into her eyes, stinging them. She didn't blink, didn't move, fearing either might cause her to lose her grip. Fire ripped through her mind, a red haze of agony she had no choice but to ignore as she battled to contain the creature.

But simple containment was not the answer. The zombie had to die, or else it would come back again and again. The creature who controlled its mind wanted Jake dead. The zombie would follow the wishes of its master until it succeeded.

Or died.

She had no choice. Slowly but surely, she pushed the creature backwards, forcing it towards the edge of the building. The creature hit the ledge, and its arms flailed. It screamed, a sound so human, Nikki hesitated.

In that instant, the creature surged forward again—

running straight for the shadows that held Jake.

Nikki gasped and dropped to her knees. She couldn't do it again. She bit her lip and hugged her body tightly. She had to. This zombie had to die, or more people would. People like Jake, who'd done nothing to Jasper except be her friend.

She forced past the pain and grabbed the creature, thrusting it back to the edge. It struggled desperately, wrenching and twisting the invisible lines holding it captive. Pain rippled through every fiber, every cell. Nikki ignored it and tightened her hold, then thrust the creature past the edge. When it had cleared the concrete edge by several feet, she let go. The creature fell, screaming.

She closed her eyes and rocked back and forth, desperately trying to catch her breath. She felt like she'd run a damn marathon—but it wasn't over yet. Two zombies still remained.

Another gunshot shattered the night. Nikki licked her lips and climbed unsteadily to her feet. MacEwan appeared out of the shadows to her left, half carrying one of his men. A zombie followed them, dragging one leg more than usual.

She clenched her fist and threw a ball of power at the creature. It staggered under the impact and stopped, giving MacEwan the chance to escape immediate danger.

Then it turned. A roar of anger bit through the night. Giving the creature no chance to charge, she sent another whip of power towards it, knocking it sideways.

She reached again, but agony locked her mind tight. She fell to her knees, fighting tears, fighting the red tide threatening to engulf her. She'd done too much, pushed too hard. Now there was nothing left. Nothing but pain and approaching death.

I don't want to die.

Not that she could, unless someone broke her neck. And she had a bad feeling the zombie knew that. That Jasper knew that.

But there was nothing she could do except close her eyes and wait.

Eighteen

The footsteps stopped. An eerie silence followed.

Confused, Nikki opened her eyes and looked up. Pain shot through her head at that smallest of movements. She blinked back tears, unable to believe what she saw.

The zombie lay on the concrete ten feet away, its neck twisted at an odd angle. *What on earth...?*

"Nikki?" The soft question flowed out of the night.

Michael. Her heart leaped, rushing heat through her body. She turned carefully, searching for him. Nothing but shadows filled the night.

"Are you all right?" Again his whisper cut through the night.

"Yes." Why didn't he show himself? Was it MacEwan's nearby presence that stopped him? Fear pounded through her heart, and she reached out to the link, only to be stopped by a wall of pain.

"Take care then, little one." His voice was distant.

He's leaving me. She squeezed her eyes shut, and tried to control the panic pounding at her pulse. This was for the best. It's what she wanted. But fingers of fear wrapped around her heart, squeezing it tight.

Tears trickled past her closed eyelids. Maybe she was a fool for letting him go, but what choice did she really have? She'd always been cursed when it came to love. Jake had managed to survive its touch, but she didn't love him the way she had loved her parents and Tommy. And now Michael.

She had to believe it was better that he left. It was the only way she could survive.

Footsteps approached. She opened her eyes. MacEwan eyed the dead zombie warily, his gun at the ready. The look on his face would've made her laugh any other day.

"The creature near the door is also dead," he said, nudging the zombie with the toe of his boot. "Care to explain how it happened?"

"One of those situations that can't be explained." God, it hurt to think, hurt to move. But she had to do both. She couldn't stay here.

His gaze was disbelieving. Nikki ignored him. She didn't

have the energy to even try to explain Michael's intervention.

After a moment, MacEwan shrugged and put his gun away. "Who am I to question deliverance? Need a hand up?"

She nodded. He clasped her arm and hauled her upright. Pain shot like fire through her brain, and she gasped, fighting the urge to be sick.

"You don't look so good." MacEwan studied her with a frown. "Maybe you should go downstairs and let one of the doctors take a look at you."

She gingerly shook her head. The last thing she needed was to be prodded and poked. She was fine. Mostly.

"Then at least let me get someone to drive you home..."

They both turned sharply at the sound of the exit door opening. More police officers. She sighed in relief.

"The cavalry, at last," MacEwan commented dryly.

"Too late, as usual." She rubbed at her temples. Would the pain ever go away? It was a white-hot fire, eating at her brain.

MacEwan gave her a wry look and waved his men over. "Would an earlier arrival have saved us? How many men does it take to kill a zombie?"

Only one—if you're a vampire. "Isn't that a bad joke somewhere?"

He laughed, a startling sound in the hushed night. "Probably." He turned as an officer approached. "Jenkins, drive Miss James home, please."

The young officer nodded. MacEwan turned back to face her. "I dare say my superiors will want to talk to you about tonight."

"You know where to find me." She glanced across at Jake, still safe in the shadows of the chimney. "Will you get a doctor up here for Jake, as quickly as possible?"

MacEwan nodded and spoke into his handset. Nikki waved away the young officer's offered arm and walked slowly towards the stairs. Every step she took sent lances of fire shooting through her brain. She bit her lip and fought the urge to sit and howl like a baby. It hurt, sure, but pain, in one form or another, was something she was used to, something she'd learned how to handle. *Something I no longer want to fight alone.*

"Nikki?" MacEwan called as she neared the door. She

glanced back at him. "If you find the man behind this trouble, give me a call."

So you can do what? It was only thanks to Michael any of them were alive tonight. She nodded, too tired to do anything else, just wanting to get home and get some sleep.

But she felt MacEwan's gaze on her back long after she'd left his presence.

***

Michael watched her walk away. His heart ached with her pain, yet there was nothing he could do to help her. Nikki had to get over her problems without interference from him. Until she did, there was no hope for them.

Maybe there had never been any hope from the beginning. Maybe he was a fool to ever think otherwise. He'd long ago stepped past the threshold of humanity and become something more. What made him think he could ever go back?

When she walked through the exit, he turned and moved across to Jake. The younger man was still heavily drugged, but otherwise appeared unhurt. He'd hate to think how Nikki would react if he died now, after all she'd been through to save him. Her dependence on him was frightening. Michael grimaced wryly. If he was being at all honest, it also made him jealous.

Which was another human emotion he could live without, he thought bitterly. That and love.

Several hospital staff came running up, and he stepped away, watching them bustle Jake onto a stretcher. As they took him back downstairs, Michael glanced at the sky. Dawn was beginning to stretch golden fingers through the night. So much had happened, yet so little time had passed. At least Nikki was now safe. Jasper wouldn't attack her with dawn so close. He would be on the run, searching for a place to wait out the day.

Michael turned and walked back to the stairs. It was time to resume his hunt.

***

The voice whispered through her brain, its touch evil, full of menace. Nikki twisted and turned, desperate to escape. But there was no running from the demons taunting her dreams.

Not even when she awoke.

She sat up on the sofa and studied the living room. Shadows hunched in the corners, but through the window she could see the red and gold tendrils of sunrise spreading across the stormy sky.

She glanced at her watch. She'd been asleep for little more than half an hour.

Evil whispered around her, shimmering through the air, filling her mind with its malice. Her breath caught in her throat, and sweat broke out across her brow. Jasper was coming for her.

She rose quickly. For an instant the room spun, and she grabbed the arm of the sofa, holding on tight. The spinning eased but not the knife-edged pounding in her brain.

Jasper was coming, and she was without any form of defense. Panic ran through her, closing her throat and making it difficult to breathe. *I can't do it. I can't face him alone.*

Her gaze fell on her boots. Silver gleamed briefly, firefly-bright in the half-light of morning. But the thought of facing the young vampire with only a silver knife made her mouth go dry. She had no idea if the knives even held enough silver to hurt Jasper. And he could so easily take it from her, without any effort, without any movement. All he had to do was command her to drop it, and she would.

Yet she had nothing else. She sat back down and quickly dragged the boots on, tucking the knives close to her shins. Again malice whispered through the silence. She clenched her fists against a wash of hopelessness.

You are mine, and I will prove it. Fighting it is useless.

Maybe it was. Maybe she should just give up. She bit her lip at the thought. She could have given up thirteen years ago, when her parents had died, but she hadn't. She could have done it when Tommy died. Maybe part of her had, and that was why she couldn't trust herself to simply love Michael and let the future take care of itself.

But she sure as hell wasn't going to give up against Jasper. Maybe he was right, maybe it was futile, but she had to try.

His laughter slipped around her, as cold as ice. She resisted the temptation to flee. Jasper would find her, no matter where she ran, no matter where she hid. The link between them was strong, stronger perhaps than the link she shared with Michael. She closed her eyes and tentatively tried to reach out to him. Pain lanced through her brain, and she gasped, blinking back tears. *In saving Jake, have I destroyed that part of myself?*

And did it matter? Jake was alive, and in the end, his survival meant more than the gifts that had caused so much trouble in her life.

She waited. There was nothing else she could do.

Open the door...

The command washed across the silence, threatening yet enticing. The urge to do as he asked stormed through her. Clenching her fist, she rose and backed away. Jasper was just beyond the front door. She could feel his heat, the sense of depravity that was his essence.

Hope flared slightly. If she could feel that, then her psychic senses weren't as dead as she feared. Her head might pound every time she moved, yet maybe, if she pushed hard enough, she might be able to defend herself.

Do not ignore me. Open the door.

No. Never. She reached down and slid one of the silver knives from her boot. Power swept around her, black wings that beat against her resistance. Where was Michael? Why wasn't he here to stop Jasper?

I have arranged a diversion for your lover. He will not arrive in time to help you.

Nikki closed her eyes and tried to ignore his mocking confidence. Jasper couldn't harm her unless she allowed him in her house. She had to keep resisting.

The zombies will delay him. By the time he realizes his mistake, I will have you.

Again hope stirred. The zombies were dead. So where the hell was Michael?

The trail is long and twisted.

His amusement slithered around her. She shivered. The only thing twisted around here was Jasper's mind. *I will never be yours.*

You are mine already, sweet thing. Shall I prove it to you?

She made no reply and backed further across the room, the knife clenched so hard in her hand her fingers were going numb. Power washed through the room, a psychic beam that wrapped around her like a chain, heavy and cold.

Open the door.

"No!" she screamed. Yet her whole body trembled, muscle fighting muscle, the urge to obey battling the will to fight.

The chains drew tighter. Cold sweat ran down her back. She wouldn't give in, she wouldn't...

He laughed. The sound stung her heart.

You have no choice. Open the door, pretty one.

Power whipped around her, beating at her resistance, searing her senses. She fought the urge to obey with every ounce of strength she had.

To no avail.

One foot slipped forward, then the other. She screamed in terror as she was slowly forced towards the door.

***

The warehouse was gutted, a blackened shell that stood out starkly against the morning twilight. Michael made his way past the fire engine, and moved on, following the trail along the docks. Jasper's scent was faint. He studied the street ahead uneasily. Something didn't feel right.

The trail led past a series of well-lit factories. There was no hiding spot here for Jasper, no hope that he could find an easy feed. The area was too full of people and light. So why had he come here? Why did he meander, when there was so little of the night left? If Jasper intended to feed, he should have done it quickly, then moved on to find shelter and wait out the day.

But he'd been away an hour, and that was a long time when you could move as fast as the wind.

Michael frowned and studied the lights ahead. The trail was beginning to take him eastward, into an area of Lyndhurst he did not know. An area on the opposite side of town to Nikki.

Michael stopped cold. *Nikki.* Revenge, it all centered around revenge, she'd said. And she was right. Jasper didn't meander. He'd played him for a fool. God, what a fool! He turned and ran back through the darkness, the night a blur and fear beating through his heart.

All he could do was hope he wasn't too late.

***

"Come in." The words were forced through gritted teeth.

Tears rolled unhindered down her cheeks as Jasper walked in, angelic and smiling.

Their gazes touched, and her heart quailed. Once his eyes had been dead, showing little emotion; now they were consumed by madness. He was over the edge and out of control—but totally in control of *her.*

Jasper walked into the living room and sat casually on the sofa. The leash loosened—but not enough to allow her to run through the door and freedom. Instead, she backed away from the door, backed away from him. She still held the knife—she might yet have the chance to use it.

"Drop it," he said quietly.

She clenched her fingers around the hilt. The silver burned into her hand, a clean fire that fought the dark chains wrapping tightly around her.

"No. Take it from me if you dare."

He smiled in amusement and locked his hands behind his head, leaning back to study her.

"You think I'm afraid of the toothpick you hold?"

She didn't think anything. She only knew it was important to keep him talking. Michael was out there somewhere. Even though the pain in her head stopped her from contacting him, surely he'd realize something was wrong. He had at the hospital. Sooner or later, he would come to her. He'd promised to keep her safe against Jasper. He'd keep that promise, no matter what.

Jasper raised a hand. Power pulsed through the silence, a fiery tendril that wrapped around her. She clenched her teeth, gathering her own energy despite the bitter ache in her head.

Jasper laughed, flicking his fingers outwards. Nikki yelped as she was lifted off the ground and flung across the room. She crashed against the wall and slithered to the floor. For a moment, she lay there, struggling to breathe against the fear locking her throat. She'd never beat Jasper. Not in a million years. He was as strong as Michael when it came to mind gifts. Maybe even stronger.

But she had to try. Or die.

She dragged her arm close to her chest and hugged the knife tightly. The cold metal burned into her skin, fighting the darkness, giving her strength.

"That...that the best you can do?" she said, when she could.

He laughed lightly. "So much courage."

Power surged again. This time, she met his thrust with her own, shoving his lance aside before rushing on, pushing him to his feet—pushing him back, towards the gathering dawn. For an instant she saw fear in his eyes and knew in that moment that Michael was right. Jasper *was* afraid of her powers.

But fire ran through her brain, and her head felt ready to explode. She couldn't hold on...couldn't...

The psychic energy slipped away. She gasped and hugged her body. Tears fell onto her arm as she rocked back and forth, desperate to shake the pain locking her mind. Desperate to ignore the laughter surrounding her, tightening the dark chains once more.

"Drop the knife."

She clenched the knife tighter, eyes closed, huddled in upon herself. Warmth spread through her hands and chest, a lone fire in the darkness surrounding her.

He took a step forward. "Release it."

The black wings of energy beat against her. Her fingers twitched in reply, and his elation grew. Still she made no move.

He took several more steps. Energy lashed at her. She quivered under the blows, but refused to move, refused to answer the growing need to obey.

Another step. The heat of his body washed over her, burning the bare skin along her arms. Her muscles twitched in agony, but she ignored it, concentrating on Jasper.

Just a few more steps, she pleaded silently, *just a few steps closer.*

As if drawn by her plea, he moved. Nikki unfolded, thrusting up in a fluid movement, ramming the silver knife into his stomach.

Jasper screamed and lashed out, smashing his fist across her face. She slid across the floor and landed in a heap near the kitchen door. Gasping for breath, she shook her head, trying to clear it of the pain falling in a red haze around her eyes. Or was it blood?

Jasper hissed. She glanced up quickly. The force of his gaze made her cringe back. Jasper was through playing games. The time for death had come.

She scrambled to her feet. He took the knife in two hands and drew it slowly from his abdomen. Small tendrils of silver fire licked against his fingers, and the smell of burning flesh filled the air. He showed no sign of pain, his eyes blazing murder.

"You will die for this," he hissed, holding the knife up in his fist. "Come to me, now!"

Sharp probes of energy lashed at her, knocking her back to the floor, filling her body with fire. It burned through every fiber, every muscle, quick, deadly and powerful. *God I should crawl to him, beg his forgiveness...*

"No!" she screamed, raising her hands in front of her face, breaking the lock of his gaze and the force of his will.

The chains of power yanked tight, and she gasped, struggling to breathe. She threw a lance of energy at him, trying to thrust him backwards, but he barely rocked back on his heels. His laughter whipped around her, cold and mocking. Nikki blinked back bitter tears, and reached for another lance. But the black wings lashed at her, and fire consumed her mind, making it difficult to think, to breathe. *If this is what Hell feels like, I definitely do not want to die...*

But maybe the choice had never been hers.

Nineteen

Energy spun through the room, and the inferno died abruptly. Nikki waited, half expecting another of Jasper's games. She refused to look up, refused to give him the satisfaction of her fear.

"Nikki, get up."

Michael's soft order seemed more a shout in the heavy silence. She glanced up quickly, elation, relief and fear tumbling through her.

He leaned against a wall near the doorway, his arms crossed, face impassive. Yet fury and death filled his eyes, and it chilled her soul. It wasn't only Jasper's death she saw in his eyes.

"Go," he said softly, still not looking at her. "Get out and do not come back."

She clung to the door frame and pulled her aching body upwards. The room spun, and she gasped softly, biting back the urge to be sick. She took a deep breath and forced herself to move, slowly edging towards Michael and safety.

Jasper's gaze burned through her soul, but he didn't move. Power whispered around her, a touch so different to the dark flames that had beaten at her only minutes before. Michael was holding Jasper still so she could escape.

She reached him and hesitated. His dark gaze met hers. For an instant the link flared to life, and their souls met in a dance that warmed her heart. Then regret flickered, and the link died, lost in a blaze of pain that made her eyes water.

She stared at him. Death rode his shoulders, and she didn't know what to say, what to do, to fight it. He reached out, gently touching her swollen cheek. She closed her eyes, leaning briefly into his touch. *Lord, I love him. I don't want to lose him.*

"How very touching," Jasper commented dryly into the silence. "Be sure that I will take good care of her when you die, Kelly."

She ignored the mocking laughter that danced through her mind. "Michael—"

He put a finger to her lips. "Leave us, Nikki. Don't come back, no matter what happens. Promise me."

Her eyes widened in alarm. "No."

"Promise me. If you stay anywhere near, Jasper will attempt to kill you."

And if I go, he will kill you. And she knew he would welcome that death. Because of her, because of her stupid fear...

"Michael. Don't-"

"Hush," he said softly. "Promise me, Nikki."

Dread pounded erratically through her heart. She closed her eyes, and took a deep breath. "I promise. As long as you make me one."

Wariness flickered in his eyes. "What?"

"Don't die."

He smiled grimly. "I promise. Now go."

Another lie. Tears filled her eyes. She stared at him a moment longer, then turned and walked out the door.

***

The door slammed shut behind her, a harsh sound in the silence. Michael listened to her fading footsteps and knew his heart went with her. But it didn't matter. Nothing did, except keeping her safe from Jasper's taint.

"I shall savor your defeat, as I shall savor your woman in your memory," Jasper hissed.

Michael pushed away from the wall and lightly shook his arms, loosening tight muscles. "You must win first, worm."

"Oh, I shall."

Michael quirked an eyebrow. "As your brother won?"

Jasper snarled in fury. Power seared the room, washing around Michael. He watched Jasper's body twitch. He wouldn't be able to hold him much longer. Jasper was close to his equal now that he'd shared some of his strength with Nikki. And maybe that was for the best.

With a snap that stung his mind, the chains shattered. Jasper howled and launched himself across the room. Michael dodged and swung his fist, smashing Jasper's jaw, knocking him sideways. It was totally unnecessary, but the sound of flesh smacking against flesh appeased some need in his soul.

Jasper shook his head, laughing as he turned. Energy gathered in the room like an approaching storm. He shifted his stance, watching Jasper warily. Madness lit the younger vampire's eyes. He'd have to be careful. Jasper was as cunning as a cobra, and, in this mood, probably ten times more dangerous. No matter what else happened here today, he had to make sure Jasper died—so Nikki could live her life in peace, without fear, without darkness.

Energy hit him, flaring around him in a red wave of heat. He flung a bolt of his own and followed right after it. He hit the younger vampire side on, knocking him backwards, closer to the window and the warm morning light.

Jasper laughed again, a high, inhuman sound. Too late, Michael felt the presence of silver. He thrust backwards, but the blade pierced his side, biting deep. White heat flared, swirling through his body, a tide that promised death.

But not without Jasper.

He staggered upright. Energy lashed at him. Michael ignored it and walked forward, watching Jasper's eyes, watching the hint of fear grow as the younger vampire backed away. Ignoring the pain pounding though his body, dredging up every reserve he had, Michael reached out kinetically. The cords of power wrapped chains around Jasper, stopping him cold.

"How long has it been since you tasted the sun?" he said quietly. "Can you remember its warmth, Jasper? Can you remember the feel of it against your skin?"

Jasper made no comment, struggling against Michael's hold, fighting with mind and body to survive. White fire ran through his mind. The knife was weakening him, weakening his ability to hold on. It didn't matter. The window was only a few feet away.

He stepped forward and wrapped his arms around Jasper, picking him up. Ignoring Jasper's struggles, ignoring the whips of energy beating through his mind, Michael thrust a cord of power at the window, smashing it. Holding Jasper tight, he dove forward, throwing them both through the shattered window and out into the sunlight.

***

Nikki stopped abruptly, her body stiffening with shock. Pain washed heat through her, almost suffocating her. Michael was hurt. Maybe even dying.

"No!" She spun and ran back to the house. Promise or not, she couldn't let him die. She'd stood back and watched

her parents die. Had watched Tommy die. She sure as hell
wasn't going to repeat the same mistake with Michael.

Glass shattered. She slid to a halt and glanced up.
Michael and Jasper tumbled out the front window and hit
the ground with bone-breaking force.

Jasper's hiss filled the air with venom, but he didn't
burst into flame, as Monica had. But she could feel his
desperation, as clearly as she could feel Michael's
determination.

He was holding onto the younger vampire, but only
barely. And with every minute that passed, he was
weakening.

Still she hesitated, needing to help but unsure what
she could do. Jasper's struggles were becoming more frantic,
his movements more desperate, but he might still have the
power to control her. She didn't want to end up attacking
the man she was trying to save.

She bit her lip and watched the two men roll down the
slight grassy incline and onto the sidewalk.

Michael's dying.

Jasper's whisper ran through her mind, full of malice.
She swore and retrieved the second silver knife from her
boot. If one didn't kill him, maybe a second would. A wash
of energy hit her, sending her staggering backwards.

"Stay...back!"

Michael's command was hoarse. Tears sprang to her
eyes. Jasper was on top of Michael, fighting with fists and
mind against Michael's grip.

Did he really expect her to simply stand there and watch
him die?

She took a step forward, then stopped. Something
glinted brightly between the two men...

Her knife, wedged deep in Michael's side. Killing him,
as she'd tried to kill Jasper.

"No!" she screamed, smashing aside the barriers of pain.
Reaching out kinetically, she ripped the blade from his side
and flung it as far away as she could. She glanced at the
knife in her hand and threw that away as well. Just in case
Jasper managed to break free from Michael's hold.

Both men were weakening. It was evident in their
struggles, in the weakening wisps of power running around
her. In a last, desperate effort, Jasper screamed, surging

upwards, smashing free of Michael's grip and staggering away. His desperation to escape the growing heat of the sun filled her mind...then he turned and met her gaze.

He smiled suddenly. Nikki clenched her fists and backed away. Energy flowed through her, a desperate shield, a last defense.

"Mine," Jasper whispered harshly, and lunged at her.

She hit him with every ounce of kinetic power she had. It wasn't enough to do anything more than thrust him away. Panting harshly, she watched him rise. Ignoring the bright beat of pain smashing at her temples, she hit him again.

This time he slammed to a halt. The link between her and Michael flared to life. His thoughts caressed hers, and their powers combined.

Now, Michael whispered.

Together, they thrust Jasper skywards, holding his struggling body up to the bright sunshine. He screamed, his white skin flaring red as he began to burn. Again energy pulsed, a thin strand of power wrapping tightly around Jasper's throat. Fear washed around them, his struggles becoming more violent as dark flames began to lick around his arms, his hands.

Nikki dredged up the last of her reserves, battling to hold her share of the psychic cage. The strand of power snapped tight, and there was a sickening crack as his neck was broken. Jasper's eyes went wide with shock an instant before death took his soul to eternal darkness.

It was over.

The last of her strength ebbed away, and she dropped wearily to her knees. Everything hurt—her brain, her body and her heart, but it was worth it. Jasper was dead.

With the strength of the psychic cage gone, he flopped back to the pavement. His skin was slowly darkening, slowly burning where Monica had burst into flame. But it didn't matter. His neck was broken, and he would not rise again. The sun was only finishing what she and Michael had started.

She closed her eyes and took a deep breath. They'd won—together they'd won. She reached out to link but it was little more than a void—as if Michael had never been a part of her.

Fear slammed into her heart. She pushed upright and

staggered to his side. He didn't move. She dropped to her knees and frantically felt for a pulse.

Nothing. No pulse, no sign of life.

"Damn it, Michael, don't you dare die on me!"

She rose and grabbed his arms, dragging him back towards her house. Every muscle was screaming by the time she reached the stairs. She hesitated, looking up in despair. Six stairs. It was all that stood between her and home, and they'd never appeared such a mountain before. He was too heavy to carry, too much dead weight...

If she gave up now, he would die. Just like Tommy, just like her parents.

She reached for kinetic energy. Warnings beat through her mind—she'd done too much, pushed too far. If she kept pushing, she might lock her mind in an eternal band of pain, never able to use her gifts again.

She closed her eyes and reached regardless. It didn't matter. Nothing mattered if Michael died.

Energy came. She opened the door, then lifted Michael up and thrust him through. The world spun drunkenly. She grabbed the banister, holding on tight. Gritting her teeth, her breath little more than wheezing gasps, she eased him to the floor. She didn't know how much time he had left. She had to hurry if she wanted to save him.

She slammed the door shut then staggered over to the shattered window, pulling the blinds closed. If he was to have the slightest chance of life, she had to make sure there was no bright light to weaken him further.

She knelt by his side and picked up his hand, holding it close to her chest, close to her heart. Reaching forward, she gently brushed dark wisps of hair away from his closed eyes.

"Come back to me, Michael."

There was no response. Tears sprung into her eyes. *I don't want to live alone any more, Michael. Please, don't leave me alone!*

"Damn it, you promised me you wouldn't die!"

And lied when he'd done so. A sob tore past her throat. She couldn't let him die. No matter what the cost, she couldn't let him slip away from her now.

But maybe he was simply too weak to live.

She bit her lip, then pushed upright and ran to the

kitchen. Michael might not drink human blood anymore, but she had a feeling he needed it to survive.

She grabbed a knife from the rack, then hesitated. He wouldn't thank her for doing this. She had a feeling his control over his bloodlust had been a battle not easily won. But her only other choice was to watch him die.

She walked back to his side.

"Forgive me if I'm doing the wrong thing, Michael, but I love you. I can't sit here and watch you die."

Leaning forward, she kissed his forehead. Then she took a deep breath and sliced her wrist. She forced open his mouth and let the blood drip down his throat. He swallowed convulsively for several seconds, then jerked spasmodically. Lunging forward, he grabbed her arm, holding her still, his grip bruising as he sucked quickly, greedily, at the wound.

He wasn't awake, wasn't even aware of what he was doing. He could drain her without knowing, and she knew it wouldn't matter. As long as he lived, as long as he broke the curse of her love, she didn't care.

Through a growing haze of pain, she formed a thin lance of psychic energy. Touching his forehead lightly, she closed her eyes and thrust deep into the darkness holding his mind captive. She plunged down, deep down into his consciousness, deep down into the shadowed areas he'd kept well hidden when their minds had last merged.

Don't leave me! she screamed through the darkness of his mind.

Something burned in answer. A single heartbeat, weak and uncertain. Elation trembled through her. It was working. Breathing harshly, she dove deeper.

"I need you! I love you! Don't leave me!"

Another beat ran through the dark silence, stronger this time. A dark haze ran across her vision. An odd sort of lethargy was beginning to creep through her body, sucking the strength from her limbs. She ignored it.

Live, damn you, live! she mentally screamed, pouring the last of her energy, the last of her strength into him.

Then the darkness claimed her, and she knew no more.

Twenty

Michael leaned a shoulder against the wall and watched the dawn rise through the lace-shielded windows. From behind him came a steady beeping—Nikki's heartbeat, recorded by the intensive care instruments that still surrounded her, strong at last.

Not that he needed the instruments to hear her heart. The demon within him had finally woken from its long slumber and was hungry to taste her again.

He shuddered and clenched his fists against the need beating through his soul. Three days had passed since he'd awakened and found her lying still and pale by his side, her life still hot on his lips.

He'd come so very close to killing her.

He'd never thought to warn her against offering her blood. It was the one thing he'd never expected her to try. She might share his life force and be impervious to most wounds, but he could still kill her. He was her maker.

He scrubbed a hand through his hair. His need to taste her again was growing. He had to get out of this hospital, had to go somewhere far away from any sort of human habitation until he could bring his demon under control. Until he could, he was a bigger risk to Nikki than Jasper had ever been.

The door to his left opened, and Jake entered. Though he still wore the thick white bandage around his neck, his movements were stronger.

"How is she?" he asked, walking across to her bed.

"Alive." Like a siren song, the pounding rush of blood through Jake's veins called to the darkness in him. His canines lengthened in anticipation. Michael swallowed and looked out the window.

"I was just talking to the doctors. They said she'd lost almost eighty percent of her blood. They have no idea how she managed to stay alive."

She was lucky she'd only lost eighty percent. Lucky he'd awakened in time to stop his demon.

"Don't suppose you'd like to explain how it happened? I mean, you don't take human blood, do you?"

He didn't have to turn to see Jake's bitterness and

sudden mistrust. It was all too obvious in his thoughts. "I was unconscious, probably dying. She cut her wrist and offered it to me. She gave me life."

"And you almost killed her in the process!"

Michael closed his eyes. "Yes," he said softly.

"What about that bastard, Jasper? He still around?"

"No. We killed him."

"Good," Jake muttered. "At least some good has come from this mess."

Maybe it had. Jasper was dead. He had his revenge. But at what cost?

He walked over to the bed and gently brushed the dark strands of hair away from her eyes. Her face was still pale, despite the strong beat of her heart. But her thoughts were finally stirring. She would awaken soon. He had to be gone before then.

He met Jake's gaze. "Take care of her for me, will you?"

Jake raised an eyebrow. "After all she's been through for you, you're not sticking around until she wakes?"

"I can't." He smiled, revealing lengthened canines. Jake took a hasty step back. "When she fed me, she destroyed the hold I had on my vampire urges. I can't stay here, can't stay near her, until I get control back."

"Good idea." Jake swallowed, then ran a hand through his hair. "But there's a lot of unfinished business between you and Nikki. I don't think fate will let you go so easily. He hesitated. "And I know for certain Nikki won't. She'll keep looking for you, no matter how long it takes."

"She can look all she likes. She will never find me."

"Want to bet on that? You've seen how tenacious she can be."

Michael smiled grimly. Tenacious or not, she wouldn't find him unless he wanted to be found. After three hundred years of existence, hiding was one thing he'd become very adept at.

And yet part of him hoped Jake was right.

Jake frowned. "What do you want me to tell her when she wakes?"

"Tell her—" Michael hesitated. *Tell her I love her. Tell I'll come back for her if I can.* "Tell her to take care."

Jake raised an eyebrow. "That's all?"

"Yeah." It wasn't fair to offer anything more, to offer

hope when there might not be any. He bent and brushed a kiss across her cheek. Breathed, for the last time, her scent.

Then, without glancing back, he turned and walked for the door.

Leaving his heart behind.

Don't Miss the Continuation of
Keri Arthur's
Acclaimed
"Nikki and Michael"
Series

Hearts in Darkness
(Book Two)
ISBN 1-893896-71-4

Chasing the Shadows
(Book Three)
ISBN 1-893896-84-6

Available from
ImaJinn Books
www.imajinnbooks.com
or call toll free
877-625-3592

Don't Miss
Keri Arthur's
Acclaimed
"Damask Circle"
Series

Circle of Fire
ISBN: 1-893896-70-6

Circle of Death
ISBN: 1-893896-77-3

Circle of Desire
ISBN: 1-893896-92-7
(Coming in July 2003)

All Circle books are stand-alone
romances and don't need to be read
in any specific order.

Available from
ImaJinn Books
www.imajinnbooks.com
or call toll free
877-625-3592

Printed in the United States
128054LV00003B/251/A